"Where did you get this?"

"From the woman to whom it was given nearly five years ago, along with the instructions whispered from her deathbed, instructions I now seek to carry out," she said, taking great care with the words.

A myriad of emotions crossed Tylir's face before it settled into a harsh frown. "Does Estrid still live? Has she traveled across the seas? Quick now. Where is she?"

"Estrid died last spring during the fever which swept our village."

He lifted a brow. "Have you traveled all the way here to inform me of her death? What we shared, we shared a long time ago, my lady Melkorka, but it vanished like the summer mist confronting the hot sun. You have done your duty. You may depart now. In peace and privacy. But I thank you for the return of the arm ring."

He was dismissing her without even listening. Mel counted to five slowly and clung on to her temper.

"What you shared produced a child." Mel gently pushed Katla forward. "A girl, this girl—Katla."

Author Note

I love reading about what happens after people have their lives turned upside down and how they restart, often going on to lead rich lives that would not have been possible if they had not first traversed the shadowy vale of tears. It gives me hope for the future when sometimes the present can seem bleak.

When the idea for Mel and Tylir's story came to me, I knew I really wanted to tell their story of how two people who had experienced severe hardship and heartache are able to find a lasting love. An added bonus was being able to set the story in Iceland, a place I visited when I was writing my first Viking-set novel. The kindness of the people I encountered there, particularly after I accidentally tumbled from an Icelandic pony, lingers long in my memory. I do hope you enjoy the story as much as I do.

As ever, thank you for being one of my readers. If you'd like to get in touch, I love getting comments from readers and can be reached at michelle@michellestyles.co.uk or through my publisher or Facebook or Twitter @michellelstyles.

MICHELLE STYLES

———

A Viking Heir to Bind Them

HARLEQUIN
HISTORICAL

If you purchased this book without a cover you should be aware
that this book is stolen property. It was reported as "unsold and
destroyed" to the publisher, and neither the author nor the
publisher has received any payment for this "stripped book."

Recycling programs
for this product may
not exist in your area.

ISBN-13: 978-1-335-59569-0

A Viking Heir to Bind Them

Copyright © 2023 by Michelle Styles

All rights reserved. No part of this book may be used or reproduced in
any manner whatsoever without written permission except in the case of
brief quotations embodied in critical articles and reviews.

This is a work of fiction. Names, characters, places and incidents
are either the product of the author's imagination or are used fictitiously.
Any resemblance to actual persons, living or dead, businesses,
companies, events or locales is entirely coincidental.

For questions and comments about the quality of this book,
please contact us at CustomerService@Harlequin.com.

Harlequin Enterprises ULC
22 Adelaide St. West, 41st Floor
Toronto, Ontario M5H 4E3, Canada
www.Harlequin.com

Printed in U.S.A.

Born and raised near San Francisco, California, **Michelle Styles** currently lives near Hadrian's Wall with her husband and a menagerie of pets in an Edwardian bungalow with a large and somewhat overgrown garden. An avid reader, she became hooked on historical romances after discovering Georgette Heyer, Anya Seton and Victoria Holt. Her website is michellestyles.co.uk and she's on Twitter and Facebook.

Books by Michelle Styles

Harlequin Historical

Return of the Viking Warrior
Saved by the Viking Warrior
Taming His Viking Woman
Summer of the Viking
Sold to the Viking Warrior
The Warrior's Viking Bride
Sent as the Viking's Bride
A Viking Heir to Bind Them

Vows and Vikings

A Deal with Her Rebel Viking
Betrothed to the Enemy Viking
To Wed a Viking Warrior

Sons of Sigurd

Conveniently Wed to the Viking

Visit the Author Profile page
at Harlequin.com for more titles.

For Gina and Rob

Chapter One

June 881, west coast of Islond, near modern-day Akranes, Iceland

'Did I hear that right? This man says Fork-Beard's sister has business with me?' Tylir Tjorson turned away from the messenger and towards one of his oldest friends, Grim the Stargazer. 'Does Helm the Fork-Beard have a sister?'

'Half-sister.' Stargazer touched his finger to his nose. 'She arrived two days ago. Bedraggled from a storm at sea with a child clinging to her skirts. Caused no end of uproar.'

Tylir did not bother to ask where Stargazer obtained his information, but he believed its accuracy. The man's ability to absorb gossip along with the general lie of the land had several times saved not only his own life but more importantly the lives of the men Tylir commanded when they campaigned in Alba. 'Indeed.'

Stargazer delicately dusted his fingertips. 'I thought the information might be useful.'

'Your intelligence on the matter is much appreciated.'

'I do my best.' Stargazer lowered his voice. 'You must have met her when you were still in the North Country. Dark red hair. Hazel eyes. Slender like a reed.' He paused and his cheeks reddened slightly. 'Or so they say.'

Tylir kept his face blank. Stargazer knew Tylir had forbidden anyone from visiting Fork-Beard's lands after the General Assembly issued their misadventure verdict about the brawl which had claimed lives on both sides, including one of his most promising warriors, but Tylir suspected Stargazer went there anyway.

The deadly brawl had happened three days after Tylir's wife's funeral. Fork-Beard swore he had nothing to do with her demise at the hot pool but unlike the General Assembly, Tylir did not believe his lies about not having seen Tylir's wife in weeks. Despite several people's testimony about his plans to work in that area, Fork-Beard swore that his plans were a coincidence and anyway he had been delayed by a sheep pen collapsing and by the time he'd finished, Ingebord's body had been discovered. The explanation was far too rehearsed in Tylir's opinion.

'Two days ago? Anything else I should know about from Fork-Beard's steading?'

'The sister's name is Melkorka Helmsdottar… And the child resembles you.' Stargazer shrugged and then hastily examined the ground. 'Or so the whisper goes.'

'And the mother?'

'You mean is Fork-Beard's half-sister the mother?' Stargazer scratched his neck. 'So they say. Why else would she have the child with her? The journey from the North Country is perilous even at this time of year.'

'Why indeed?'

* * *

Tylir frowned. He had no recollection of this Melkorka Helmsdottar. He preferred bedding a certain type of woman—raven wing's hair, soft curves and a pleasing manner, never a redhead or someone as thin as a reed. And if the woman's personality was anything like her half-brother's, she would be arrogant beyond the point of obnoxious. He gazed out at the whitecapped wavelets on the sea loch and tried to puzzle the mystery out.

Any visit from this Lady Melkorka would bring trouble and discord. He knew that in his bones as surely as if he'd seen several ravens flying at midnight.

'What does your master want?' he asked, turning to the messenger. 'What does Helm Helmsson the Fork-Beard require from me?'

The man lifted his chin. 'Does Melkorka Helmsdottar have permission to travel here unmolested? And leave when she wishes?'

Barely restraining his temper at the direct insult, Tylir glanced left and right to the men ranged behind him. 'Have my men threatened her? Ever? Have they threatened anyone from Helm the Fork-Beard's steading since the last General Assembly?'

'Helm considers his half-sister's business could be completed at the next General Assembly.' Fork-Beard's messenger puffed out his chest. 'But Melkorka Helmsdottar wishes to put the business before you sooner, and in private. I am here to facilitate that request. It is why the question is being asked. Will you give safe passage and vouch for your men to do the same?'

Tylir rubbed a hand along his chin. Helm's explanation for Tylir's wife's death was that it must have been an accident. The same excuse given for the brawl—just a misunderstanding and his men did not make obscene gestures during the funeral. Tylir's men simply misinterpreted the hand signals.

'Tell Melkorka Helmsdottar that she may travel here without delay. We discuss the matter in private. Safe passage. I give my word on that. I have never knowingly harmed a woman and do not intend to start with Helm the Fork-Beard's sister.'

The man's tongue flicked out like a snake's. 'In that case, my master informs you that his half-sister will not expect any ceremony. Discretion will be best for all parties, according to Lady Melkorka.'

Tylir fingered the hilt of his sword. What game was Fork-Beard playing now? He sensed the treacherous undercurrents in the messenger's statements. Why wouldn't the woman expect any ceremony? In his experience, women lived for the mundane ceremonies which made up their lives. His late wife certainly had. Everything a ritual until he had trouble breathing. This unknown with a child intrigued. Anyone who tried to play a game with him would lose and lose badly.

'I will take the advice under consideration. Tell your master, the woman comes alone.' Tylir nodded pointedly towards the man's boat. 'Now go in peace while you still can.'

The man bowed low. 'It will be as you request, Tylir the Sunbear Berserker.'

Melkorka Helmsdottar hated the way her stomach roiled. She should never have come to this place, not like this and not with this little girl clinging to her hand. Not on her own, without any of her half-brother's men, except for the man who'd rowed them across the sea loch. And he'd refused to leave the boat, claiming a direct order from her half-brother to ensure discretion. Melkorka wished she'd never used the word in her argument with Helm. He seemed to have taken the idea to extremes.

More than anything she wished she had not given her solemn promise to Katla's dying mother. She knew what it was like to be foisted on an indifferent father and his family and she didn't want that for the little girl she'd grown very fond of.

'Promises must be kept, even when it is hard.' She whispered her mother's old saying and tried to keep from showing any nerves. Mel knew the child was nervous enough for them both.

The faint smell of rotten eggs tainted the air and she strained to hear any looms clacking or the sound of wool being carded inside the formidable longhouse.

The men working in the fields surrounding the farm simply regarded them with curiosity before returning to their task.

'Aunty Mel?' Katla asked, her forehead puckering. 'Can we go? Now. Uncle Helm said that if no one opened the door, not to go in as the monster would be waiting to eat me up. I don't want to die. And the boys agreed.'

Mel tightened her jaw and cursed her half-brother and her two nephews, aged eight and ten years, for putting ideas in Katla's four-year-old head. Monsters indeed! If she asked Helm about it, he'd claim that it was a joke and wonder aloud why the child remained such a frightened rabbit.

'We shall soon see the great berserker warrior, Tylir Tjorson the Sunbear. Do you remember the stories I told you about him?' Mel concentrated on keeping her voice light. She'd embellished the snippets she'd heard, but they had kept Katla entertained on the long sea voyage when the waves crashed over the prow and all they could see was the dove-grey sea meeting the ash-grey sky. 'You liked those stories, didn't you?'

'The ones about Sunbear who saved an army and the kittens? They were exciting! I didn't think he could possibly be real. Do you think he still has Freya's kitten? Could I meet it? I don't like dogs much, but I do like cats.'

'It was a long time ago. The kitten will be grown now.' Mel tucked a strand of dark red hair behind her ear and tried not to think about the other stories she'd heard about Tylir's ferocity in battle and his ruthlessness with the men under his command, or the secret Katla's mother revealed right before her death—instead of the gentle elderly jarl Katla revered, the famed berserker was Katla's actual father.

'Won't that be a good treat to meet him?' she continued when Katla's face became even more uncertain. 'Finally, to be here like your *mor* instructed me you should be. She would be proud of you in that gown she embroidered. She wanted you to meet him.'

Katla's eyes brimmed with unshed tears. 'I don't want to meet him. I want my *mor*.'

Mel patted the girl's hand. 'You will make a new home in Islond. We both will.'

'Why can't I stay with you for always?'

'You are with me now,' Mel replied.

Katla scrunched her face and appeared close to a full-blown wailing, something she'd done frequently back in the North Country. The last thing Mel required. She had no wish for Tylir to refuse the girl on grounds of difficulty. Or much worse, to decide that Katla needed to be schooled in the proper way to behave. Mel's father had kept her mother a Gallic slave on a separate small farm some ways away from his main hall. Mel's peaceful childhood came to an end when her mother died after a short illness, and she was sent to live in the main house. Her back still bore the scars from Helm's mother's heavy belt.

A good first impression could make all the difference in how Katla was treated. Silently she prayed to any god who might be listening but particularly to Sif, the goddess of family, that she'd made the right decision in bringing the child here.

'Uncle Helm said…' Katla whispered.

Mel squeezed Katla's hand. 'My half-brother and his boys love to tease. Remember I told you on the boat—pay him no more attention than you pay to the cawing crows.'

The little girl bit her lip and gave an uncertain nod. 'Will you go away as well?'

'Once I get my own farm, you must visit. Anytime.'

'To talk and sing songs all day?' Katla appeared hopeful. 'Like we did on the boat?'

'Yes, like that.'

She gave Katla a hug, breathed in, savouring her fresh little-child scent. Katla with her blond hair carefully tied in bunches, a clean gown and pinafore and her big blue eyes, was a sight to soften any man's heart. Mel did not want the little girl to suffer the pain of rejection.

She clearly remembered how it felt after her own mother died and she arrived at her father's estate, dirty faced and with a torn apron. A bad first impression and she'd never really recovered from that.

That child will never be pretty, therefore she must be made to be useful, her father's wife had proclaimed with a curled lip.

Young as she was, Mel understood the woman meant to banish her to the back of the weaving hut or be given menial tasks in the kitchen, so she shouted out to her father that her mother's final wish was for her daughter to become a healer. Not strictly true as her mother had simply wished someone could have healed her bone-racking cough. But the slight ruse worked, and she was allowed to concentrate on learning to heal people with herbs, tonics and ointments.

Mel wrenched her mind away and smiled down at Katla. 'Be good, sweetling. Be good for Aunty Mel. Let me do the talking. Do your late mother proud.'

Katla sniffed loudly, brushed a single tear away from her cheek with the back of her hand and promised she would be.

Mel whispered a prayer to any god before she raised her hand to knock.

Before her knuckles connected with the wood, the door swung open, revealing a giant of a man with a distinctive puckered scar running down the left side of his face and fearsome dark blue eyes. Tylir Tjorson the Sunbear. As great and as terrible as the rumours said he would be. Yet she could see the ruined handsomeness of his features—like a god come to earth was how her late friend had described him.

Katla retreated a step before burying her face in Mel's skirts.

Mel tilted her chin upwards and tried to begin, but no sound emerged from her throat. Her long-practised speech vanished from her mind like ripples on a storm-tossed sea.

'May I assist you, Melkorka Helmsdottar?' The deep voice rumbled over her. 'You have taken considerable time in deciding whether to knock or not.'

Mel blinked several times. 'You are Sunbear the Berserker?'

'I prefer Tylir Tjorson, jarl of these lands. My fighting days lay across a sea and several moons ago.' A faint smile touched his full lips, but his eyes lost none of their glacial blue. 'Your brother's messenger emphasised your wish for privacy and desire to speak only to me.'

'Kind of him,' she said and wondered what other instructions the messenger had imparted. She had merely told her half-brother that she wanted to explain the situation to the jarl Sunbear first before shouting it in the General Assembly.

'You have something to tell me, I believe. Something important from the North which cannot wait until the next General Assembly meeting.' His lips turned up in a sardonic smile, the sort which said he knew he was a powerful warrior and she an ill-favoured widow and that she had no business staring at him like he was some sort of tempting morsel.

Mel swallowed hard. 'Yes, I do. That is... I thought

it best for the matter to be dealt with swiftly. Privacy is good for all sakes but mostly for the child's welfare.'

'Well then, woman, say your piece. Then you can be on your way as if we have never met. Better for all concerned.'

Mel straightened her spine and glared at the imperious warrior. Be on her way as if she was some sort of servant. She understood the implication. He had decided that she was unimportant and thus did not merit even a pretence of hospitality.

She wondered if her brother's message had indicated that sort of behaviour was acceptable, or if he decided the fact on his own. Had to be the message. No one would be that intentionally rude. If she mentioned the lack of hospitality and inquired if it was because of the message when she returned, her sister-in-law would argue that it was her own fault, and she should be aware of her precarious position in society. Despite her change in circumstances after inheriting her late husband's estate after their young son died, in the eyes of her half-brother and his family she remained the despised daughter of a Gallic slave girl.

'That man shouts, Aunty Mel,' Katla said in a loud whisper. 'I want something to drink. Please. You promised when we arrived, the women would come out and give us something to drink. Like they always do.'

Mel patted Katla's hand. The promise had seemed straightforward back at her brother's. 'Soon, sweetling.'

'Why does that little girl stare at me like I have grown two heads?' he asked, lifting a brow. The stubborn set of his jaw echoed Katla's. If Mel had doubted her friend's tale about Katla's parentage, she knew the truth from the mirrored expressions. 'State your business and go. I'm sure we both have things we'd rather be doing—you and your little friend, including finding her a drink.'

'My little friend expected the traditional welcome which does include a thirst-quenching drink when a stranger comes in peace as did I, but obviously we were mistaken.' She quirked her brow upwards and prayed her hands would not tremble and betray her nerves. 'My brother's message did inform you I came in peace, didn't it?'

His eyes flickered over Katla. 'You are hardly likely to bring a child with you if you do not come in peace. The message emphasised the need for privacy. I have given you privacy. Do you seek to question my hospitality at the General Assembly?'

'No one wishes that!' She tried to peer behind him, wondering where the women were. She'd feel better if she could meet anyone who would be looking after Katla. 'Katla and I are unused to Islond customs as we have lately come from Viken. I was merely trying to explain why a four-year-old child might expect a drink and that she was not being rude.'

'I regret I am out of practice.' A faint rose hue coloured his cheeks, making him appear much younger and less forbidding. He ran his hands through his hair. 'If you and the little girl care for refreshment, it can be arranged after our business is completed.' Each word appeared to be chipped from ice. 'Will that suffice for the niceties, my lady?'

'I am thirsty, Aunty Mel, but…he frightens me. Can we go now?' Katla hid her face in her skirts, clearly overawed by the giant confronting them.

'This should not take long.' She put a hand on Katla's shoulder. Though she hated to admit it, deep in her heart, she hoped he'd deny the girl. Katla deserved to grow up in a place where she'd be loved, but the law of the land decreed a child legally belonged to her father. She had to give the man a chance, even though she guessed he didn't deserve one. 'Once I am finished, Katla, the jarl will surely get you something to drink.'

He made an elaborate bow. 'As you wish, my lady. I know better than to argue with one such as you over customs.'

'Are you mocking me?' she asked.

He made a pointed cough. 'Polite custom and I are strangers, my lady. That is all. I meant no disrespect to you or your child. All I wish to do is live in peace with my neighbours. I've seen enough war.' Although his words held a faint note of warmth, his eyes were as cold as ever. 'I'm perplexed about what your business with me might be. I do not believe we have ever met. I left Viken and the North behind four years ago. Your brother and I have little in common. Does that serve for an explanation?'

Katla started to speak, but gently squeezing Katla's shoulder to warn her to keep silent, Mel reached into her pouch and extracted the arm bracelet. The intricately worked gold-and-silver piece gleamed in the early-morning sun.

'Do you recognise this piece?'

He took it from her, regarding it as if it might bite him. Something flashed in his eyes but was quickly masked, so quickly Mel wondered if it had been a trick of the morning light. Hard lines settled on his face.

'Where do you get this? How did one such as you acquire it?'

'From the woman to whom it was given to nearly four years ago, along with the instructions whispered from her deathbed, instructions I now seek to carry out,' she said, taking great care with the words. Ever since Katla's mother whispered the truth to her, she'd half hoped he'd deny ownership of the bracelet. It would make life far simpler in many ways. Mel had at first wondered if her friend was hallucinating when she insisted on the bracelet and Katla being taken to him. 'She told me that you had given it to her, and she felt it was time for it to be used for good, rather than being stored in an iron-bound trunk.'

He watched the arm ring as if it might bite him. 'For good?'

'She asked me to beg your forgiveness for not doing so earlier, but she had been under the impression you were dead.' A polite lie. Katla's mother had her own reasons for marrying the wealthy jarl who commanded a large estate.

A myriad of emotions crossed his face before settling into a harsh frown. 'Estrid is dead?'

'Alas, yes. Estrid died last spring during the epidemic which swept our village.'

He lifted a brow. 'Have you travelled all the way here to inform me of her death? What we shared, we shared a long time ago, my lady Melkorka, but it vanished like the summer mist confronting the hot sun. You have done your duty. You may depart now. In peace and privacy. But I thank you for return of the arm ring.'

He was dismissing her without even listening. Mel counted to five slowly and clung on to her temper.

'What you shared, produced a child.' Mel gently pushed Katla forward. 'A girl, this girl—Katla.'

His eyes blazed with cold fury. 'A child, my child? Estrid hid my child?'

'Her last words: "Take Katla to her true father, Tylir Tjorson the Sunbear, after my husband departs this earth. Show Tylir this bracelet. Ask him to forgive me. I believe some good for Katla will come of it." I had no reason to doubt a deathbed request.'

He gave a noncommittal grunt.

'You have identified the bracelet as belonging to you.' She hated how her heart clenched and how she had to force the words from her throat. 'Do you claim the child as your own? Or must she look elsewhere for survival?'

His eyes showed less warmth than a midwinter's day. 'It is custom in the North to send any children to their real father as soon as they are weaned. Why didn't she send word as soon as the child was weaned?'

'You would have to ask her mother that, but...' Mel allowed her voice to trail off.

His mouth took on a sardonic twist. 'Dying, she remembers I live and wishes to send the child to me, provided her husband has also died. How convenient for all concerned.'

'Not necessarily convenient for me.' Mel crossed her arms and glared. 'Once my question is answered, we can proceed.'

His eyes slowly roamed from the top of her couverchef over her nearly nonexistent curves to the tips of her sturdy boots. She was aware that a strand of hair had escaped from her couverchef and rapidly pushed it back. He gave a nod before hunkering down so that he was at eye level with Katla. 'Let me have a closer look at the child. Then we shall see what can be done.'

After peeping at him, Katla buried her face deeper into Mel's skirts. Mel put a hand on Katla's shoulder and tried to prise her away from the fabric. 'Look your father in the eye, Katla. Let him see your prettiest smiles like we practiced on the boat.'

'Not my father,' came Katla's muffled reply before she stamped her foot. 'My real father is back in Viken.'

'The child disputes your words. She has a father. Left them destitute, did he? Is that why you brought her here?'

'She is yet to come to terms with her loss. Why would I lie about something like this?'

He gave a half nod and rose, his face as unreadable as ever. 'I've given up wondering about what goes on in women's minds.'

Katla tightened her grip on Mel's gown. Mel's jaw clenched. She'd done this poorly. She should have gone on her own without Katla, but last night it all seemed simple. He would have to see the girl to make the determination, and she didn't want one of her nephews to start pinching Katla's arm again.

'Her mother married before she gave birth to Katla. Everyone assumed Katla was his. He died two weeks after Estrid.' Mel forced her voice to remain low and steady. 'He gave Katla many gifts before he died. Katla is far from destitute if that is what you are worried about. If you refuse to acknowledge her…'

His face became fierce in a precise imitation of Katla's expression. 'Never have I turned away from my responsibility. Why should I begin today?'

The back of Mel's neck eased, but her heart panged slightly. He was going to claim her, even if he had failed to say the exact words, the words Viken custom required. She supposed the precise formulation didn't matter because they were in Islond, not Viken. 'You appear very certain of your responsibility.'

His mouth became a thin white line. 'She has the look of my sister, and in a certain light of my mother. That tight pursed smile when she considered me unhospitable was my mother brought to life. I will not deny the arm bracelet or the parentage. I cannot.'

Mel hated how her heart fell to the top of her boots. She realised then that she expected him to deny it and to leave her with Katla and the plans for the two of them she'd worked out on the boat. 'I see.'

'I hope you do.'

'Katla, do be good now and greet your new father with a smile.' At the arched brow from Tylir, she swallowed hard. 'I mean your real father. Go on. Best smile.'

'My new father?' Katla asked, peeking up from Mel's skirts. Her cheeks and Mel's gown were stained with fresh tear marks. Mel's heart sank. 'He can't be.'

'Tylir Tjorson has claimed you.'

A fresh tear slipped from the corner of Katla's eye. 'Oh, no, not him. Don't leave me with him, Aunty Mel. Please. He is a frost giant, I'm sure of it. Frost giants eat little girls. The boys…your nephews…told me.'

Mel winced, hating her nephews' teasing had made Katla terrified of Tylir. First impressions were important and now, she had an uphill task in getting the girl to accept her new home. When she returned to Helm's farm, her nephews would get a piece of her mind about unnecessarily frightening a little girl. 'Katla, mind your manners.'

Tylir's face could have been carved from ice. 'You had best come in, the both of you. We will speak there. This business will take longer than I first imagined. I will see about that drink the little girl wanted.'

Mel gritted her teeth. She hated that Helm may have been right—she should have stayed well away from this place and this man. Katla should have had a safe place to grow up. No one would have known. She paused. She would have known. She kept her promises.

'Her name is Katla. She is not a dog or an inanimate object. She is your daughter.'

'Surely the custom in the North is for the *father* to give the child a name.'

With a curl of his lip when he pronounced *father*, he turned on his heel and strode back into the longhouse with a pronounced limp in his left leg.

Mel swallowed hard. Without truly acknowledging it to herself, she had gambled on Tylir denying the girl or at least declaring that he did not want to be burdened with her. Her dream of making a new home in Islond with Katla tasted like three-day-old ash in her mouth. She wanted to curl up in a ball and cry until the tears ceased to come. But crying never helped. Instead, she concentrated on making her voice sound cheery. 'Come, Katla, your father has invited us in. He is going to find us something to drink. Isn't that lovely?'

The words sound false to her ears.

'My name will always be Katla Gormsdottar.' Her face suddenly brightened. 'Let's run away, Aunty Mel. You and I together. This one won't mind.'

'I will explain slowly. We are not going to run anywhere.' Mel knelt so that her face was level with Katla's. 'The man you thought was your father died, but your real father is here and alive. He claimed you as his daughter. You will be living with him in this wonderful longhouse with all these green fields rather than in Viken, which had that horrible mud with nothing growing and everyone getting sick.'

Katla gave a briefest of nods. 'But that Sunbear man won't be my really real father. Ever.'

Mel forced her lips into a hopeful smile and tried for a light voice, even though internally she wanted to weep and then weep some more. 'I will always think of you as Katla, no matter what. When you think of me, I shall be thinking of you.'

Katla scrubbed her eyes with the back of her hand and her smile bordered on bravery. 'Truly?'

'When we meet, we can speak of our old life in the North if you wish. I promise, but now you must meet your new life with your chin held high.'

She stood and gestured towards the hall.

'But,' Katla whispered, hanging back, 'the boys were right—he looks like a frost giant.'

'Tylir Tjorson is no frost giant. Stop pretending.' She searched her mind for what she knew of the former legendary berserker. She wished she could promise he wouldn't alter the child's name. 'Remember the stories I told you. He is a brave warrior by all accounts. And he has built this magnificent longhouse for his family...for you.'

Katla put her hand in Mel's. 'You won't leave me, will you? You need somewhere to live as well. You could stay here with me. Maybe you could marry...'

'I will make sure you are safe.' Not the same thing, but it was the best Mel could offer. She silently prayed to her mother's God that everything would work out for Katla. As for her situation, one marriage had been enough for her. She knew her growing fame as a healer as well as being the mother of her husband's only child were all that had saved her from being abandoned by her cruel husband. And she'd lost both in the epidemic which had swept through the village.

'Promise?'

Tylir appeared in the doorway. His face was harsh planes and sharp angles. He nodded towards where some of his men gathered in a field and were frankly gawping at them. 'Melkorka Helmsdottar, I've no intention of discussing my *intimate* business where all can hear.'

Mel curled her hand tighter around Katla's and straightened her shoulders. She was going to find a way to make it easier for Katla...somehow. 'We must follow your father's request.'

Chapter Two

A daughter! He and Estrid had a daughter. Shortly before her death, his wife, Ingebord, consulted a soothsayer about her inability to produce a living child and discovered it was not her fault. Instead, the soothsayer proclaimed he was cursed for ever by his mother to be the last of his line for enjoying life snug in his jarl's hall when he should have been protecting his family from the raiders and later all the suffering they endured. He had accepted the soothsayer's word as the truth.

He knew in his heart when he discovered the bodies that he should have not accepted the message that they had all survived and were fine without going himself to check. However, now it appeared that the soothsayer had been wrong about the curse—he had a living child, one who had been born after his family perished.

He wanted to shake Estrid hard for not sending the girl until now but also to silently bless her memory for finally sending the child.

Tylir concentrated on containing his anger and shock as he regarded the carved door to the longhouse. Stargazer's rumour about Helm's sister bringing his daughter to Islond was partially correct. Helm the Fork-Beard had obviously not believed the rumour, or he wouldn't have allowed the girl to travel here. He would have held her for payment or worse. After Ingebord's death, Fork-Beard had shown how truly devious he could be.

He put his hand on the doorframe and tried to focus. He had no idea why his enemy's sister, Melkorka, had produced the child in the way she had, keeping her parentage a secret from her blood kin. Until he knew, he proceeded with caution.

He flung the door open and entered the deserted hall. Before Melkorka's arrival, he'd taken the precaution of sending the women to the weaving huts, explaining that he would let them know when they could return to their ordinary duties, but he needed them working on the new sails for his fleet. A slight bending of the truth but a necessary precaution. The hall, which he normally avoided as much as possible on principle, now appeared lifeless and a bit worn around the edges with platters and bowls left from breakfast on the tables and the pregnant spaniel gnawing on a bone in front of the smouldering fire.

The child clung to Melkorka with a death grip which double punched him in the stomach. He was not meant to be a father. Perhaps his child could sense this.

'Aunty Mel?'

'I'm here, dear.' Melkorka patted the girl's back.

Reining in the urge to bellow that he was determined to be a good father, Tylir gestured towards where a pitcher and several beakers sat. 'Let us be civilised about this. We can be civil, can't we?'

Melkorka rolled her eyes. 'Depends on your definition of civilised.'

He inclined his head. 'The ordinary definition will suffice.'

'Do you intend to take the child then?' Melkorka asked, keeping tight hold of the girl's hand. 'Raise her properly, I mean. The girl will need a nurse to look after her, not just be allowed to roam free and grow wild.'

Tylir permitted a thin smile to play on his lips. 'I hardly expect her to find her own food or shelter.'

'There is more to raising a child than simply providing food and shelter.' Melkorka's hazel eyes flashed with barely supressed fire. Tylir raised a brow. The woman obviously had a temper as fierce as her dark red hair. 'You can't leave her for the wolves to raise.'

'Wolves do not exist in Islond except for the two-legged variety. I would never allow any of my family near them.'

She blinked rapidly. 'They do in the North. Two-legged as well as the four-legged varieties are both plentiful.'

'Just as well we are in Islond then.' Tylir struggled to contain his temper at the situation: Melkorka, the woman with the dark red hair, was standing in front of him, a knowing expression on her face and possessing a penchant for stating the obvious. Wolves indeed! The only wolf near here was Helm the Fork-Beard.

Melkorka looked about her glumly.

He gave a long sigh. Was Melkorka like his wife, devoid of a sense of humour? 'A feeble attempt at a joke, my lady.'

Her long lashes swept down over her eyes. 'Is that

what you call it—a joke? Do you think a child's welfare a joking matter?'

The woman appeared to think that he was some sort of wild animal. Or had bad intentions towards the child. Nothing could be further from the truth. He gritted his teeth and clung on to the shreds of his temper.

'Your suggestion that I would not care about my child's welfare was absurd. I answered it with equal absurdity, my lady.' He tried again in a calmer tone. 'Do not make the situation more difficult. The child is no longer your concern. Even I know that much about the law of this land.'

Melkorka looked at him with unconcealed disdain. He knew instantly she was the sort of woman he instinctively loathed. She had already condemned him as an inadequate father before he had the chance prove himself. 'I see.'

'There can be no doubt the little girl is mine and will be looked after properly,' he said, trying to keep hold of his temper and sanity. Surely, she would find a reason to depart quickly, and he could get on with finding a suitable nurse and whatever else the child required. What did little girls like? What did they need? 'You will be able to visit her often. I'm sure she'd like that.'

The child watched him with his youngest sister's piercing eyes. He concentrated on breathing steadily.

'I am glad to hear that.' Melkorka's tone became a trifle less arched.

'I take it she has no other relatives and that is why she is travelling with you,' he said, attempting to reassert control.

He had never expected this mess when he received

Fork-Beard's message, despite the gossip Stargazer had repeated. He'd expected more mischief from his near neighbour but not the sudden appearance of a child who was truly his blood kin. He pinched the bridge of his nose. By Thor and all the gods, he never considered that a child might have come from that magical time four years ago.

When he learned of the girl's mother's marriage to a much older and hugely wealthy man, a man he considered an inferior warrior, he had a passionate affair with an incredibly beautiful but highly ambitious woman and married her too quickly to rid his mouth of the bitter taste. And the less said about that particular folly the better.

'I will ensure you are compensated for delivering her to me. Will I have to worry about the husband's relations? I seem to recall he was quite a powerful man in Viken.'

'Estrid's husband knew of my stated intention to travel to Islond. With his dying breath, he gave her into my care. His relations agreed it was the best solution.'

Tylir stared up at the rafters. He could well imagine how the interview went. The man's kin were cowards and cost many men's lives before later claiming a great victory in the most recent war in Alba.

'Did he know about the child's parentage before her mother informed you of it?'

'He never said and I never asked.' All light vanished from her eyes. 'Nobody questioned my decision. The epidemic took nearly everyone in our small community. People understood why I wanted a fresh start.

They were simply grateful not to have one more mouth to feed when I explained I was taking Katla.'

Tylir gulped hard. Nearly everyone dead and undoubtedly food scarce. He'd lost far too many to illness and war. And he knew that when there was vast sickness, crops were left to rot, causing starvation in the next winter for the survivors. And some of those who could, raided other farms.

He should have never stayed away that winter, attempting to gain favour with his new jarl and enjoying the plentiful meals and the discussions about where to ply their trade next summer. He should have returned home after Jul and been there to defend the farm when the raiders came and took the final precious mouthfuls, leaving the family to starve. He should have never made the excuse that his father would want him to gain glory for the family.

His throat closed and he all could do was stare at the little girl who looked back at him with his youngest sister's eyes, eyes he never thought to see again.

'Do you have much experience with children?' Melkorka asked in a conversational tone, banishing his memories of his now vanished family. 'Or perhaps I could meet with the mistress of your house before I depart. Helm's oarsman will be anxious to be off, but I want to ensure Katla has the proper care. I've no wish to trouble you for longer than I must.'

'I am a widower,' Tylir said through clenched teeth, wondering what Fork-Beard had said about him. Mistress of his house! He had sworn never to marry again nor to allow a woman free rein over his household after his late wife and her imperious ways. He'd been shocked at how the women were treated by her when he learned of it after her death.

'I see.' An overly extravagant sweep of her arm seemed to take in all the deficiencies of his longhouse and more importantly of himself. The house was fine for him and as a feasting hall when required, but it lacked tapestries and gilt on the wooden pillars, all the things which should have proclaimed his status as one of Islond's most important landowners. His late wife had been quite vocal on why he should demonstrate his status through adorning his hall, rather than concentrating on replenishing his merchant fleet. He could almost hear her voice buzzing in his ear in triumph that others thought as she did.

He firmed his jaw and struggled to control his temper. 'Why does my home and its perceived defects matter to you?'

Melkorka's cheeks coloured slightly, making her almost pretty. 'I've grown very fond of Katla. I care about what happens to her. I merely observe that little girls tend to flourish where there are women.'

'Children flourish where they are well cared-for,' he replied, stung.

'That is what I meant. Men seldom take responsibility for their children…in my experience.'

'Here you go, child. Drink up.' He went over to the pitcher and poured a drink for the girl. Her experience could go hang. He would be a proper parent.

The child screwed up her nose and reluctantly grasped the beaker. She took the barest of sips.

'Drink up.'

'Not thirsty now.'

Lady Melkorka continued to watch him with that hooded expression which seemed to peer into his soul and see all his failings as a leader, a husband and now with a certain inevitability as a father. And he wanted to shout to give him a chance, that he was much more than that.

'Don't you want a drink, Katla?' Melkorka said in a low voice.

The girl screwed up her eyes, pursed her mouth and turned her face away.

'She said she was thirsty,' he said as the feeling of being out of his depth washed over him again. Stargazer might have an idea about a suitable nurse whom he could turn her over to when Lady Melkorka left, but Stargazer had gone to the eastern fields to solve a problem with the sheep and was unlikely to return, leaving him to sort Fork-Beard's sister's mysterious business out on his lonesome. Said with a wink and tap of his nose as if he knew the idea of Tylir being involved with such a woman or indeed having a child was nonsense.

'Katla is working herself into a temper,' Melkorka said with a superior upwards tilt to her mouth. 'She can be stubborn when she wants to be. Now, Katla, your father has poured you something to drink. Behave.'

The girl took another small sip before placing it down. 'Done now, Aunty Mel. Not thirsty now. Want to go. Hate it here.'

'Hush, child, you will settle here in time.'

At that heartbeat, the loathing for Melkorka and her oh-so-calm ways choked him. It was as if the little girl peeked into his soul and discovered how dark it was, as if she knew why he preferred to be alone with the ghosts rather than having a noisy being thrust on him. He wanted to tell Melkorka to take the girl with her as he wasn't worthy of looking after the child, having already failed to protect his family. He should have been there when they died of hunger instead of being away trying to curry favour with his new commander.

But he could not deny this child, not looking the way she did, precisely like his youngest sister. That Katla too had had a temper and delighted in provoking him. Who said the gods did not have a sense of humour?

'So what is your plan to be?' Melkorka asked in an arched tone.

'That is none of your concern!' he yelled, trying to regain control of the situation and his wayward thoughts of his long-dead family. They belonged in another, happier time. Once Melkorka was out of here, things would be simpler. He would find a nurse of a sort from the weaving shed. 'I am her father. You brought me the arm bracelet. I claimed her as my blood. Your task is done. We part in peace.'

She gave a half nod and a perfunctory curtsey. 'Your father has formerly claimed you, Katla. My task here is complete.' She grasped the child's hand. 'We will meet again, Katla. I promise you that. Soon, Katla.'

She kept saying Katla like she expected him to correct her. The name had opened the place where he stored memories of his sister, but they did not hurt like he'd expected them to.

Despite his scar itching, he kept his face still and willed for her to turn and go.

His daughter held on to her hand much as a dying man hangs on to a spar. Tears streamed down her face.

'Stay. Don't leave me here, Aunt Mel. Not yet. Frost giants walk in this place.'

She began to howl in earnest, and his pregnant dog joined her. So great was the noise that he wondered if the puppies might have started to arrive.

The continuing noise pierced his eardrums and made it impossible to think. He could clearly remember his sister doing precisely the same thing for hours and hours until he gave in. His scar throbbed and lights flashed before his eyes, a sure sign that one of his blinding headaches was about to start. The last thing he required was another one of those. The last time he had not been able to see straight for three days.

'Can you stay? See the girl settled?' Tylir swallowed hard and pushed the pain away. 'Please?'

Melkorka's eyes spat hazel fury. 'The child has a name she is accustomed to—Katla.'

'I heard it. I know the name.' He examined the rushes and willed the great hollow ache in his chest which always developed when he thought of his long-dead family, in particular his youngest sister and his mother, to recede. He'd allowed his temper to get the better of him in the yard and here, in the hall, he hoped to do better. That would not happen if the pain overwhelmed him. 'I had no intention of changing it. But she will be known as Katla Tylirsdottar from now on. Only proper.'

He pinched the bridge of his nose and willed the ever-so-correct Melkorka to see sense. The pain in his head made his knees start to buckle and he put out a hand to steady himself on the table. Missed.

'Katla, did you hear Tylir?' Melkorka rested her hand

on Katla's quivering shoulder. 'He was teasing earlier. He isn't going to change the important part of your name. He just wants everyone to know that you belong to his family.'

Katla instantly stopped howling and peered at Melkorka. 'I want my mother,' she whimpered.

'She left this doll for you.' Melkorka reached into her pouch and withdrew a tiny wooden figurine wrapped in a blue shawl. 'I promised your mother to give it to you when your father acknowledged you and not before. One last gift for her daughter. She named the doll Freya, but you can call her anything you like.'

Katla's eyes gleamed. She took the small figurine and started to rock back and forth, crooning to it. 'Good. The goddess Freya looked after my mother all her life.'

Melkorka stroked the little girl's hair. 'Yes, that's right. Freya will guard you.'

'Stay with me, Aunty Mel. Please. For always.'

'Impossible, sweetling. Your father wants you with him. You belong with him now.'

Katla opened her mouth again.

Tylir braced himself for a renewed bout of shrieks. This time there would be no new doll. Or the next time. Or the time after that. He had no idea how he was going to deal with this little girl if she worked herself into one of those screaming fits his sister had excelled at. Once his sister had held her breath until she turned blue and fainted, narrowly missing the fire.

He wasn't sure how he felt about becoming a father, but he simply knew he did not want anything to happen to the little girl. Or for her to become a quivering wreck if he spoke abruptly. Or accidentally chose a nurse who would harm her in some fashion. He needed time to adjust to this new situation and find the right woman to look after her. And to do that he needed this woman, even though he hated being beholden to any of Fork-Beard's kin. 'Please. Please stay, Lady Melkorka. Stay until my—until Katla is settled.'

Katla instantly closed her mouth and her eyes widened.

Melkorka tilted her head to one side like an inquisitive bird. A flash of something like hope appeared in her eyes. 'How long are you asking me to stay for? The day?'

He thought about Fork-Beard's message. It had been slighting towards Melkorka. *My half-sister, Melkorka Helmsdottar, says she has business with you. It will not take long. She will not expect any ceremony. I expect our truce to hold.*

In turn, Melkorka had kept the secret of Katla's parentage from her half-brother... Now why was that? What bad blood lay between these two and what was he wading into the middle of by having this woman remain here?

A prickle coursed down his backbone, like the sensation he used to get before battle.

'Until Katla is firmly settled on my farm.'

Her tongue moistened her bottom lip, turning it a deep rose hue like cloudberries on a midsummer's day. He suddenly realised he was staring at it and wondering if it would be as sweet as ripe cloudberries. He wrenched his gaze away. Melkorka was Fork-Beard's sister and hopefully now his daughter's temporary nurse, not his bed mate for this evening or any other evening. What was he thinking? She wasn't even his type, although there was admittedly something intriguing about her fiery locks and even fierier tongue…

'You are speaking about days or even weeks,' she said in a low voice.

Tylir watched her from under hooded eyes. 'Will your brother permit that, Lady Melkorka?'

Her hand plucked at her gown, twisting the fabric between her fingers, but then she straightened her back and stared him directly in the eye. Her hazel eyes held a myriad of colours. 'My half-brother does not dictate where I go. Never has done. I am a respectable widow, but I am no lady, just Melkorka. My mother was a slave girl. Helm knows that quite well. He used to remind me of that every chance he got.'

Interesting. Stargazer's rumour from yesterday had not mentioned any rift between the siblings or indeed Melkorka's status. And she certainly carried herself like a lady. He held out his hand. 'Well then, just Melkorka, will you help settle Katla, my acknowledged daughter?'

'I accept your kind offer.' Her fingers curled about his for a brief heartbeat. He was surprised at their strength and the pulse of warmth which travelled up his arm. Up close, her features were far finer than he'd considered. He firmed his mouth. The woman was the half-sister of the man he held responsible for his wife's death. There could be nothing between them. He forced his fingers to let go.

'I will arrange for your trunks to be sent,' he said in a tone which most had the sense not to answer back to.

She blinked rapidly. 'My trunks? Shouldn't I go and collect them? Explain to my brother?'

'The child must remain here. Therefore, you must remain with her, or she will panic.'

He waited, with crossed arms and readied himself for her refusal. Lady Melkorka would show where her true loyalty lay. It bothered him that a part of him wanted her to prove him wrong, to prove that she was better than all the other treacherous ladies he'd encountered. He wanted her to show integrity and honour.

She slowly shook her head as the child's eyes darted from him to her and back again. 'I have given my word. I stand true. I will send a message telling my brother and his wife that I shall remain here for the foreseeable future.'

'Standing true, a refreshing change from your brother, who blows with the wind and tells any tale which will give him advantage.'

'Half-brother,' she said with a decisive nod which made him aware of the slender length of her neck, the length of her fingers and the way her gown skimmed her curves, details he'd missed earlier. 'I must assure you, Tylir Tjorson, I do know what my half-brother is like.' She held out her hand. 'You may count on me to keep my side of the bargain we have made.'

On impulse, he raised her hand to his lips. Her skin tasted like a warm sea breeze on a summer's day. His mouth wanted to sample more and for the first time in a long time, his body reminded him that he did have a sexual appetite, one which had not been fed recently. He let her hand drop and she watched him with her large hazel eyes. Not what he expected at all. There were many reasons why becoming involved with this woman would be a serious mistake.

'I shall hold you to that promise.'

Chapter Three

The enormity of what she'd agreed to do hit Mel the next morning after she had dressed and had breakfast with Katla in the small alcove which served as their sleeping quarters. It had been kind of Tylir to arrange the meal of bread and cheese last evening while the overwrought Katla had been able to get used to her new home. Someone had kindly left further food this morning.

She'd allowed her mouth to run away before she engaged her brain. She'd told him her parentage and even hinted at her problems with Helm, problems Tylir the Sunbear did not need to hear about. Finally, she'd held out her hand and he kissed it, causing a warm pulse to travel up her arm as if she was some young maiden rather than a widow who'd been discarded by her husband after she had given him his longed-for son and heir.

She sank down onto the bed and tried to consider her next move, because her earlier daydream of claiming Katla as hers after Tylir refused her had come to nothing. She understood why she and Katla must remain here and wait for the trunks to arrive. Helm might behave oddly once he learned the identity of Katla's true father. His temper had become uncertain after he took that blow to the head when they were young. The last thing she wanted to do was to cause renewed friction between neighbours. And she knew how her half-brother could behave around anyone whom he saw no use for. Somehow, he'd find a way to blame her for this.

'I'm pleased you stayed, Aunty Mel.' Katla laid her head in Mel's lap, all shy smiles and laughter. Now that Mel had encountered the Sunbear, she could see Katla's resemblance to him beneath the network of scars which etched his face. 'Is it true he used to be a famous berserker?'

'Why, his nickname has the word *bear* in it.'

Katla wrinkled her nose. 'Good, then maybe Freya will not have to be frightened anymore. We have a great big bear to protect us.'

'I didn't know she was frightened.'

Katla pursed her lips. 'She was, but she is better now because you are here. That man looks like he can use a sword against the frost giants which lurk in the wood near the hot pool.'

'Frost giants will not come here. And Tylir isn't a frost giant either. You must not believe everything those nephews of mine told you.'

Katla held the figurine to her ear. She nodded. 'Freya said you wouldn't have stayed if he was a frost giant in disguise. You do like him, don't you, Aunty Mel?'

'He is your father, sweetling. My views on him do not matter.'

Mel absolutely refused to think about the jolt she'd

experienced when his hand touched hers or the way his eyes crinkled when they took in her figure, or rather, lack of a figure.

She was not in the market for a bed partner, and Tylir would be after someone who had far more standing as a wife. The evening before she left for Tylir's, her sister-in-law had whispered that if she didn't set her sights with any future husband too high, she was certain Mel would find one. After all it was not as if her looks had improved with age. Said with that tinkling laugh of Helga's which grated like sand in the toe of a slipper.

'Will everything be all right, Aunty Mel? Freya wants to know.' Katla hugged the figurine tight to her chest.

'Everything will be just fine. See what a lovely place you have for your private chamber. Very few little girls have such privacy. Soon we will go and meet the other children who live here. They are bound to like you.'

Katla wrinkled her nose. 'I want to live with you… because you know everything.'

Mel forced her lips to turn upwards. Too late for regrets. 'I promised to see you settled. Your mother wanted you to live with Tylir. It is why she sent you here with me.'

Katla frowned. 'Will you tell me a story about my mother? Freya and I want to hear about her. Maybe the one about the feast where she sang and caught my…my old father's eye. He fell instantly in love with her, and they lived happily ever after.'

Mel kissed Katla's forehead. 'Soon. Maybe after we meet the other children.'

Katla sighed and went back to playing with the figurine, but she seemed content. Mel tried to decide if she should wait for Tylir to appear or if they should go explore Katla's new home.

'I've brought you some furs for your bedding like the jarl Sunbear ordered,' an elderly woman said, bustling in with a huge pile of fine furs, far more than Mel had expected to see. 'I see you ate the breakfast I left.'

Mel thanked the old woman for the breakfast, remarking about how thoughtful it had been while she took the furs. The old woman gave a derisive sniff.

'Freya's tired,' Katla declared. She slipped under the top fur and closed her eyes. Mel's heart squeezed. Despite her relatively easy sleep the night before, the poor little mite must be exhausted.

Mel carefully spread a fur over the girl. When she finished, she noticed the woman remained in the doorway, with an expectant expression like she wanted to impart some important morsel of gossip.

'Can I assist you with something? Katla needs to rest.' Mel raised a brow and waited for the old woman to make her excuses and go.

'Is it true what they whisper?' the woman finally asked, glancing at Katla with curiosity. 'Can she really belong to the Sunbear? Is that why he is keeping her and you prisoner in here?'

'Aunty Mel!' Katla sprang up with alarm. 'Are we prisoners here?'

'No, Katla,' Mel replied firmly. 'This old woman is confused. Rest now.' Reluctantly Katla settled herself back amongst the furs and her eyes quickly began to droop despite herself.

The woman laughed harshly. 'Just repeating what everyone is saying.'

'Who is saying anything?' Mel asked, keeping her voice steady.

The old woman sneered. 'That the little girl is Sunbear's child. He intends to keep you as a hostage because you were the one woman to bear his child and break the curse his mother uttered with her dying breath. There, I have said it. All the women in the weaving hut are gossiping about it.' She tapped the side of her nose. 'Old Virin knows a thing or three about keeping her ears open, you know.'

Mel didn't believe in curses. 'Why would the Sunbear keep me as a hostage when Katla is not my daughter? The woman who bore him a child is dead.'

Virin's mouth open and shut several times. 'Well then, it must be because of the fight between your brother and the Sunbear. Everyone knows about the enmity they bear each other. It was barely settled at the last General Assembly. It is why the women decided to be elsewhere yesterday when we heard of your impending visit. We knew that his orders about needing a new sail in double-quick time were rubbish. And then he told us to keep away from this here alcove.'

A finger of ice crept down Mel's spine. She should have expected something like this. Nothing was ever straightforward with her half-brother. Like his mother, Helm had a habit of collecting enemies and then wondering aloud about how it had happened. It was why he and his family had left Viken and sought a new life in Islond.

'Neither have mentioned it.' Mel smiled and silently cursed her half-brother. 'Helm would have hardly permitted me to travel here without an armed escort if he considered such a thing to be a possibility. My half-brother and I have had our difficulties, but he would never knowingly put me in harm's way.'

She silently prayed that it was the case. Helm could have also decided to teach her a lesson about why she needed to be guided rather than following her instincts. It could explain why he had not appeared last evening, frothing at the mouth.

'You sound very sure of that.'

'I often find the truth is far less interesting than weaving room gossip.'

Virin shrugged. 'True enough. The men love to tell tales too, so I know neither Sunbear nor Fork-Beard was satisfied with the General Assembly's decision.'

Mel tilted her chin upwards. The thought of her being held as a hostage to ensure Helm's good behaviour was ridiculous. He'd sooner throw her to the wolves than change his ways. But when she returned, she didn't doubt he would mention the situation and take the credit for her becoming free. The fact that she could walk out and had volunteered to look after Katla would make little difference in Helm's world.

'I gave Katla's mother my word to see her settled properly and I will. I keep my word. I asked for my trunks to be sent as well as Katla's. Tylir the Sunbear agreed to my request. I'm grateful not to have to confront my half-brother with that fact as he can be difficult. Cowardly of me but that is siblings for you.'

Virin wrinkled her nose and her eyes appeared to take in all Mel's deficiencies, the ones her late husband delighted in reciting every time he visited after their son was born. 'If you intend to stay, you should know Sunbear has declared he will not marry again. Too many young girls think they will capture him, but they won't. He remains devoted to my late mistress.'

'I have embraced widowhood.'

'Is old Virin bothering you, Melkorka?' Tylir loomed into view. His scar made his frown appear particularly fierce in the morning light. 'I know about your tricks of trying to frighten newcomers, Virin. You promised it would not happen again.'

Virin went scarlet and mumbled an apology before she slowly sidled out of the room.

'I understand you have done as you promised and sent a request to Helm for the trunks, Jarl Tylir,' Mel said in a loud voice to cover the awkward silence. 'Makes it easier for everyone to my mind. What a pity that people prefer gossip to the actual truth. Some appear to think we might be betrothed or some such nonsense. As I explained to the old woman, I have embraced widowhood. In fact, it suits me far better than marriage ever did.'

'Sending for the trunks seemed the best way. And I take note of what you say about your widowhood.' He gave a sudden smile and Mel glimpsed the handsome warrior who wooed Estrid before his face was ruined, the one whose memory made Estrid's blood race and sent her cheeks pink in her final days. 'It accords with my views on marriage. Once was enough for me.'

Mel dropped a slight curtsey and tried to ignore her churning stomach. 'I am pleased we have that out of the way and can safely ignore all rumours to the contrary.'

'Always best to ignore rumours in that regard.' He glared pointedly at Virin, who stood watching just outside the door, codfish mouthed and not bothering to disguise her interest. 'Virin, don't you have something else to be doing? Now?'

The woman mumbled something, picked up her skirts and fled.

Tylir raised a brow. 'My late wife's nurse enjoys stirring trouble even when her intentions are good. Saves her from getting bored, my wife used to claim.'

'She managed to frighten Katla.'

'The child sleeps peacefully so it can't have been that bad of a fright.'

Mel crossed her arms. 'You only met Katla yesterday. You have no idea about what frightens her, what she dislikes or indeed what she likes.'

'True enough. Her late mother withheld that pleasure from me until now.' He raised a brow. 'My late wife thought the world of her old nurse. I refuse to have her banished because my newfound child takes a sudden dislike to her.'

Mel gulped hard. 'I never asked for banishment.'

'My hall and lands and my rules. Old Virin knows that. Remember that as well and we will get on, Melkorka.'

Mel pinched the bridge of her nose. His late wife's nurse. Did he intend for the woman to be Katla's nurse as well? Katla would never settle if that were the case.

'Can we speak about this somewhere else?' she asked, nodding to Katla's sleeping form. Katla murmured something incoherently about needing magic to save her aunty before turning over. Mel mentally sighed and prepared herself for one of Katla's terror screams like she had had on the boat. But in one breath, Katla softly sighed, hugged the doll tighter and turned over.

'Your voice disturbed her.'

Tylir's cheeks faintly coloured causing the scar to stand out. 'I'm sorry. There is much I don't know about being a father.'

'Katla can be a light sleeper,' Mel explained. 'And she can be prone to night terrors. It caused a problem on the ship.'

'My sister had those as well. We will go elsewhere.'

Tylir gave a nod and led the way back to the main hall. The fire had been relit, which helped with the dank smell. A half-dozen women were readying the hall for the main meal.

Her heart thudded. He had kept everyone away for their initial interview. He had expected trouble and had sought to protect his people. It gave her hope that in time he would protect Katla.

At his sweeping glance, everyone stopped what they were doing. The room emptied, leaving them alone except for a pair of wolfhounds and the pregnant spaniel lolling in front of the now-blazing fire.

Mel wrapped her arms about her middle and tried to concentrate on the dogs, rather than her growing disquiet about the dispute and Helm's role in it. Why had he not disclosed the trouble to her before she came?

Helm could be like his mother in that respect. The trouble was she had inadvertently stumbled into a fight where she had little idea about what the rules were and who was in the right.

Now she was in Tylir's house, where his rules would need to be obeyed. And the little girl she'd grown so fond of belonged to him.

A long sigh emerged from her throat. Her ability to mess up was unsurpassed today. She just needed to figure out how to explain the situation and why Katla required someone who would understand and gently guide her rather than an old woman who wanted to frighten her into submission. To do that would destroy her spirit.

'The little girl reminds me of my youngest sister, also called Katla. My sister was wonderfully brave and never shrank from anything until she met hunger and starvation in the depths of a Northern winter,' he said in a low voice before she could give voice to her growing concerns. 'You should know that I'm unwilling to put any member of my family in danger if I can avoid it. I may lack experience as a father but I will watch over my daughter.'

The words condemning him died in Mel's throat. She blinked rapidly. His youngest sister was named Katla.

'I can only assume Estrid chose that name to honour our connection and to give me a clue should she ever require it.'

Mel examined her hands. She wished she had thought to ask Estrid why she had given Katla that name.

Tylir sighed. 'Katla must be well-treated. She is my only known child. I want to be a good father, certainly a better father than I was a husband, but she fears me.'

'She is young and alone.' Mel spread out her hands and tried to get him to understand. 'She will come to see the goodness beneath your gruffness in time.'

A dimple flashed in the corner of his mouth. Looking like that, she could understand why Estrid had whispered that he'd been the only man to truly satisfy her.

'My lady?'

Feeling the heat rise in her cheeks and aware that he had said something, Mel rapidly examined the rushes scattered on the floor and tried to keep in the forefront of her mind the long litany of her failings which her husband recited after their son was born. Top of the list that she was far too determined and persistent in wanting her own way. Too wrapped up in her herbs and potions to be a good wife, hostess or even mother.

When she finished the litany, she glanced up. His smile had grown. 'What?'

'Thank you for coming here, and for showing such strength of character, my lady. A change from most of the ladies from Viken I've encountered.'

She tapped her foot against the rushes. Why did men always resort to sarcasm when a woman with a strong personality confronted them? Strength was not something men looked for in a woman, and she could never do the 'please rescue me' with fluttering lashes like Estrid excelled at. Estrid had even managed to die prettily. No, she had to accept and embrace what she was—a woman of some means who could live an independent life, rather than one searching for the next husband or bed partner.

'I will take your word for how ladies of the Viken court behave. I have never had the pleasure of attending the queen.'

'Your brother's message said surprisingly little about your status. I apologise again for the welcome not being what you expected. My reasons were sound but flawed due to the half-right rumour.' He frowned. 'I also did not think he would be this long in having the trunks delivered.'

'No such thing as a half-right rumour.' She lifted her chin and caught the blueness of his eyes.

'It mentioned the child.' His warm gaze travelled down the length of her, taking in her meagre curves, and lingering slightly. Mel resisted the urge to cross her arms over her suddenly tingling breasts. 'However, I knew we had never encountered each other intimately.'

'Your woman spoke of my being taken hostage. I came here of my own free will. I wish to be able to leave whenever I choose.' The words came out more forcefully than she intended, but the way he pronounced *intimately* did strange things to her insides.

His laugh boomed out again, completely transforming his face. 'That is an excellent reminder of what we need to be speaking about, my... Melkorka. The future, not supposed intimacies in the past.'

Mel raised her brow. 'I fail to find it a laughing matter. Helm left Viken to start afresh after he quarrelled irrevocably with his neighbours. I have no control over what he did or did not do in this new life. Now it possibly threatens my future.'

Tylir sobered. 'It is my daughter's future that I am concerned with.'

'Meaning?'

'You gave Katla a promise to see properly her settled. I expect you to hold to that promise because otherwise my daughter will complain. And her shrieking shatters my calm. It made my head pound. I had to lie down for several hours to recover. My sister perfected the trick years ago. Now it would appear that my daughter has inherited it.'

'It should not take long to settle her in.' Mel waved a hand. 'A day or three. A week at the most.'

'It takes as long as it takes. My daughter guides us. I

want her to be happy, Melkorka. She is the future. I do not plan to have more children.'

Mel assessed him under hooded lids. His blue eyes stared deep down into the dark places of her soul. 'Your woman mentioned something about breaking a curse. I don't believe in them.'

'You are braver than some then.'

'A woman like me has no time to ponder such things like curses. I am too busy trying to survive.' And it hadn't been a curse which made her child and husband die. It had been a sickness which she lacked the skill to cure, even though she had bragged her skill with herbs and tonics was such that she could cure almost anything. It had been her fault. She'd seen the accusation in the survivors' eyes.

'Hopefully now you understand why I cannot permit you take Katla anywhere near my sworn enemy's hall now her true parentage is acknowledged. The temptation to hold her for his own personal gain would be ever likely to overcome Fork-Beard.' He paused and gave an ironic smile. 'Your half-brother lacks a certain control… in my humble opinion.'

Mel silently swore. Tylir spoke true. It was when Helm angered the very powerful jarl whose lands bordered their father's old estate over the seduction of the jarl's mistress that Helm had fled the North. And here he was making powerful enemies again in Islond.

'I'd no idea about the problem between you and my half-brother. I've certainly no wish to cause further dispute between neighbours.'

Tylir studied the rushes for a long time. 'The General Assembly decreed the matter of who started the brawl between us settled as a misadventure. Helm would do well to let the matter lie, but I fear that is not in his quarrelsome nature.'

Mel gulped hard. The matter was far from settled then. 'Are you comfortable with me being here? I could be a spy.'

'But you are not.' His smile increased as he slowly examined her from head to toe, seeming to linger on her meagre curves.

She folded her arms over her suddenly aching breasts, determined not to smile back at him. 'How can you be sure?'

He covered the distance between them in two steps. So close that their breath intermingled. He put a finger under her chin and lifted it so she stared into his starlit blue eyes. He looked at her for a long moment and then let go. His hand fell to his side. 'Instinct.'

Her mouth ached as if he tasted it. She gulped hard. Wishing for that would lead to her humiliation. *Useful, not pretty.* Lesson remembered. 'I appreciate your trust.'

A sudden shout followed by a blast of a horn drowned out his reply.

'What is it?'

His eyes blazed cold fury. 'My early-warning system. It appears your brother decided to take matters into his hands and has ignored my warning not to travel here.'

Mel clutched her throat. 'He has come here?'

'Armed and ready for war. It is what the blast of that particular horn means—Helm the Fork-Beard has arrived with his men.'

Chapter Four

When Mel reached the loch shore a few steps behind Tylir, her half-brother glowered from his boat, their father's favourite sword gleaming in the midmorning sunlight.

She only hoped that she'd hidden the gold in their trunks well enough as Helm would have pawed through them and, like his mother, he could never resist a shiny object. That gold—Katla's inheritance and her own— was essential for both their security and protection in an uncertain future.

'I demand to see her,' Helm said in his high nasal tone and jabbed his finger towards one of Tylir's men. 'Immediately. You can't keep her from me.'

Tylir merely looked at the much smaller man. A mighty full-grown bear to a jumped-up bantam cockerel. 'Or what?'

'You know what! Produce her!' Helm's voice rose on the last word.

She rolled her eyes heavenward at the remark. Trust her half-brother to overlook where she stood in full

view of everyone in favour of making some grand pronouncement.

'I am here, brother, or don't you trust the evidence of
your own eyes?' Mel said, crossing her arms.

'Melkorka, I didn't see you there.'

She should have guessed that Helm would have gone
about alienating his neighbours just like he had done
in Viken. Part of the reason why her father married her
off was to smooth over a growing feud which Helm had
started. 'Quite unharmed and breathing freely. You have
not become blind like our father did in his last years,
have you?'

When he said nothing, she gave an uneasy laugh in
the sudden silence.

Helm, who had raised his finger, clearly in anticipation of haranguing the onlookers further, lowered his
arm. 'Melkorka with your usual wit and charm. How
unexpected and yet how apt. Everything you do ends
up in a muddle. Be pleased I am here to rescue you and
that child you insisted on carting over from Viken.'

'I explained where I was going. You wished me luck
yesterday.'

Helm's face contorted into a precise imitation of his
mother before she ordered Mel to be beaten. Even though
Mel knew the woman had been dead for six years, ice
still crept down her spine.

'Not that you intended on staying for an indefinite
period, Melkorka, and sending for your trunks. What
was I supposed to think?'

'That I had everything under control like I normally
do, brother.'

'You waded in without regard for consequences. You

now must suffer those consequences. I will not allow you to bring shame on my family. I will not hesitate to repudiate you, Melkorka.'

He gave the word *Melkorka* the exact same pronunciation his mother had always done before beating Mel's back with what object was handy to ensure proper punishment. Even after all these years, her back still tensed, waiting for the blow.

Mel raised her chin several notches higher and glared back at him. She'd ceased being the ill-favoured daughter when she married. Currently, she was a widow of independent means. He had no power over her.

'Katla is Tylir's daughter,' she said in a firm voice.

Helm looked between Tylir and her. The scowl on his face deepened, setting into hugely unattractive lines. 'You hid things, Melkorka.' He nodded. 'But now I can see why you decided to travel to Islond. Good luck in your quest for a new husband. I sincerely doubt that Sunbear will be willing to have one such as you as a wife.'

His men gave sneering laughs. Tylir simply stood there, his face carved from stone, but his right brow arched.

'You are oblivious to many things, brother.' Mel allowed her anger to show. Let Helm chew on that remark. He and his wife had always dismissed her looks and importance, but she had no intention on remarrying.

'I claimed Katla as mine when Melkorka produced evidence from her mother. Your sister has kindly agreed to remain here to help her settle. My daughter recently lost her mother and the only father she knew. I will not have her bereft of friends.' Tylir came over to stand beside her so that their bodies touched.

Helm's eyes shifted from her to Tylir. The colour went from his face. 'You claimed her?'

'The girl bears the look of her father once you see them together. I wonder you did not see it before, Helm.'

He scratched his chin. 'I merely thought it a saucy rumour. Everyone knows about the curse Sunbear bore.'

'Funny how supposed curses vanish so readily,' Tylir remarked. 'And I dare say that you, Fork-Beard, have no idea of the kind of woman I would *actually* desire as a wife.'

Mel felt herself redden. Surely, Tylir was simply trying to get under her brother's skin somehow, and it was working. Helm looked positively furious, yet he held his tongue.

'You did bring Katla's trunk, didn't you, Helm?' Mel asked, as to her surprise Tylir snaked his arm about her middle and pulled her closer. Her body hit his hard muscle. 'Or did you simply decide to come and rescue me?'

'Why didn't you tell me all that you knew?'

'I had no idea if Tylir would claim the child as his blood kin and had no wish to trouble you with my concerns.'

She waited, acutely conscience of Tylir's bulk and the heat of his body, protecting her, making her feel safe in a way she had not felt safe for a long time. An illusion, but one she unaccountably wanted to cling to.

'I see.' Helm's face contorted. 'How like you to get it the wrong way around. You always did this when we were children.'

Mel clung to the remnants of her temper. Screaming at him would only provide amusement for the onlookers and fodder for the gossips. But his furious reaction showed her that she'd been right to keep Katla's parentage a secret. She had known nothing of the feud, only of Helm's general untrustworthiness. For that, she was grateful, since he would clearly have used the girl for his own schemes in some way.

'I intend to keep my promise to Katla, Helm.' She ensured her voice betrayed no hint of emotion. 'I gave my solemn word to see her safely settled.'

'Who to?' Helm asked. 'I don't believe a word you are saying, Melkorka. My mother always said you blink rapidly when you lie.'

'Fork-Beard, I warn you. Melkorka is a guest under my roof and therefore under my protection…' Tylir said in a warning rumble.

Mel stepped away from Tylir's warm hand. The last thing she required was some false declaration. A great hollow of sadness opened within her and threatened to overwhelm her.

'Her mother was Estrid. You must remember her. She lived on the estate next to my husband's. Every man within two hundred miles seemed to pant after her. You know Katla is not my child.' She clenched her fists and bit out each word, determined not to burst into noisy sobs.

'Now that you mention her, I do recall the woman. But why are you interested in helping her child?'

Her half-brother refused to remember the existence of her son, who had celebrated his seventh birthday a few months before the sickness took him. Even now, months later, she wanted to fall to her knees and rail against the gods who had taken him instead of her. Those very same gods who had shown her that despite her proud boasts before the sickness hit that she had no real skill as a healer, not when it really counted.

'My young son died in the epidemic. You like to forget about him, but I don't. Not for one heartbeat. Elkr, son of Elkr. Seven years at his death. A death which occurred three weeks after his father's.'

She straightened her shoulders and stood with her head proud. The only sounds were the seagulls cawing as they circled and the waves from the loch hitting Helm's boat.

Helm licked his lips with a pointed tongue. 'I'd forgotten. I am sorry for your loss, sister. But I don't understand why you and you alone had to bring this child to this place. She is not of your blood or mine.'

'But she is an innocent child, one that I can help, though I could not help my own child. For me, that is enough.'

Tylir stepped forward, his eyes blazing with a fierce fire. 'I'm grateful to Melkorka for her actions and for agreeing to settle the child in my home.'

'The child is several years beyond a babe in arms,' Helm said, obviously intent on stirring up trouble. 'Surely the mother should have acted sooner but that is not a failing on my family's part. You have no right to detain my sister for her part in this sordid affair.'

'What the mother did or did not do matters not at all. The woman died,' Tylir said in a tone which did not allow for arguing. 'I have never run from my responsibilities. Your sister has agreed to assist me in making sure the little girl feels comfortable in her new home.' He lifted a brow when Helm did not answer. 'Do you require this in simpler words?'

Helm's face contorted with barely concealed rage, and he raised his fist. Mel instinctively took a step backwards and half stumbled. Tylir's warm fingers went under her elbow and steadied her. She smiled up at him. He nodded back and somehow things were easier. She wasn't a young girl without friends.

'What are you going to do afterwards, Melkorka?' Helm shouted. 'My mother always warned me that you played games. What game are you playing now?'

'Are you deaf?' Tylir said. 'Your sister promised to get my daughter settled in her new home. A selfless act to my mind. What Melkorka does afterwards is up to Melkorka, but she will have the protection of my house for as long as she requires it.'

Tylir glared at Helm as if daring him to say differently. Helm gulped twice. 'If you say so…'

'I am pleased you see the necessity, Tylir.' Mel made the barest of curtseys and tried to regain some dignity. She stood on her own two feet and did not look for rescuing. She'd learned the hard way that the only person who was going to rescue her was herself. 'And allowed the promise to be made to a very frightened little girl. Katla will be the better for it.'

Tylir gave her a speculative look with hooded eyes. The look was enough to make a warm place grow inside her. 'My gratitude is immense.'

Helm pursed his lips as if he'd encountered a sour plum. 'Afterwards, when the child is settled, Melkorka, what then? Have you considered that? What will a poor widow like yourself do?'

Mel crossed her arms. She might be a widow, but she was not poor. Her son had inherited his father's wealth.

When he died, she had received the wealth in her own right as was the custom in the North. Had Helm ever thought about her son, he might have thought of that.

As he hadn't, she'd simply allowed him to assume certain things about her circumstances, like that her husband's death had only left her with her widow's portion. Estrid would have laughed at her caution, but there always had been something mean and greedy about Helm when he was a boy. And his eyes always shone when he spotted gold.

Mel firmed her mouth and pushed the thought away. She had to hope the gold remained well hidden in the trunks and that Helm would give up those trunks without a protest. The last thing she wanted was bloodshed or to be swindled out of her inheritance.

'As my husband died, I am a widow. How could I deny it?'

Helm narrowed his eyes. 'Why are you behaving in your usual headstrong fashion with no thought for the future?'

Mel tugged at the sleeves of her gown, an old habit from her childhood which she did whenever anyone confronted her. 'The present concerns me. The future will be faced when it comes. All the plans I made this time last year came to nothing because the sickness arrived. I am sick of weeping over futures which will never be.'

Helm drew himself up to his full height and gave a smug smile. 'You won't be able to return to my steading unless you return with me today. I am prepared to wait for you to say your goodbyes.'

Helm's words were a sham. Return with him and

break her promise to Katla? Helm knew she'd never do that. His words were a way of ensuring that she could not bring a claim against him for failing to provide shelter. Not that she'd ever do that. She understood he had an obligation towards her as she had sheltered him and his wife before they left for Islond. At that time, he clung to her hands and promised with tears in his eyes that he would always find a place at his hearth for her and her blood kin should it be required.

How quickly that promise was forgotten. But Mel decided to be the bigger person. She refused to stay where she was unwanted.

'I have not planned that far ahead, but I accept your decision. I release you from any obligation of blood.' Mel curled her fists and tried to hold on to her temper.

'If you starve to death, you will only have yourself to blame, Melkorka. Even in a backwater like Islond, few wish to take a chance on a widow of limited means and no family connections.'

She filled her lungs with air. Helm had not found the hidden gold. She was willing to wager on it. 'My future is a bright one, Helm. The gods will smile on me.'

Helm rolled his eyes. 'Just as well that I brought your trunks then along with the girl's.'

'Saves anyone going to fetch them.' She lifted her chin and kept her gaze firmly from Tylir even though every particle was aware of how closely he watched her. Had he guessed what might happen? Did he suspect her fears about her half-brother's honesty?

Helm casually snapped his fingers and pointed. The men began to unload the trunks. She counted the trunks as they were dropped on the foreshore. Her neck muscles eased. All the trunks were there, even the small iron-bound one which had belonged to her father.

'That's everything then.' She gestured towards the loch. 'Don't let me keep you.'

'I wager you'll regret this decision, *sister*. You know nothing of this man you seem hell-bent on hitching your wagon to.' He gave a half smile. 'I can't imagine why you're so impressed by him.'

Mel cleared her throat. 'Goodbye, Helm.'

'My men will take the trunks up to the longhouse,' Tylir said, capturing her elbow and pulling her close. His breath caressed her hair. 'You stay however long you desire. You have my word on that. I will never abandon a woman to that creature.'

Mel gave a tight smile and knew his gesture was for Helm's eyes, something to taunt him with rather than because he had any attraction for her. But even still a warm thrill went through her. 'Thank you.'

'My pleasure.'

His hand fell to his side, and she stepped away from him.

Helm saluted smartly. 'I wish you well with your choice, Melkorka.'

He and his men laughed at another quip of his which Mel failed to catch. Mel knew it had to have been coarse and about her looks.

A sort of tightness settled in her chest. And she pretended to take no notice of it. She knew her looks were past their best. Her husband claimed she had never recovered the few ones she had after her difficult pregnancy. His abandonment of her bed and preference for other women hadn't mattered so much when she had her son and a strong belief in her power to heal with herbs. Now, she was determined to forge her own life and to create somewhere where people felt valued for who they were.

Once the trunks were unloaded, the boat pulled away from the shore with Helm's men rowing frantically.

'I doubt they could row any faster if a frost giant chased them,' she said with a light laugh and waited for the others to join in.

Nobody said anything. Tylir and his men simply looked at her and the trunks with bemused expressions.

Mel's heart sank. The world suddenly seemed to be a much lonelier place with that ship fast disappearing on the horizon. Even if she did not particularly like Helm, he remained blood kin.

'My life has taken a different turn from what I expected this morning.'

'I'm grateful you decided to stay despite everything,' Tylir said with a wry smile.

'I gave Katla my word. Without holding fast to that, what do I become?' She gave a small shrug. 'My half-brother knew which choice I'd make before he made the ultimatum. He wanted to make a point.'

He raised a brow. 'Fork-Beard seized the chance to get rid of you.'

Mel examined her hands. He didn't need to know everything about her and her fraught relationship with Helm. 'I rather like that name for him—Fork-Beard. His beard does have two points now that I think on it.'

'Forked-tongue more like,' one of the men called out.

'Keep it civil, boys.' Tylir put a hand on her upper

arm. 'This lady will be staying with us for some time to come. And you are under my protection for as long as it is required. Remember that. No matter whatever anyone else says.'

'I'm no…' The words died in Mel's throat. He was making a point for his men. 'I'm grateful.'

'Why did you really come here, Melkorka?'

'I needed to fulfil my promise to Estrid. My half-brother had made certain promises before he left Viken which led me to believe there would always be a place for me at his hearth.'

It was a half explanation, but it would serve. She was here now, hoping for a fresh start, and not looking back to what might have been if she had managed to cure the village from the sickness like she had thought she would when her husband first fell ill. She'd been overly proud. And she refused to believe Estrid's husband when he confided his belief that there were some things which no healer could ever cure.

'I find Fork-Beard's promises to be easily made and easily broken.'

'I wondered if time had made me remember things differently,' she added. 'Helm lived down to my expectations.'

His soft laugh filled her ears. She suspected he was trying to be agreeable, but she almost liked him better when he was being grumpy. Yet his eyes did have a pleasant twinkle to them. 'Did he?'

'Worse than I thought.' She nodded towards the trunks and attempted to take control of her wayward thoughts. 'Katla will be awake soon. If she wakes alone, she will panic. Can I leave them with you?'

'The trunks will be brought up without delay. My new daughter's comfort is most important.' Tylir waved a hand, dismissing her.

Tylir watched Melkorka sprint off. Her gown lifted slightly to reveal a slender ankle. Her long legs were far shapelier than he'd first considered.

He gave a wry smile. Everything about the woman was more than he'd first considered. He had not expected her to stand up so forcibly to Fork-Beard. She was not the stuck-up little mouse he'd first thought, but a grown woman who was willing to fight for what she believed in. She had a fire in her belly, as his mother used to say.

Stargazer whistled next to him. 'Quite the unexpected bundle of fire and passion. I wonder why no one mentioned that in the whispers I heard about the woman.'

'What are you talking about, Stargazer?'

'I'd heard that she was awkward and ill-favoured, but someone lied.' Stargazer kissed his fingers. 'That woman is all passion underneath a touch-me-not exterior.'

'The woman is my daughter's guardian while she resides with me and will be treated with respect.'

Stargazer clapped him on the back. 'How long do you intend for the current situation to continue?'

'For as long as my daughter wants it, Stargazer.'

His friend burst into raucous laughter. 'We speak of two different things, old friend. A woman like that is going to be snapped up. Did you see how her dress swayed when she walked?'

He made the shape of Melkorka's bottom with his hands.

'Melkorka is a respectable widow,' Tylir said quickly, far too quickly.

A white-hot anger surged through him at the thought of any wandering hands near Melkorka, particularly ones like Stargazer's during any feast. He'd given his word that she'd be safe and that included being safe from his men and any stranger who happened to appear, panting for a woman to warm his bed and clean his hearth.

'This is Islond. Men require women to keep them warm at night, and many are not too choosy. She will be taken from under your nose.' Stargazer gave a dirty laugh. 'Not all men are like you, Sunbear. Keeping such urges buried with their dead wives. A pleasant enough woman your late wife, but she is with the gods now. Time to move on. That curse of yours is well and truly at an end. You have blood kin after all.'

Fresh anger rushed through Tylir. The Stargazer's reputation for seducing women was common gossip. Some even whispered his seduction technique was why he had so much access to titbits of gossip.

'Melkorka will be treated with the same due care and reverence like you would treat my daughter.'

The Stargazer adopted an I-am-innocent pose with his hands stretched out. 'Did I say anything different? I merely remarked on a fact, Ty. The lady Melkorka has a great many physical attributes. Shall I work on finding your daughter a proper nurse?'

'I hate the name Ty. Always have done.' Tylir gestured to the pile of netting on the shore. 'Did you fix those fishing nets like I requested two days ago?'

Stargazer laughed. 'I see you, Tylir Tjorson. Don't say I never warned you.'

Chapter Five

When Mel returned to a fast asleep Katla with her thumb in her mouth, she stopped abruptly, and her lungs struggled to fill with air.

She had severed all ties with her half-brother and thrown her lot with a former berserker, one whose exploits skalds sang about. Something she'd thought she'd never do when she was back in the North hit Mel straight in her stomach.

Not that there was any remote chance of anything happening between them like that soothsayer had once claimed—one day you will meet a berserker who will alter your life for ever.

She had laughed it off at the time because she knew soothsayers said enough to be mysterious and to claim to have foretold the future accurately. The woman who helped her to learn more about herbs and the way they worked explained it to her when she first took Mel under her wing. But what if that had been accurate?

Mel kept her mind resolutely away from the intermingling of their breath just before her brother's arrival and the warm pulses which had infused her. Or later when Tylir had his arm about her waist to tease Helm. Helm's scandalised expression as he glanced between her and Tylir had been a moment to treasure. It was almost as though Helm had considered that there might be something between them. Her and a man who could have his pick of women, if Estrid's stories were to be believed. As if he'd look at someone like her, even now with that ruined face of his and the limp. But by Freya, a very large part of her wanted him to.

She sat down next to Katla's slumbering form and started laughing until tears streamed down her face. Her laughter held a faint hysterical edge to it.

'What's wrong, Aunty Mel?' Katla tugged at Mel's sleeve.

Mel wiped away the tears with the edge of her sleeve and tried to think sobering thoughts. If she didn't start believing the innuendos or any light flirtation he indulged in, no harm would come of her being slightly attracted to the jarl.

'Nothing, sweetling.' Mel pressed a kiss on Katla's damp hair. 'Uncle Helm brought our trunks. Wasn't that kind of him? We can now get changed out of our best clothes.'

Katla opened her eyes wide. 'Did the boys come? Did they say anything about magic?'

'I suspect they stayed with their mother. They have a lot of chores to do. You will see them one day. We can ask your father about it.'

Katla scrunched up her nose. 'Tylir is not my father. My really real father is dead.'

Mel pressed her lips together. The words had slipped

from her tongue. Better for her to hear the words from her rather than from Tylir or whichever nurse he found.

Time to adjust was all Katla needed. Mel had to convince Tylir to give Katla that time and not to rush things and insist she call him father. Only she did not have any idea how to go about it. A problem for the future, not right now. Particularly as the trunks had arrived, courtesy of Tylir's men.

Katla watched the pile of trunks grow with round eyes. Mel waited until the men departed before she opened any of the lids.

'I think we should look at my trunks and see how they survived the sea voyage,' she said in a bright voice. 'I wonder if that necklace Elkr gave me last Jul is still at the bottom of my third trunk. Do you remember helping me pack it?'

Katla's eyes swam with unshed tears. 'Your trunks are here as well?'

'I do need to be able to change my clothes if I am to stay with you.'

Katla threw her arms about Mel and hugged her tight. Mel savoured the little-girl scent.

She raised Katla's chin and saw fresh tears tracking down her cheeks. 'Hey, what's all this? Tears?'

'Happy tears. I'm like my mother.' Katla smiled. 'It means you are going to stay and be my...my companion for ever. How wonderful is that, Aunty Mel? Magic can work provided you make the proper payment.'

Mel patted Katla's back and put Katla from her. When the time came to leave, she knew she'd leave more than a piece of her heart behind. But leave she would; she'd made a vow to keep her independence no matter what on the day her unlamented husband breathed his last. 'Your friend who lives in her own house. First, we must find you a proper nurse, someone to look after you and to keep you from mischief.'

Katla frowned. 'I don't want a proper nurse. I want you. That isn't how the magic was supposed to work.'

'What magic are you talking about, Katla? What isn't working like you thought it would?'

Katla put her hands on her chin. 'You promised my mother you'd look after me. And my new... Tylir, he isn't married, and I thought...the magic could work that way, couldn't it?'

'Let's open your trunk,' Mel said in a bright voice. She had no idea what this magic was that Katla kept referring to. She hoped it was nothing that her nephews had put her up to. Back in Viken, they had once tried to lead her son astray when he was barely eighteen months old. She'd given Elkr a lecture about always telling a grown-up before doing anything rash like climbing up to the roof of the longhouse. 'Do you remember the treasures we packed away in Viken? Shall we name each one as they come out?'

She quickly worked the lock and threw open the top.

Her heart sank. It was obvious that the clothes had been rifled through. The few gold coins in a leather pouch which she'd placed under Katla's best dress had vanished. She was certain the only other person who knew the secret of the complicated lock was Helm. Proving it was another matter entirely.

She hurriedly opened the other trunks and found the same had happened to them. Worse, her mother's gold torc was gone.

Luckily though, no one had touched the gold she secreted in the false bottoms. She still had enough to buy a sizeable farm. She had her independence gold, her inheritance from her son. She wished he was there instead of the gold, but she vowed that she would create a place where people could feel safe, just as Elkr had wanted to do one day. And Katla's inheritance from her father remained at the bottom of her trunk.

'Something wrong, Aunty Mel?' Katla came to stand beside her. 'You are staring at the trunks with such big eyes.'

She slammed the trunks shut and scrubbed the back of her eyes with her hand. 'Nothing, sweetling, just my half-brother living down to my expectations more than usual.'

'Is everything how it should be, my lady?'

Tylir stood in the entranceway, his broad shoulders nearly blocking out the light. Shoulders a woman could lean on and which would support her. A quick jolt of heat went through her. She pushed it away. She leaned on no one ever again.

Mel forced her lips upwards. 'I never expected my half-brother to forbid his hearth to me. Today is a day of surprises.'

He shrugged. 'I understand. But you are welcome here. How long you stay is up to you and my daughter.'

Katla leaped off the bed and clasped her arms. 'Oh, thank you. The magic does work better than I hoped it would.'

Mel and Tylir exchanged puzzled glances.

'What do you mean by that, sweetling?'

'Aunty Mel needs to stay here for ever. Please say she

can. She needs somewhere to live. Her husband and son died. She has no one in the world 'cept me. Everyone in the village turned their back on her, even though she saved lives. Maybe she will save your life as well with her herbs and potions. Or at least make you limp less.'

'Katla.' Mel fixed the little girl with a hard stare. 'Little need to tell Tylir my life story. And it is rude to mention someone's infirmity.'

The last thing she required was gossip about how the putrid throat arrived in her old village with her late husband and why she hadn't become ill. She had done, but she had not had it as badly as everyone else. She had considered it the tonic she took, but the tonic had not really worked for the others. And she had paid such a price. Her son dying, gasping for air. Her best friend dying. Everyone she loved gone in a matter of weeks and all because her husband had returned ill, expecting her to look after him. After Elkr's birth seven years before, her husband spent most of the time in Kaupang, or in the arms of other women, only returning if he was injured or ill.

A fine healer she'd turned out to be. She was through with making such claims. She had planned to turn her back on such things like tonics and potions.

'But you must stay, Aunty Mel. For ever.'

Tylir's face became carved from stone. 'How could I deny you something like that, little one? We have been without a healer for a long time. But I fear I will always limp.'

Katla twirled on one foot. 'Aunty Mel will have an idea on how to make it better. My mother said that my...

well…my other father only lived because of Aunty Mel's ointment.'

'Someone is getting above herself,' Mel said. For ever? No, only until she was certain Tylir could look after the child properly, then she would set up her own farm and live her life as she pleased. She'd lived too long under the thumb of someone. A small shiver went down her back as she remembered her late husband, who insisted on doing everything his way when he was around. He wanted a docile wife who never answered back or told him what he was doing was wrong even when it clearly was.

Her reputation as a healer had reflected on him, and she carved a little freedom that way. She had been re-lieved to bring up their son as she wanted with minimal interference from him.

His dying words, telling her that it was all her fault that the illness spread, echoed in her mind.

'Pay no attention to Katla's fantastical stories. My ability to heal is…well…less than ideal.'

Tylir laughed. 'My sister Katla was like that. Always brimming with ideas and stories. Always wanting to be the first to tell some good news.'

Katla's smile shone.

Mel pressed her lips together. Father and daughter did appear to be getting on. Hopefully it would be a start and she could leave sooner rather than later. Before her heart became too captured by something which never could be. It was a lesson she'd learned early—never to count on dreams, and instead to be aware of the slimy underside and how quickly one could lose everything.

The time to be aware of disaster was when everything was going smoothly.

'I stay until it comes time for me to leave. I wish to be clear on this. I want my own farm.'

Both faces fell.

Tylir recovered first. 'Of course, that is what I meant. Until you wish to leave.'

'But you are not going today, Aunty Mel? Or tomorrow or the next or...'

'I will let you know long before I leave, sweetling.' She looked over Katla to Tylir, who nodded. 'I gave you my promise to keep you safe.'

'Shall we do a tour of your new home, Katla?' Tylir said.

Katla rushed over and held Mel's hand. 'Only if Aunty Mel comes too.'

Tylir gave a slow smile, one which warmed Mel straight down to her toes. 'Of course.'

It bothered her that he knew precisely what he was doing. Flirtation because the man was a natural-born flirt with women. She tried to remind herself of the explanation Estrid had given on her deathbed as to why she had chosen a far steadier and gentler man as her husband and father for her unborn child than this famed berserker. But when he smiled at her in that way, she found it difficult to think straight.

The tour of his home farm proceeded far more smoothly than Tylir had anticipated. His new-found daughter seemed to delight in the horses and asked to stay and watch them being exercised. To his surprise, Melkorka readily agreed.

He'd been tempted to correct Katla once or twice about calling him Tylir or Jarl Sunbear instead of Father, but Melkorka put her finger to her lips as if warning him not to mention it.

He had to remember Katla was a little girl and had no idea until recently that he was her father. But having discovered he was her father, he wanted to be that father in truth. He had longed for a child for so long and had thought the rumours of a curse were true when his wife failed to fall pregnant after miscarrying twice and then having a stillborn son, a child brought forth well before his time.

'My men will look after her.'

He led Mel down towards the bathing hut. The sun remained high in the sky, but the days were already rapidly drawing in. 'We need to speak about what happened at the jetty.'

Melkorka's brow knit. 'My half-brother can be impetuous, but he rarely stays angry for long. He will come around in time. He will not forbid me his hearth for ever. And Katla will settle.'

'We might be speaking of different people. I have found your brother to be petty and inclined to bear grudges.'

She waved an airy hand. 'I have a lifetime of dealing with him. I thank you for your kindness and ask for your patience while I sort this mess out.'

Kind? Him? Sometimes he felt he had no kindness left within his body. It had been wrung out of him years ago when he discovered his family dead of starvation while he had feasted and laughed with his new jarl. More leached out when Estrid refused to wait for him, saying she wanted more than ambition. The final drop went when he found his wife's body and had known the rumours which swirled about were true—she had dalliances which went beyond flirtations designed to make him jealous.

Rather than confessing, he opted for a less-revealing truth. 'Estrid put you in this position.'

'Estrid? She became one of my best friends. I was happy to do this after her many kindnesses.' Her tongue wet her lips, again turning them the precise colour of cloudberries. He wondered if they tasted as sweet as the berries he remembered from his youth. He forced his glance upwards. He'd simply been far too long without a warm body. A natural reaction of any man to a beautiful woman. And Melkorka was beautiful.

He'd been wrong when they first met. Melkorka possessed an inner luminous quality to her skin, fire in her eyes and an unstudied sensual grace to her movements. He silently cursed Stargazer. Perhaps Stargazer was correct in more ways than one—he'd been too long without the warm embrace of a woman, but all desire for coupling had vanished after he discovered Ingebord's naked body in that pool. Vanished until he encountered Melkorka.

'You serve as my daughter's protector when many would have refused,' he said, trying to drag his mind away from the length of her neck.

'Protector?' She gave a small laugh and her mobile mouth twisted upwards. 'Some protector. I can't swing a sword. And I certainly can't save anyone from the sickness despite what Katla claimed. My son died, Tylir.'

'You managed to get her here across an ocean. I

handle the sword-swinging duties from here on out, but she requires something more…' He allowed his voice to trail.

'I won't leave until I have found a suitable woman to look after her. It may take some time. I mean to be picky.' Her brave smile faltered. 'Nevertheless, I have no wish to become an imposition.'

He raised a brow. 'I, too, keep my word. My intention is to offer my protection for as long as necessary.'

'Your protection.' Her hand plucked at her skirt, twisting the fabric beneath her slender fingers. An irrational hatred against all who had hurt her swept over him. 'I can say hope I never need it. I pride myself on being self-reliant.' She nodded towards where Katla had disappeared. 'Your daughter will require me soon.'

He put his hand on her elbow. 'Something upset you with those trunks. I wanted to ask you privately about it, rather than upsetting Katla. Confide in me, Melkorka. What is missing from the trunks? Will it make my daughter upset when she learns?'

'Upset Katla?'

'Yes, my daughter.'

The air rushed from Mel's lungs. Her mind had leaped in the wrong direction again. Protection because she was looking after Katla, not protection because he wanted to make her his concubine. Her cheeks burned as if she had been sitting for too long in front of the fire. She hoped he would think that she was embarrassed about feeling upset rather than her mistake about his intentions. 'Why would you think that?'

He reached out and touched her flaming cheek. 'You appeared to have been crying.'

She took a step backwards. She barely knew this man, but her body thrummed from his touch. The last thing she wanted was to become a warm body in the night or to accidentally offer herself as a concubine. 'Tears of laughter at my half-brother's antics. No need to be concerned.'

'You now belong to my household. If your half-brother has dishonoured you, I will make representations at the General Assembly. We are a nation of laws here.'

'*Belong* is a strong word.'

'You are free to go when you wish. I simply want you to know that you have a place at my fire. A thank-you for what you have done.'

A place at his fire. Something inside Mel shrivelled. She was glad she had not leaned into that touch or offered up her lips for his mouth. She had done that sort of thing before, mistaking someone's kindness for desire, only to discover her mistake too late when he rejected her and chose another woman.

She had been certain he was going to make a marriage offer for her, boasting of it to her father, and had worn her best dress in anticipation. She still cringed from the cruel laughter of the man and his intended as they entered the feast and learned of her pronouncement. Later she learned Helm had set her up as a cruel joke.

The experience had led to her marriage as her father decided that she could not be trusted to behave properly.

'I will stay until Katla seems settled. Despite what my brother believes, I inherited gold from my late husband. I intend to buy a farm and run it properly.'

He lifted a brow. 'Would you like me to keep anything safe until you do leave?'

Mel gulped. 'I hadn't thought that far ahead,' she admitted.

'The offer is there, but no one from my household will touch your trunks without your permission.'

Mel gulped hard. He guessed that someone in her brother's household had removed certain items. The last thing she wanted was for that to cause more strife.

'I have Katla's inheritance as well,' she said in a rush. 'I kept it hidden from my brother and his wife.'

His eyes narrowed. 'Did it arrive with the trunks?'

'Most of it.' Mel carefully shrugged. 'A small pouch of gold has gone missing from the trunk. It was there yesterday morning but now is gone.'

He seemed to grow several inches. She could understand why he'd been so feared as a warrior. 'You should have trusted me earlier. And I should have considered that she would be an heiress. Estrid had very little when I knew her but she always dreamed of being a great lady. One of the reasons why she married her husband—he already had land and men.'

Mel raised her chin. Estrid's rejection continued to bother him. He must have loved her a great deal. 'Estrid made a good life for herself. She and her husband wanted Katla to live comfortably.'

He turned his palms upwards in a gesture of submission. 'I did not claim Katla because she might have an inheritance, Melkorka. I've wealth enough from the sweat of my own brow and have no need to covet anyone else's.'

'Regardless, you may rest assured that I pay my way

and my debts. I will ensure Katla has her full inheritance.'

'Do you want to do anything about the missing gold?' he asked in a quieter tone. 'Do you wish to bring it before the General Assembly?'

She pinched the bridge of her nose. 'Helm will deny it. I would have to prove it was him. Or that it even existed in the first place.'

His scar throbbed on his temple and her words dried up. 'My daughter has no need of gold from anyone. It was not your fault, Melkorka.'

'It feels like it,' she whispered to the rushes. 'It shouldn't but it does.'

'Anything else?' He captured her chin and raised it so she was forced to look him in the eyes. A woman could drown in the deep pools of thawing blue. 'I can tell something else is missing.'

'He took my mother's torc, but she hated it as much as my father's wife coveted it. However, my father gave it to me when I married, part of my dowry. A sign perhaps that my father did care for me in his own fashion.'

She wet her lips and tried to think of something beyond the compassion she thought she glimpsed in his eyes. It was far too easy to mistake these things. Once she considered her late husband must be kind because he helped her to gather the herbs she needed for the ointment which eased her father's aches and had remarked on how nettles must sting her hands.

She held her body completely still and concentrated on breathing steadily. 'I left the torc on the top of my gowns. Hoping that if he did steal from the trunks he'd take that and not consider that there might be more.'

'And he did.'

She wrenched her chin away and wrapped her arms about her aching middle. Given the slightest encouragement, she'd lay her head on his chest. When would she learn that leaning on anyone for anything was wrong? Self-reliance was her goal.

'Yes. I'd hoped better of him. I gave him and his family shelter before they left for Islond. He promised me that he was going to change but he is the same old Helm.'

He made a cutting motion with his hand. 'I give you my word—no one will touch your gold from now on.'

'Thank you.' She held out her right hand. 'I believe you.'

He grasped it and raised it to his lips. The soft touch sent a warm pulse thrumming through her again. Her mouth ached as if he had kissed it. 'I'm grateful for the trust, Melkorka.'

The way he said *Melkorka* was nearly a caress. She tried to keep her mind focussed. There would never be anything between them. He gently tugged her hand as if to bring her closer to him. If she lifted her mouth the merest breath, their lips would meet.

She withdrew her hand. It took all her self-control not to curl fingers about the palm and hold the kiss in like her son used to do. 'I've no wish to give Katla any ideas. I want you to know that I've no intention of ever marrying again or indeed becoming involved with a man.'

His soft laugh ran down her spine. 'You are most unusual, Melkorka. Forthright.'

'Good. Tomorrow, Katla and I will take our meals with everyone else.'

'I will keep your words under consideration.'

Suddenly Katla rushed up with the pregnant spaniel waddling after her, chatting about the horses and how much her doll Freya wanted to learn to ride. The intimacy vanished like mist in the summer sun.

'Your charge has returned.' He turned on his heel and strode away.

It was only later when she was lying in bed with Katla curled into her side that she realised she kept turning Tylir's words over and over in her mind. She cradled the palm he kissed. She banged a fist into the pillow. The last thing she was going to do was to start panting after a man like Tylir.

'Face forward. Think about the longhouse you are going to build and the garden you are going to plant, rather than wishing for impossible things,' she whispered, but she suspected her dreams would include a pair of broad shoulders, strong arms and eyes in which she glimpsed a soul as tortured as her own.

Chapter Six

The longhouse lay wrapped in stillness when Mel and Katla went in for breakfast the next morning. Normally Mel liked to be up and doing things, as the morning was the best time of the day for getting things accomplished, but she had allowed Katla to sleep in after the restless night of dreams the young girl had had. Her own dreams had been full of faceless warriors chasing her until she found sanctuary in a strong pair of arms.

Estrid had sworn by portents and dreams as a means of figuring out what truly ailed a person, but Mel refused to consider what the dream might mean or if it indeed meant anything beyond the piece of hard cheese she'd consumed for supper. Things like ointments, tonics and elixirs cured people, not interpreting their dreams or other forms of magic.

'People will like me here, won't they?' Katla whispered, clinging to Mel's hand. Her other hand was wrapped tightly about Freya. Mel doubted if Katla had let go of the doll all night. 'I dreamed of frost giants last night. I needed to fight one to keep everyone safe.'

'You are a very brave girl, Katla. And anyway, frost giants would melt before they reached here.'

Katla's face shone up at her. 'With you here, I do not fear them. I know you would fight any monster that crossed your path.'

Mel's heart twisted. She learned the hard way that she couldn't fight monsters, not the real ones like disease. She'd tried and failed. And yet she wanted to keep this little girl from all harm. 'You are in your new home. Safe.'

Katla rolled her eyes. 'As long as you are here.'

Virin, the elderly woman who had tried to make trouble yesterday, appeared to be the sole occupant of the hall, and she was sitting down, fanning her face with one hand while the other drew patterns in the ash with a stick. A quick glance about the hall showed Mel at least a dozen jobs Virin could be doing instead of drawing with a stick in the ash. But Mel swallowed the pointed comment. It was far from her place to remark on such things. She was going to leave soon, and she did not need to make any enemies; she had enough of those as it was.

When Virin spied Katla and Mel, she put the stick down, gave a distinct sniff and muttered about late risers, charity and how things were different when her mistress was alive. Katla's face crumpled, and she clung tighter to Mel's hand.

Mel schooled her features. Obviously, a reason existed why Tylir tolerated such a person, but she refused to have Katla discomfited in the way she'd been. In her case, it had been her father's wife who had taken against her, but she was under no illusions that this woman could cause trouble.

'Doesn't your new home look lovely in the morning light, Katla? Breathe in and appreciate.'

Katla wrinkled her nose and gazed about the room, tapping her leather boot on rushes past their best. 'My mother would not like this place or its hospitality. Dirty and disgusting, she'd say.'

'The cheek of it.' Virin added a disgusted tut. 'In my day, elders were respected. You should curtsey when you come in. You will learn once that person leaves.'

Katla stuck her tongue out. Virin's furious look made Katla shrink closer to Mel. A distinct sliver of fear ran down Mel's back. Virin confidently expected to be named as Katla's nurse. Mel silently vowed to find a way to get Katla someone else.

'Katla states what she believes to be true. Her mother had very exacting standards and it is wonderful Katla seeks to uphold them,' Mel said in a firm voice. 'As the daughter of the house, she will have to be the mistress soon rather than later. Unless Tylir Tjorson acquires a new wife.'

'The jarl Sunbear will never take a new wife. He buried his heart with my late mistress, Ingebord.' Virin pointedly coughed. 'So many women have made fools of themselves over him, but he will not yield in his determination. He can't bear to say her name or to have anything changed in this hall.'

Mel fought against the urge to laugh. The foolish woman thought she had designs on Tylir and wanted to become mistress of this hall, a suggestion which was quite frankly absurd. She was through with all men, particularly those who might be husbands.

Mel plastered her best smile on. 'Isn't it lucky that I have no intention of remarrying either.'

'You're not planning on marrying again?' Virin's eyes bulged. 'How will you survive? A lone woman in a strange land?'

Mel schooled her features. The woman had already decided that Mel was one of those silly fluttering women who sought refuge in the arms of men as their only chance for survival.

'My most fervent wish is to see Katla properly settled into her new role as Tylir's daughter before I depart,' Mel said, pointedly altering the subject. 'Her mother schooled her well in the twin arts of hospitality and household management. There must be a way to tidy up this hall and make her feel more at home. A small-enough ask.'

Virin curled her lip and gave a distinct sniff as if tidying the hall was beneath her. 'Katla is awfully young and small. She seems a long way off from becoming the mistress of anything.'

'She is growing every day.'

Katla stood up on her tiptoes to make her seem as tall as possible. 'Yes, ever so much.'

Virin rolled her eyes. 'Sunbear needs careful managing as my lady Ingebord found to her cost. Many times, I discovered her weeping after his petty cruelties towards her.'

Mel frowned. Virin was supposed to be a trusted member of the household. She should not be gossiping in this way to a stranger about the man who gave her shelter. All she could think was that Virin exaggerated about Tylir for her own purposes.

She forced a smile. 'As I never met the woman, I am unable to comment.'

Virin sniffed. 'You and the little girl will need to learn about how he likes his hall kept and what happens to those who fail.'

Katla balled her fists and took a step closer. 'My mother taught me well, old woman. I won't fail.'

'You certainly have his temper. Someone needs to rein you in. Your new nurse will be the ideal person to achieve that miracle.' Virin smiled, a nearly toothless smile.

Mel bristled. Virin had wanted to make Katla lose her temper. She wanted to show that she was uncontrollable so that Tylir would be forced to find someone to keep her in check. Mel knew that game. Helm's mother had played it with her. Too spirited and needing taming, she complained over and over until her father finally gave in.

'Currently I stand as Katla's protector.' Mel stepped between the pair. 'Katla is a young girl who recently lost her mother in dreadful circumstances.'

Virin sniffed long and hard. 'Many people lose their mother.'

'My mother was special. She had standards.'

'Yes, she was.' Mel gave Katla's hand a squeeze. Estrid had been fastidious in tidiness and very strict about what Katla could and could not do. She clearly remembered Estrid's sighs when Katla went chasing after Mel's son with a wooden sword. Mel did not see the harm in the play, but it disturbed Estrid, who thought little girls should be learning how to spin and to keep house. And that they should certainly not play rough-and-tumble games with boys. 'But this is your father's house and your new home. They will do things differently here.'

Virin gave a distinct sniff. Mel resisted the temptation to ask if she had a cold.

'My mother would be in tears at the rotten rushes and how the fire is banked,' Katla whispered, tugging at Mel's skirt. 'Truly shocked and disappointed as she used to say.'

'Your mother had high expectations,' Mel murmured, putting a finger to Katla's lips. 'Best to hold your tongue until we know everyone better. Honey catches more flies than sour milk. Your mother wouldn't have wanted anyone to think you were made of sour milk.'

Katla nodded, tucking her chin into her neck. 'I want my *mor* to be proud of me wherever she is watching me from.'

Mel ruffled Katla's hair. 'Sweetling, she was, and she is. She knew this would be the best place for you. It is why she sent you here, where she expected you to be polite and not rude.'

Two bright pink spots appeared on Katla's cheeks, and she gave a solemn nod.

'I am sorry, old woman,' Katla said with a curtsey. 'I didn't mean to seem overly proud, but I must honour my mother's shade.'

Rather than making another cutting remark, a spark of mischief which Mel distrusted appeared in Virin's eye. 'That one has some spirit. I will remember for the next time. Perhaps look around the hall and see if anything else is amiss. You might want to inform your father that his hall, the hall which he so proudly built with his own hands, is only fit for pigs.'

Mel gave the woman a hard stare. Virin had tried to cause trouble yesterday when she proclaimed Mel a hostage and now she was up to something else. Virin hurried away, muttering that the weavers needed seeing to and that the leftover pottage was there for any straggler, Sunbear's standing orders.

'Katla, we should see about your food growing cold. Your stomach has started to rumble.'

Rather than sitting down and attacking her food like Mel expected, Katla marched around the room and ran her finger over the rough tables.

'Dust and dirt, Aunty Mel. Dust and dirt everywhere.' She sighed and put a hand to her heart, resembling her late mother. 'Lots to keep me busy, Aunty Mel. I doubt I will have time to ride or play games like I used to.'

'Wait until we have spoken with your father…with Tylir,' Mel said and made a mental note to speak to Tylir about finding out which of his women would be in charge of Katla. Virin was clearly unsuitable.

Katla gave a dramatic sigh and flopped down on a bench. 'Freya will be unhappy. Very unhappy. But I am not afraid of hard work.'

Katla's stomach rumbled. Again. Loudly.

Mel carefully schooled her face. Her son had always been fractious before he ate. 'We had best see to your food before we put the world to rights. It might prove to be a different place once your belly is full.'

Katla gave a solemn nod. 'All right then.'

Mel went over to the pot and procured two bowls of

the pottage from the pot which bubbled over the dying embers. Pottage was never her favourite food, and this one looked more than a bit lumpy, but it should be nourishing. 'Here you go, sweetling.'

Katla wrinkled her nose and pushed it away without trying it. 'Not hungry.'

'What did I say about being polite? Food is hard to come by.'

Katla pursed her lips up. 'Fit for the pigs, that is. My *mor* would never ever have served it.'

'We are in your father's house. Your new home.'

Katla tilted her chin in the air. 'My real father always gave me soft bread when I asked.' Katla drummed her heels against the bench. 'Always. I want it now. I want to go home, Aunty Mel. And I don't like those smelly dogs. They have no place inside a house.'

The dog began to howl. The door to the longhouse swung open with a loud bang and the dog went instantly and eerily quiet. The back of Mel's neck crept.

Without even glancing behind her, she knew who had arrived, who Virin had obviously scurried off to summon—Tylir. She held out her hand and Katla gripped it with fierce fingers.

Mel's heart sank and her mind flashed back to when she was a little older than Katla. Three baskets had fallen out of the storage hut and spilled precious grain on the ground after she witnessed a game of chase between Helm and a cat.

She explained the situation to a maidservant who ran off to find Helm's mother, who refused to believe a word against her darling boy and whipped Mel for telling lies about who spilled the grain. Her father had sided with Helm's mother and told that she was being difficult as it was obviously her fault—everyone said so. He did not listen to her protestations that the mess had had nothing to do with her. And everything to do with Helm chasing the cat. Ever after, it seemed he always took Helm's mother's side in a dispute, however wild her claims.

She pinched the bridge of her nose and tried to concentrate. Katla wasn't her as a little girl and Tylir, despite his gruffness, wasn't her capricious father.

'Katla, how good to see you awake and your lungs in good working order,' Tylir's voice rang out. 'How is your first breakfast in my hall?'

Instantly Katla stopped drumming her feet against the bench and watched him with big eyes. He quirked a brow upwards, making his scar appear even more fierce. Katla put her feet back on the ground and sat up straighter. She rapidly picked up her spoon and forced a mouthful down, gagged and forced another one.

'Katla, can you greet your father?'

'Busy eating,' came the mumbled reply.

'Then I shall have to do it for you.' Mel pasted a bright smile on her face. 'So wonderful to see you this morning, Jarl Tylir. Katla, as you can see, is busy with her breakfast.'

Her spoon dangling midway between her mouth and the trencher, Katla watched the exchange with big eyes.

A half smile tugged at Tylir's face. 'And you, Melkorka. I do see how busy Katla is with her breakfast.'

His bulk filled the doorway and then he strode forward, vitally alive, hair gleaming from a wash.

A warm pulse coursed through Mel as she remem-

bered how he'd featured in her dreams. She swallowed
hard and examined the knot in the tabletop, trying to
get her thoughts in order so she could protect Katla.
She refused to be attracted to this man. She was here
because she'd given her word to Katla and her mother.
A little voice in the back of her mind whispered, *Liar*.

'Katla is a growing girl. Her appetite is something
fierce.' Her voice rang falsely cheery to her ears.

He stopped and his gaze roamed over her from the
top of her couverchef past her nearly nonexistent curves
to the tips of her boots. He gave a slow smile as if he
knew she'd dithered over which gown to choose. 'And
Melkorka, looking positively refreshed from her night's
sleep. What more could I ask for—my daughter eating
and your conversation.'

Mel winced at his apparent mocking. She was not
about to become a panting female or to start dreaming
impossible dreams about handsome men developing a
sudden passion for her like her mother had once predicted. She knew about her lack of charms, while Tylir
could have the pick of his women.

'We are just having our breakfast,' she said more
sharply than she intended. 'It was kind to leave the pottage for us. The bed was so comfortable that we overslept. I can't remember when that last happened.'

'I can see—in peace and quiet. I thought it very good
earlier.' He nodded to Virin, who had sidled in after
Tylir. 'I had some kept back for you specially. Virin has
a wide experience of children and what they like and
thought it would be appropriate. Next time, though, you
can have meals with the household.'

Virin stood up taller and patted her hair. Mel pressed

her lips together. Her mind raced. She had to find a way to avert this looming disaster for Katla.

Katla pushed the lumpy pottage about with her spoon.

'I want soft bread,' she whispered in a fierce voice.

Mel stared directly at Tylir and willed him to understand. 'Children can be fractious before their bellies are filled.'

'Apparently the little girl fails to appreciate my special pottage.' Virin drew back her upper lip to reveal her gnarled teeth. 'I've never seen the like. Most children gobble it up. My late mistress swore...'

Tylir made a cutting motion with his hand. 'Understood.'

Katla's lower lip stuck out. She put her spoon down with a bang and crossed her arms.

'Children when I was their nurse ate what they were given or went hungry,' Virin continued. She gave Tylir a significant glance. 'Tylir knows what a good job I did with Ingebord.'

'My late wife was always very grateful to you,' Tylir said. 'It is why you will always have a place at my hearth.'

Virin gave a triumphant smile. 'You see...'

Mel made a mental note to find some bread and cheese for them both later. Virin obviously expected to be confirmed in the position or at least to have lots of input in Katla's rearing. She had to hope her instincts were wrong. 'Remember the hard tack, Katla, on board ship and how it hurt your mouth until you became used to it.'

Katla picked up a spoon and tried a bit more. 'Burnt.'

'Is it?' Tylir came over and peered at the bowl.

'See—black bits.' Katla gestured with her spoon. 'Freya thinks they taste awful. I agree.'

He tried a finger full and made a face. 'Katla, I believe you are right.'

He raised a brow at Virin. 'I asked you to ensure my daughter could be fed whenever she appeared.'

'Hardly my fault if she rises long after everyone else.'

'I take full responsibility,' Mel said. 'Please stop blaming the child, Virin, and blame the person who is looking after her.'

Virin gave a long sniff. 'I need to see about the spinning. The women gossip if someone does not keep an eye on them.'

She hurried out of the room. The muscles in Mel's neck relaxed.

'I don't like her,' Katla whispered, holding out her hand. 'She is always cross.'

Mel squeezed her hand. 'I will find a solution.'

'I will get you some cheese and bread,' Tylir said. 'Accept my apologies. My late wife swore by Virin.'

Katla swung her feet in a pleased manner. 'Thank you, Tylir. I like soft bread.'

He left the room.

'Be sure you are grateful to your father, Katla,' Mel said. 'Any bread would be wonderful.'

Katla began to sob. 'He isn't… I want to go back. I want my mother.'

Mel gathered Katla to her chest and held her tight. The storm of tears was far greater than she'd seen before.

When Tylir returned with a large plate of cheese

and bread, Katla's tears had subsided to mere sniffles. She gave a watery smile when she spotted the mound of food.

'Plenty for the both of you.' He placed the platter down on the table in front of Mel. 'I've no intention of forcing my child to eat burnt pottage.'

Mel rose and took the platter from him. 'Thank you. Katla needs to be gently led rather than browbeaten into submission.'

'Katla is stubborn like my sister used to be,' Tylir said in a fond voice. 'Ran rings around my mother for the most part. She needs to keep her spirit, not have it broken.'

A bubble of hope filled her. Perhaps all wasn't lost. For Katla's sake and for the sake of the little girl Mel had once been, the one who'd longed for someone, anyone to stand up for her.

Mel leaned forward so that her face was close to Tylir's and whispered, 'Thank you for thinking of Katla.'

His breath intermingled with hers. And the blue in his eyes deepened to a summer's sky.

'I brought enough for you as well. Should I have asked first?' The corners of his eyes crinkled, and he turned towards his daughter. 'Where are my manners today, Katla?'

She wet her parched lips. She was intensely aware of Katla watching them with intent eyes.

'I'm very grateful you thought of me.' The words came out far too quickly and breathlessly for her liking. She took a deep breath and was aware that her breasts nearly skimmed his chest. She put her hand over her mouth and leaned backwards. 'That came out all wrong. I don't expect you to think of me at all.'

'Melkorka.' Tylir reached out and captured a lock of her hair, before brushing it back from her forehead. 'I must apologise.'

Mel all but collapsed on the bench. 'You do?'

'I thought Virin would do for Katla's nurse to enable you to start your new life, but I see now it will be impossible.' He paused and gathered her hand in his giant one. 'Forgive me. You will have to remain in charge of Katla for a while longer.'

Mel tugged and he instantly let go. Her entire body thrummed from the brief contact.

'Nothing to forgive. I value my promise to Katla and her mother too much to put my desire for a new home before ensuring her happiness.' Mel carefully shrugged while her heart hammered.

There were so many reasons why she ought to leave immediately, starting with becoming too close to Katla and ending with her growing attraction towards Tylir, but she'd given her word. When was she going to learn that men were not interested in her, not in that way?

Mel nodded to Katla to begin eating the bread and cheese she put before her, rather than keep staring. Katla rapidly took a bite of the bread and made delighted noises.

'While I remain under this roof, I want to be able to look after Katla how I see best and not have to suffer from undo interference.' She crossed her arms and waited.

He drummed his fingers on the table. 'Do you mean

I am to have no say in the raising of my daughter while you are here?'

'I mean other women, in particular Virin. I want your word that I am in charge. If my approach differs from yours, we have a discussion without little girls listening.'

Katla's eyes moved quickly from her to Tylir and back again as she stuffed her mouth full of cheese.

He seemed to assess her under his eyelids. 'A nightly discussion?'

Mel hugged her arms about her waist. 'If necessary...'

'A nightly discussion it is. I wish to learn how to be the right sort of parent.' Tylir's blue eyes seemed to drill down to that hidden place in her soul.

Mel felt her face burn. Could he be flirting with her again? Impossible. 'Only if necessary. I presume you are a quick learner.'

'I intend to be the most intent pupil.'

Mel wet her suddenly dry lips. Definitely flirting. Why? What did he require?

'Any nurse must be suitable to me.' Katla wiped the back of her hand across her mouth. Only a few crumbs from the bread and cheese remained. 'I'm the one who is most important here.'

Tylir's eyes danced. 'Out of the mouths of babes. I defer to...my...' Katla frowned and pushed her trencher away. 'To Katla.'

Mel glanced between the two. They wore identical conspiratorial smiles. That had to be a good thing that father and daughter were getting on. 'Did I say differently?'

'We have ruled one person out. Progress.' Tylir made a sweeping gesture with his hand. 'Virin may go back to her well-deserved retirement and her great love of weaving.' He gave a half shrug. 'She enjoys a certain reputation in the weaving shed. I suspect some of the women will not be overly pleased that she has returned. Several of them had suggested her for Katla. I felt I had a duty to try.'

Mel felt vaguely sorry for Virin and the women she bothered. It sounded like a difficult situation for all concerned, but the solution was not Katla. 'I've no doubt that she was an excellent nurse to your late wife but that was a long time ago.'

'What do you have planned for today, Katla?' Tylir asked, clearly moving the subject away from nurses. 'Making mud pies? Drawing in the ash? Seeing if my spaniel, Sif, has finally had her puppies? I bet you would like a puppy of your own.'

'I'm not supposed to get dirty. Puppies aren't for little girls.' Katla wiped her mouth fastidiously.

Tylir's laugh boomed out. 'Who says that about you getting dirty? Children attract dirt.'

Katla screwed up her face and gave a long sigh, a perfect imitation of her mother. Mel's heart constricted when she saw it. 'My mother used to. I bet that sour old woman would say so as well. How girls are supposed to behave—spinning, weaving and sewing. Boys get to train dogs to hunt, not girls.'

'Every child I've ever met likes to get dirty, jump in puddles and make mud pies. Part of being a child. And my sister Katla taught her dog to do lots of tricks.'

Katla's eyes widened. 'She did? What sort of tricks?'

Tylir banged his fist on the table. 'To follow her, to fetch and carry her spindle and to walk on her hind legs. Spaniels are very clever dogs.'

Katla scuffed her feet on the rushes. 'I've never met a spaniel before. Maybe I could peep at the puppies once they arrive.'

Mel put an arm about the girl. From what she could remember, Estrid had disliked dogs intensely.

'I last saw Sif in the stables, making a nest in some straw, a sure sign that her time is near.'

Katla's eyes lit up. 'Can I go see the puppies, Aunty Mel? Freya likes puppies. Very much. I promise not to touch them. Just to watch like a good girl.'

'Who is Freya?' Tylir asked, a confused expression appearing on his face.

'Her new doll.' Mel tapped the side of her nose. 'Katla and Freya have very similar tastes, I believe.'

'Yes, we tell each other everything.'

Tylir gave a huff of a laugh before clicking his fingers and telling one of his men to take Katla to see if the spaniel puppies had arrived. The man gave a wide grin and said he'd be delighted to.

'Stay and finish your food, Aunty Mel.' Katla waved an imperious hand. 'You two talk and get to know each other properly. I can find the pregnant dog with this man.'

She paused at the door and gave a pleased smile. 'It takes time for the magic to work, you see.'

A sudden suffocating hush descended after Katla left. An uncomfortable intimacy. Tylir appeared to be about to say several things but then thought better of it. Mel examined her bread and cheese. Talk and get to know each other. She had the uncomfortable feeling that Katla was trying to do some matchmaking. Estrid had taken great delight in indulging that sort of behaviour, claiming it was better to have a couple properly suited rather than leaving matters to random whims.

'Katla knows her mind and doesn't mean to cause offence,' she said to break the sudden silence.

'None has been taken,' Tylir said, stretching out his hands in front of him. His brow quirked upwards. 'What did my daughter mean about getting to know you?'

She inwardly cursed, one of the curses her father used to use. It had been too much to hope for that he would not notice Katla's artless words. Her plan was sweet but entirely self-interested.

'Katla didn't mean anything about us getting to know each other better,' she said quickly, far too quickly. Her cheeks flamed. 'She merely echoed the words her mother used to use. She is trying to be the good hostess like her mother was.'

She silently prayed to any god who might be listening that she told the truth.

'Ah, Estrid.' Tylir rubbed the back of his neck. 'She really did not like dirt or untidiness. Used to berate me for muddy boots, spending too much time on the practice field and always having a dog at my heels. But by Var was she beautiful. We were both young.'

Mel stood and started bustling about, anything to keep her hands busy, anything to prevent her from hearing a confession from Tylir about how much he'd cared for Estrid. Towards the end, Estrid had spoken about how much she regretted ending the relationship the way she had and how much she had loved the man. Mel had no wish to be both people's confidante. 'Katla is completely unlike me when I was that age. I liked to be quiet as a mouse and unnoticed. Saved on the beatings.'

'Beatings?'

'I failed to please Helm's mother after my own died. My father was…changeable. He preferred an easy life without young girls complaining they were unjustly treated.'

Tylir captured her wrist and gently prevented her hand from reaching the bowls. A great warmth radiated out from his gentle touch. His thumb rubbed the inside of her wrist. Once. Twice. Three times. 'Melkorka.'

Her mouth went dry. 'What?'

'Leave it. My servants will clean up.' His smile sent tingles coursing down her spine. 'You're safe here. Sanctuary until you create your own.'

'Safe?' Her mouth ached. She was anything but safe here. It would be easy to fall into his arms. One simple tug and she'd be there. She pulled her hand away. 'Do you think I am that concerned about safety?'

He watched her from under hooded eyes. 'Yes, I do.'

She was tempted to cradle her tingling hand to her but allowed it to fall to her side and concentrated on breathing steadily instead.

'Katla's safety is my only concern. I don't mind clearing the bowls. Things are best done straight away. Saves time.'

'You wish to save time. In everything?'

She licked her parched lips, certain he could hear her heart beat. 'Always seems to be the best policy.'

He watched her mouth for a long heartbeat. Her tongue flicked over her lips again. A slow smile tugged at his scar, making him heart-stoppingly handsome. A man to have erotic dreams about, Estrid called him on that final day, and Mel could understand why.

'I will remember that.'

'Good.' She chose to think they were speaking about the housekeeping, rather than flirting. Men did not flirt with her unless they wanted something. Not to do with her body but something else, a special potion or other favour. Tylir had no need of those from her. They weren't flirting. She dampened down the little protesting voice in the back of her brain. 'Katla idolised her mother. She wants to be the hostess Estrid was. You should have seen the feasts Estrid used to give. Legendary.'

She exhaled. She had safely moved the subject on. He frowned, glancing about the hall as if seeing its ruined and half-finished state for the first time.

'My late wife was one such as Estrid,' he said in a low voice. 'People used to flock to our hall. Fork-Beard and his wife were frequently guests as Ingebord wanted to be seen to be a good neighbour to people who had recently arrived on Islond. For my late wife, appearance was always more important than substance.'

Mel pressed her hands together. Whatever had happened between Helm and Tylir obviously had happened after his wife's untimely death. And perhaps he was not in love with Ingebord as much as Virin had implied. 'Give Katla a chance. She likes to be busy, and the hall does need a thorough clean.'

He ran a hand through his hair. 'I haven't had the heart to change the hall since my wife's death. That's my excuse anyway. Surely, Katla will understand.'

His eyes crinkled at the corners. It would be easy to

tumble into his gaze and convince herself that he was attracted to her. In the back of her mind, she heard her stepmother's condescending laugh—*Poor Mel, never fall for a man simply because he seems kind. That is my tip to you.* And this man was very much off limits what with one thing and another.

'A reasonable enough excuse but it does need a thorough clean as people from all around Islond will find an excuse to visit if only to look at your new-found daughter.'

'If you say so, O guarder of my daughter.'

She examined her hands. A smudge of dirt was on the knuckle. And she suspected there was one on her face as well. 'I must find Katla's whereabouts if I am her guardian. Children have a way of finding trouble.'

He waved a hand. 'I've lost track of how many people asked about her. They are very excited that I have a daughter.'

'And that this curse you were under is broken.'

'Curses are something other people believe in.'

'Indeed. I prefer to take responsibilities for my own mistakes, rather than blaming fate or some soothsayer's curse.'

'An interesting idea.' He took a step closer. 'Do you have any more words of wisdom for me?'

'Many, I'm sure. I figure I have more experience at being a parent than you do.' She dusted her skirts down. She refused to dwell on past mistakes. Time enough for that when she lay awake at night. Keeping her mind active helped to keep the shadows at bay. Her face had to be towards the future.

He lifted her chin. 'On that we can agree.'

She turned her face, hating that her breath caught in her throat. 'Can we?'

He stepped away and the cool air rushed between them. 'I need to go away for a few days. Problems on the top meadows. It is why I hoped Virin would be acceptable and you could teach her about Katla's little ways. We will sort out another nurse on my return.' He stopped and gave a smile which tugged at his scar. It was the sort of smile which she doubted he used often. 'And my parenting lessons.'

'Do I have your permission to clean this hall?'

He lifted a brow. 'If Katla insists on it, then it must be done. However, I suspect she will be far more interested in the ponies or following my spaniel about to see when she gives birth.'

'I will inform Katla.' She started for the door, wanting to put distance between her and this man. He made it far too easy to confess the troubles in her soul.

She had very nearly offered herself on a permanent basis, which was nonsense. She had plans of a farm of her own, a cosy house and people who respected her. The inheritance meant she would not be a servant in anyone's house ever again, and she refused to think about marriage. She had made a mess of her first one. The one shining part—her son, Elkr—had slipped from her fingers.

He put out a hand and caught her elbow. 'Tell her I say goodbye as well.'

She glanced at his fingers, and he instantly let her go. 'If you wish, I will do so but she might like to wish you a good journey.'

His eyes slid away from her. 'I've no wish to interrupt her and whatever mischief she might be up to. You tell her goodbye from me. There will be time enough to get to know my daughter when I return.'

Mel firmed her mouth. Why were men always the same? Her late husband had said the exact same words to her about Elkr more times than she'd liked to count. And each time, she had seen Elkr's little face fall when he learned that his beloved father had gone without saying goodbye. 'I see.'

'I trust that you do.'

He was a coward, and he knew it even before Melkorka turned on her heel and strode out of the halls with her skirts giving a disapproving swish.

Tylir stared at the half-carved post which helped to hold up the roof. Ingebord had berated him for not finishing it in time for the hall-warming feast she'd meticulously planned so that she could put up all the foils she'd carefully hoarded from everywhere she had feasted at the last possible moment. She had demanded that it be kept up like that as a testament to his many failings including the curse he'd visited on her, which had resulted in two miscarriages and the stillborn baby boy.

Keeping his gaze on that column returned his sanity. He had nearly kissed Melkorka. He'd nearly asked her to stay and look after Katla permanently. The woman wanted freedom and sanctuary, not an embittered former berserker.

As he picked up the handkerchief she dropped in her hurry to get away from him, Tylir told himself he wanted to keep Melkorka around for his daughter's sake. In the back of his mind, a little voice whispered,

Liar, you are going to find an excuse to keep her here because you want to see if her mouth tastes as sweet as it looks.

Chapter Seven

Mel discovered Katla sitting on a step outside the large barn, watching the bustling yard with a cross look on her face. In contrast to when they arrived, the place hummed with men going about their business, but she noticed the women seemed to confine their activity to the weaving sheds rather than ensuring the hall was tidy or attending to a thousand other jobs she'd expect to see happen on a well-run farm.

'Has the spaniel had her puppies?'

'Freya said we should wait for you.' Katla jumped up. 'We can go now and see them again. But they are very tiny and have their eyes tightly shut. Sort of boring, I guess.' She peered intently at Mel. 'My *mor* always said that a woman who has pink cheeks had a good conversation with a man. What did you and Tylir talk about?'

'We spoke about how he needs to attend the sheep in the top meadow and is going away for a few days. He told me to tell you goodbye. He will start being a proper father on his return.'

Katla tapped a finger against her mouth. 'That is no good. He needs to be here. My mother used to say—'

'Katla! I am here until you get a nurse and no longer. And I've no wish to marry anyone ever again. I want my own farm where I can bolt the door.'

'But—'

'The colour of my cheeks has nothing to do with Tylir.' Mel pressed her lips together. She had not meant to say that aloud. Katla had a little girl's notion about marriage. Little point in explaining why she refused to marry again. She knew how Estrid used to play at matchmaking every chance she had. 'Stop this match-making nonsense.'

'Me? I am too little.' Katla held Freya up to her ear. 'Freya agrees though. Tylir should be here at the hall instead of tending those fields. How can I get to know the man? How can I ensure that he will like me?' Her voice caught on the last word. She held out her hands. 'Why didn't he come to say goodbye? Is he angry about the pottage?'

'He asked me to tell you. It is very sudden.' The words tasted like ash in her mouth. 'No time.'

Katla gulped twice. 'I understand. Truly I do, Aunty Mel.'

Instantly a wave of remorse swept through Mel. The same sort of fear haunted her when she was a child. Not that Katla, with her blonde hair, and sunny smile, had any of the awkwardness Mel suffered with. No need for Katla to be practical and concentrate on healing or weaving unless she wanted to. Katla would be sought after when the time came.

'All in good time.' Mel patted Katla's hand. 'While he is gone, we can sort the hall out and show him how useful you can be in making that hall a true home.'

Katla scrubbed her eyes with the back of her hands. 'Can we see the tiny puppies before we start work? They're sweet, Aunty Mel, even if their eyes are shut.'

'I thought they bored you.'

'I was trying to be big and grown-up,' Katla said, tucking her chin into her neck. 'I remembered something important, Aunty Mel. Last year, my other father said I could have one when I was bigger, and I'm bigger now.'

Mel crouched down so her eyes were level with Katla's. 'We can see them on the way to get the clean rushes. Maybe you should get to know them and pick your favourite for when he returns.'

Katla instantly brightened. 'I think Tylir is very handsome. Do you?'

'It doesn't matter, but yes he is quite pleasant looking.'

Katla gave a catlike smile and hummed a little tune, the sort her mother used when she wanted to make people do things. 'I miss my mother and Elkr. Do you mind much if I speak about your son? I know sometimes you cry at night.'

'Everyone cries sometimes.'

'Not for your old husband, I don't think. My mother said he was a cold fish, but I thought he looked more like an angry walrus. Elkr agreed with me—his father had walrus moustaches and made walrus noises.'

Mel put her hand on Katla's back. She had not realised that Katla had overheard the sobs. The image of her late husband as an angry walrus made her smile. Her late husband with his long moustaches did have that sort of look about him now that she thought about it. 'You may be right about how he looked.'

'Maybe one day, I will get a new mother like my new father.' Katla glanced up and fluttered her lashes. 'Do you ever think you will get a new child, Aunty Mel?'

'Let's go find those puppies,' Mel said around the sudden lump in her throat. Explaining she didn't want a new child was beyond her. She wanted her old one and she could not have him. Her fault. Her mistake for believing she could find the right herbs to cure him. Nothing had worked.

'Puppies make a day better.'

'They certainly do, little one. They certainly do.'

'I can't make up my mind, Aunty Mel. Should I ask for the one with the spots or the little girl one with a black nose?'

'Shall we wait until their eyes open?'

'It might be best. May I hold one?'

'When they are older. Right now, they need their mother.'

'I need my mother, Aunty Mel. Not a father. Like they do.'

Tylir heard his daughter's voice wobble as he went to get his horse. The men he intended to take with him had already gathered in the yard and were mumbling about everything and nothing while they waited for his orders.

He stopped for a moment and allowed the sound to wash over him. His little girl. His blood. Who desperately wanted a mother instead of a father. He clenched his fists. Would it have been better for the child for him to deny her? The dull ache of wanting a family but knowing he didn't deserve one engulfed him.

A shaft of sunlight revealed the gold in Katla's hair

as well as the dark copper of Mel's. Their heads were bent together examining the newborn puppies. Katla laughed at something Melkorka said, her distress about not having a mother momentarily forgotten. He forced his fingers to relax. A great and unexpected longing to be part of the happy scene swept over him. He did belong to someone. He might not deserve this child, but he intended to be the best father he could be for her.

'I promise to be the best parent possible,' he whispered, absently rubbing his scar on his left thigh, the one which always seemed to pain him these days.

'Sunbear, here you are. I thought you had left. You do need to see the flooded fields for yourself. You gave your word.'

Tylir firmed his mouth. Stargazer was right—he had given his word. 'And I am not in the habit of breaking it without good cause.'

Stargazer gestured towards where Mel and Katla could be heard, speaking softly. 'Are they a good cause? Or an encumbrance which will blunt your sword?'

Tylir swung himself up on his horse and signalled to his men to move, rather than answering. His happiness would have to wait. Duty had to come first. He'd learned that lesson a long time ago when he discovered the bodies of his family. He had to hope Katla would be more understanding than his late wife was.

Mel readjusted her hold on the reeds and listened to Katla's chatter about the puppies. They were finally about to start clearing the hall after Katla spent a long time cooing over the tiny puppies and being unable to decide which one she wanted. Mel was determined to use this time to show Katla how much work was needed to create a hall which exuded friendliness.

Estrid's wall hangings and her own languished in the trunks and they needed to be aired if only for a little while to recover from the voyage. She clutched the reeds tighter. Katla might enjoy seeing them hung in the hall as a reminder of her home while she checked the tapestries for any damage. In this way, Katla would see that simply screwing up her nose and proclaiming a space dirty was not as effective as hard work.

'They told that two pretty things had arrived to beautify the place.' A tall man with a bushy moustache stepped in front of them and blocked their way.

'It would appear gossip has been flowing readily,' she said when the stranger appeared disinclined to move out of her way after a brief mumbled greeting.

The man bowed low. 'Grim Larson, also known as Stargazer on account of my love for heavenly bodies.'

'Are we supposed to know you?' Katla asked, tilting her chin in the air.

Stargazer gave a smarmy smile, the sort which said, *I'm indulging you because I think you might be useful to me.* He puffed out his chest. 'I am one of Tylir's best and oldest friends and you, young lady, are his new daughter. I wonder that he kept you under wraps for all these years. Never so much as a peep.'

Katla made a considering noise. 'Never heard of you.'

'Ah.' Stargazer's smile did not reach his eyes. Mel instinctively distrusted this man because there was something about him which she couldn't quite put her finger on. 'I am sure we will become great friends. Shall we go for a little stroll and leave the others to do the hard work?'

Katla shrank back against Mel. 'I need to help Aunty Mel.'

'What are you two up to this fine morning? No good? Or is it women's talk with the others in the weaving shed?'

Mel gritted her teeth. 'We are about to change the reeds in the longhouse. Katla noticed they could do with changing.'

A watchful wariness came into his eyes. 'And Sunbear agreed?'

'He gave his permission. Why not ask him if you don't believe me?' Mel fixed a smile on her face. It was fine wanting to keep things as they were, but certain standards had to be met. And wall hangings mouldering in trunks did not do anyone any good, and they would not be up for very long.

Stargazer held up his hands. 'Think out loud, that's all. Your aunty is going to work you hard, little one but don't worry I won't tell if you want to play later. Shall we put a little wager on you deciding to give up early and enjoy yourselves?'

He winked at Katla. Mel frowned. The man was the sort that she instinctively distrusted. He had the look of one who had supped regularly with Loki, the god of tricksters. Elkr had been such a man—showing one face to the public and another, very different one in private. Mel forced her face to be bland.

'We need to be going, Katla. The rushes must be attended to. Lots to do before Tylir returns.'

Stargazer's moustache quivered. 'Sunbear will be

gone for several days. I wonder he did not tell you. But he can be like that—careless of his family duties.'

Mel gritted her teeth and held back saying the words that she thought Tylir cared a great deal. She had seen how he brought Katla breakfast after the pottage was ruined. But she had the distinct impression Stargazer was trying to get a reaction from her and to gauge how much she knew about Tylir's plans. 'He told me all that I was required to do was my job. I am only here to look after Katla until a suitable nurse is found.'

'One day I'm going to be a great lady,' Katla declared, gesturing with her right hand in precise imitation of how her mother used to gesture. 'My house will be the finest for miles around. Just like my mother's was. To be the finest requires the elbow, my mother used to say.'

Stargazer tugged at Mel's sleeve. 'Does Sunbear know about the girl's ambition?' he asked in a low voice. 'He doesn't like to speak about the girl's mother. Always gets cross with me. I reckon he left a great deal of his heart behind.'

Mel's heart sank. She put a hand under Katla's elbow. 'Let's not get ahead of yourself, young lady. We have a hall which needs to be made presentable.'

'I'm going to show Tylir that I can be the lady of his house. When I do, then he will give me the present I want. The magic will work.'

Mel stifled a smile. Katla seemed determined to prove herself to Tylir. That was something. She tried to remember if Katla had ever talked much about magic before she arrived in Islond.

Stargazer's eyes danced. 'And what magic is that?'

Katla put her finger to her lips. 'Wait and see. The magic doesn't work if you know what is coming.'

A shiver went down Mel's spine. Katla was talking about matchmaking, had to be. She wanted to scream at Katla and tell her not to get her hopes up with something like that.

'I wait with bated breath and much anticipation to see your progress.' Stargazer touched his fingers to his brow. 'Ladies.'

Mel endured another top-to-toe scrutiny in silence before he strode away, whistling.

There was something about the way Stargazer looked at her which made her feel unclean, like she had been catapulted back to just before Elkr made the marriage offer. Sometimes she wondered if Helm's friend hadn't humiliated her, would she have accepted Elkr's offer? There again her father and Helm's mother had been in favour of the match as they doubted she could do any better. Too late to worry about that.

'Shall we get to work, Katla? Tylir might be gone for a few days, or he might get back early.'

Katla shifted her small bundle of rushes to her other hip. 'I don't like that Stargazer. He looked at you funny.'

Mel tightened her grip on the rushes. Hopefully Katla would have forgotten all about the incident by the time Tylir returned. The last thing she wanted to be accused of was seeking to make trouble. Her late husband had accused her of that when she was his bride and she'd objected to having her bottom pinched as she was trying to pour the ale. 'You are talking nonsense, Katla. I am a widow whose best days are behind her.'

Katla snorted. 'You are the same age as my mother.

I think you are very pretty. Jarl Tylir thinks so as well. His eyes follow you everywhere.' She cupped her hand to the side of her mouth. 'And I saw his shadow watching us when we examined the puppies. Honest truth.'

Mel nearly dropped the rushes. Tylir had been watching them? 'How do you know it was Tylir?'

Katla puffed out her chest. 'Freya told me. And he is going to be back early, early, early.'

'She just knows that as well?'

'She is clever like that.'

'Freya should keep her thoughts to herself.'

It was good to be back home. For the first time in a long time, Tylir found an excuse to return before the work of draining the field was completely done. The problem with the flooded fields had been quicker to sort than he first considered. He swore his men puffed themselves up with pride at the thought of being trusted to accomplish the job without supervision.

When he entered the yard, several people had made it their business to tell him that Melkorka had changed the rushes, given the hall a thorough clean and put wall hangings up. Tylir did not remember agreeing to wall hangings. Virin said it as if Melkorka was committing some great act of treachery, but others remarked how pleased they were at the development.

Tylir frowned. His hall. He should have known Melkorka would go beyond. Women always did. She had probably discovered the wall hanging that Ingebord wanted up—the ones which had gold thread and silver thread so they would shimmer in the torchlight.

He threw open the door with a huge force. The fresh

scent of a hay meadow wafted out, taking him back to his youth. A great longing swept over him. In that heartbeat, he wanted to be back on the farm, coming home to see his sisters and mother, knowing that there would be good food and ale to drink as well as a warm welcome. He screwed up his eyes and bade the feeling to go. That sort of welcome belonged in the past, to before he had ignored the message about them surviving the raid, to a time when he deserved some peace.

He stood and allowed his eyes to adjust, tensing his body in anticipation of seeing Ingebord's wall hangings again.

Wall hangings did adorn the walls but they didn't shimmer the way Ingebord promised. Worse, Katla and Melkorka were busy tacking foils to the unfinished pillar. Foils. And they were laughing about it.

A great fury surged through him.

'Who said that this could happen?' he roared. 'Who dared alter this hall?'

The entire hall fell silent immediately. The solitary sound which remained was a sharp cry which he knew had to have come from Katla. Instead of a merry face, his daughter now stared at him with big eyes and an open mouth. The fury flowed from him instantly but the ache inside him remained.

'Who dared do this?' he asked in a quieter voice. 'Were my words not clear? I like my hall as I like my hall.'

'I did it, Tylir,' Katla said in a loud voice, her fists balled. 'I was the one. This is my hall as well.'

'Katla? But why did you? Why were you allowed to?'

Melkorka stepped in front of Katla, her eyes blazing.

A Valkyrie defending her charge. 'You are back sooner than I expected.'

'My business did not take as long as expected. Who gave you permission to hang those up?'

'My wall hangings and Estrid's needed airing after the sea voyage. I thought it a good idea to hang them up and inspect them,' Melkorka said in a firm voice. 'I will take them down when they are dry. I see little reason why they should rot in trunks for weeks on end.'

Tylir stared again at the wall hangings. An uneasy prickle crept down his spine. He had not seen them before. 'Your wall hangings?'

'I assumed you did not have any and I wanted to show Katla what the hall could look like. I planned on taking them down after they were dry and I had repaired the various pulled threads.'

Tylir frowned. The wall hangings were in muted colours and far more practical than the ones Ingebord had commissioned, the ones which he had had packed away. They reminded him of the ones his mother had had. Practical and warm. 'They can stay for now.'

'Thank you.'

He narrowed his eyes. 'Where did you get the foils?'

'Katla thought the hall could do with some brightening up. Her late… Estrid's late husband had several made for her in tin so she could give them off if they visited anywhere.' Her lashes swept over her eyes. 'He did indulge Katla something shocking. My late husband used to say there was time enough for Elkr to earn the right to have his own foil.'

'They are beautiful and to have them up honours the guest,' Katla said in a low voice.

Tylir's heart squeezed. Honouring the guest. Out of the mouths of babes. 'But did they have to go on that particular pillar?'

'Katla thought the pillar looked sad. Is it no longer the fashion in Islond to honour your guests?'

Tylir's Adam's apple worked up and down, but no sound emerged. He swallowed hard and tried again. 'The pillar looked sad? Maybe it did. It remained unfinished to serve as a testament to the losses my late wife suffered. Two miscarriages and a stillborn son.'

'We can take them down,' Melkorka said in a quiet voice. 'I understand completely and apologise.'

'No, keep them up. The pillar looks better this way with Katla's foils on.'

'I don't mind sharing as you haven't had many people visit,' Katla said in a small voice. 'Just me and Melkorka by my reckoning. But you shouldn't mind as you will soon have guests. Freya told me it would happen because the hall smells so pleasant now.'

He stared at the little girl in astonishment. 'People have visited the hall.'

'Then why are the foils not up? Were they bad men? Why?'

'Because.' Tylir sighed. 'Because I said so.'

'Melkorka's idea,' Virin shouted in a shrill voice. 'I had nothing to do with it. The woman would not listen to reason. Ingebord—'

The other women murmured their agreement like twittering birds. He frowned at them. Melkorka was right—seawater rotted cloth very quickly unless proper precautions were made. And the wall hangings did make the hall seem cosier, more like a home rather than a banqueting hall fit for a king as Ingebord had wanted. Had he allowed too much to slide in the hopes of just forgetting what had happened and what he'd endured? How the hall looked now made him feel warm inside.

'Hush, Virin. My daughter and her attendant have done fine work here.'

'You like it? All of it?' Melkorka asked, plucking some straw out of her hair. His fingers itched to do the job for her.

He gave a genuine smile. 'I failed to realise how badly the rushes needed changing. The air smells far fresher. And I had not realised how cold the room could be.'

'And the wall hangings?' Katla asked even though Melkorka motioned for her to be silent. 'Aunty Mel's were ever so wet when we took them out of the trunk.'

'They are fine, but I have some others which can go up when yours are dry.' He forced a smile. 'You will need yours at your new hall in due course, Melkorka. I should not like to impose.'

Melkorka rewarded him with the briefest of nods. 'I agree.'

Katla stood up a little taller. 'Then you are not angry with Aunty Mel and me?'

He hunkered down so that his face was level with his daughter's. 'How can I be? You live here now. Your foils are precisely what that pillar needs.'

Katla nodded to where the women stood like carved figurines.

'They said you would be and that you'd throw us to the frost giant you keep—' She stopped and put a finger to her lips. 'I wasn't supposed to say anything, was I, Aunty Mel?'

'It is all right, sweetling,' Melkorka said. 'I told you that Tylir—'

'Her father,' Tylir said through clenched teeth. He knew what he was. The child would have to accept it. Eventually. 'I'm Katla's father. She is the daughter of this house. I won't have anyone saying differently. And I've no idea where this nonsense about a frost giant started, but I've never had any dealings with such creatures, despite what the sagas say.'

Melkorka's lips turned up into a faintly triumphant smile. He had tumbled into the trap. Or rather allowed her to make a point. 'You see, Katla, why I said you mustn't listen to the gossips. You *are* the daughter of the house. Your father has said so. And he doesn't know any frost giants.'

'Not any?' Katla seemed vaguely disappointed.

'They only exist in the tales told to frighten on a winter's night. Some people enjoy frightening others.' Melkorka's voice was light, but her eyes conveyed a serious message.

'I think it is the mark of a coward to try and frighten little girls,' Tylir said fiercely.

'Glad to hear it,' Melkorka said. 'Something we agree on.'

'Must I call him Father?' Katla asked in a loud whisper.

'Tylir is fine for now from Katla but in time, I hope to earn the title Father,' he said, watching the pair from under his lashes.

Melkorka gave him one of her looks which made him feel like he was a better person than he was. It bothered him that he wanted to be the person she thought he was when he knew of all the mistakes he made.

He watched her mouth and wondered idly what her lips might taste like, but he also knew that he shouldn't think such thoughts. Melkorka was his daughter's guardian, not his potential bed mate.

'We will see where the fatherhood takes us.' He gave a careful shrug and pushed all thoughts of kissing Melkorka to one side. 'I've no idea if I will be any good at it. But no one in this household should doubt that I claim Katla as my daughter and will raise her as such.'

Melkorka smoothed her apron down, accidentally highlighting the curve of her breasts. Tylir forced his gaze upwards.

'We need to get cleaned up, Katla. There should be time before the evening meal.'

Katla put her hand over her mouth. 'I nearly forgot. I have a special welcome-back present.'

Katla raced off before he could hold her back and tell her that it was not necessary. He lifted a brow. 'A welcome-back present as well? You've been busy.'

'A little something that Katla discovered in her trunk. Please accept it in the spirit given.'

'You intrigue me.'

Katla rapidly returned with a small stone jar. 'I found this. My mother swore it helped…it helped…'

'It helped her husband's bad leg,' Melkorka finished for her. 'An ointment I used to make. Katla thought it might help.'

He opened his mouth to say that nothing would help with the limp or the dull ache, but a look from Melkorka made him swallow the remark. 'Worth a try.'

Katla's eyes glowed. 'Really?'

'I'm honoured.' Tylir reached down and took Katla's hand. He was surprised at how soft and warm it was in his and how small. He knew the gift would probably not work, but the very idea of it made him feel like someone actually was concerned about his welfare for the first time in a long time. 'Take your time getting changed. Supper will wait until you are ready.'

'Will it be something good?' Katla whispered.

Tylir exchanged a look with Melkorka. If he wasn't careful the little girl would twist him around her little finger and while he wouldn't mind, he'd seen the result with his late wife, a woman who was incapable of doing anything constructive. 'Something nourishing. I always find solid food helps after working hard.'

'I did work hard, didn't I?' A mischievous spark appeared in Katla's eye. 'Aunty Mel did most of it. The others watched and gossiped behind their hands. I don't want any of them to look after me.'

Melkorka pressed her lips together. 'The search for a nurse may take time, Katla, but we will find someone suitable.'

Katla's bottom lip trembled. 'But Tylir said that I could have a say and I am having my say. You worked hard, Mel, and the others didn't. I want a nurse who isn't afraid of hard work.'

Tylir struggled to keep a straight face. Katla had obviously decided that Melkorka should be her nurse.

'I've no doubt Melkorka did. She should wash as well.'

Katla cupped her hand about her mouth. 'Aunty Mel prefers Mel. Someone mean used to call her Melkorka when she was little.'

'Katla!'

Tylir lifted his brow. His daughter was quite blatant in her attempts to get Melkorka as her permanent nurse. It was a pity that Melkorka was independently wealthy and couldn't be enticed, but that was life. He bowed slightly. 'Mel it is. Katla has spoken.'

She tilted her head to one side, revealing a shadowy place at the base of her neck. He wondered why he'd been blind that first time he saw her—she wasn't awkward or overly proud or not worth a second look. Something fascinating about her, particularly now that she had a spot of dust on her nose and forehead, existed, and he had to keep examining her in hopes of discovering precisely what it was. But he suspected it had something to do with the goodness of her character.

Mel broke the eye contact first. 'Wash time, Katla. Now.'

She turned on her heel and strode away. Tylir let her go.

The world seemed a new place after the bath in Tylir's well-appointed bathing hut. Mel had forgotten precisely how hard and dirty changing the rushes was.

'Can I see the puppies? They were asleep the last time,' Katla asked as they walked back towards the longhouse.

'Later. We mustn't keep hungry people waiting.'

'Maybe you can think about which one you'd like,' Tylir said from where he leaned against a wall. He had also changed and his hair glistened with droplets of water.

Mel swallowed hard and tried not to think about him bathing in the loch. 'It is kind of you to wait for us.'

His gaze travelled the length of her. She felt absurdly pleased she had changed into the dark green gown at Katla's request.

'My pleasure. I wanted to thank you for the ointment. It does make my leg feel better. Perhaps Katla will choose a puppy as her present in return.'

Katla's eyes shone, but the joy quickly became masked. 'My *mor* didn't think a puppy would be right. She told me before she died—little girls should not be playing in the dirt with puppies.'

Tylir's face became remote.

'She doesn't mean to be disrespectful,' Mel said. 'She simply says what is on her mind.'

'Why is everyone so worried about my temper?'

She stopped and blinked. 'Berserkers have a certain reputation for being unpredictable.'

'I know the difference between war and my home.' Tylir rolled his eyes. 'Has someone been telling tales about me?'

Mel gave a wry smile. 'When Virin saw us putting up foils in the hall, I swear she was positively salivating at the thought of you losing your temper.' She forced a half smile. 'For a heartbeat, I thought you'd throw me out with the hangings following after, but then... all was fine.'

The blue in his eyes deepened to a summer's sea. 'Throw you out? Your imagination rivals my daughter's.'

Mel examined the ground. It would be easy to like him. All the more reason why she should think about going as soon as possible. Every day she stayed, she risked more of her heart. 'Shall we get to your home-coming feast?'

'Hardly a feast, but you are correct that one is needed. It has been far too long. All the foils will need to be attached to the pillars before then.'

She blinked rapidly. 'You are determined to have a proper feast?'

'The hall was made for feasts.'

'A feast, a feast.' Katla gave an excited squeal. 'And will there be riddles? I am awfully good at them. Elkr taught me a couple of good ones just before…just before—' She clapped her hand over her mouth. 'I'm sorry, Aunty Mel.'

'Think nothing of it, sweetling. I like that you remember him.'

'Elkr was your son, yes?' Tylir said softly.

'Yes. He would listen out for riddles and share them with Katla. He enjoyed the tongue-twisting ones the best.'

'He sounds like he was a fine boy.'

Mel kept her eyes on the ground and concentrated on a small pebble. A lump grew in her throat. Tylir had not said anything about how sorry he was or how the pain would stop in time; instead he'd spoken about Elkr as if he were a person. 'That is the kindest thing anyone has said.'

'Why?'

'Mostly they turn their faces and mumble their apologies,' Katla said in a loud voice. 'Most annoying. They do that about my mother as well.'

'Is there anything else I should know?'

'Aunty Mel weeps at night when she thinks I'm asleep. She needs another child to look after.'

'Katla!' Mel put her hand on her hip.

'I'm tired, Aunty Mel. Pick me up and carry me into the hall. I want to see what my foils look like by torch-light.'

'I'll do that.' Tylir caught Katla around her middle and swung her up onto his shoulders. Katla gave a surprised squeak but settled down, holding Tylir's hair like reins.

'We should go more quickly.'

'Yes, my lady,' Tylir said with the quirk of a smile.

'And what do you say of the riddles that Elkr taught me, Aunty Mel? Can we say them tonight as well as at the celebration Tylir promised?'

'Yes, there will be riddles. Tonight and when you want them, little one.'

Katla gave a whoop of delight. They set off up the slight incline to the hall. Mel's heart panged a little. Katla appeared happy with her father, far more than she had dared hope. How long until she knew in her heart that she was not wanted there and needed to go? Her husband used to complain that she always lingered for too long.

'Will it just be one meal at this feast of yours?' Katla asked. 'Or will there be more? My mother used to say that if you are going to celebrate, you might as well do it properly.'

Tylir shrugged, sending Katla bucking on his shoulders. Katla tightened her grip. 'Why not? Why not have a proper gathering? Several days of feasting and games. Stargazer keeps telling me I should do something like this to show I'm not a recluse.'

'With everyone in the neighbourhood invited?' Katla asked.

Tylir lowered Katla down. His glacial blue eyes met Mel's over Katla's head. 'People can be asked but they might have other things to do. Best not to hold it against them.'

Katla nodded solemnly. 'My *mor* used to say that as well.'

'Your mother was a wise woman.'

Katla lifted her chin. 'Aunty Mel says that my *mor* was the love of your life. You may give me a kiss now.'

Tylir retreated a step. 'A kiss? Why?'

'On my forehead. My…other father used to when I said something rather sweet. And I have done.'

Mel sighed. Sometimes, Katla really tried to see how far she could push someone. Kisses for saying something rather sweet. 'Katla! Enough. Stop tormenting poor Tylir.'

'Not something I had considered.' Tylir leaned down and brushed his lips against Katla's hair. 'Is this how a kiss for sweetness is done?'

Katla scrunched up her nose. 'It'll do. Suspect you will improve in time.'

Tylir laughed, a deep masculine laugh. 'You remind me of my sister.'

'Now, kiss Aunty Mel. Properly.'

'What?' Mel rapidly stumbled three steps backwards. 'Katla, hold your tongue!'

Tylir caught her arm. The heat from his hand seemed to radiate up her arm. 'The child meant no harm.'

Mel tore her elbow away and wrapped both arms against her middle. Her mouth ached as if he had touched it. He might think she had encouraged the little girl to say these things.

'Katla needs her food and then an early bed.' Her voice sounded far too breathless for her liking.

'But you will return after you put her to bed. We have much to discuss.'

Mel wet her lips. His voice reminded her of honey sucked from a honeycomb—rich and sweet. 'If it is appropriate.'

'Very appropriate. I must insist, Mel. After Katla is safely asleep.'

Mel was aware of how his gaze roamed over her figure and her figure's many shortcomings—too long legs, too slender with no curves to speak of save for her stomach. Her late husband had been very vocal about the deficiencies. And yet there was something about his gaze which made a warm tingle start in her middle and radiate outwards. She dismissed the feeling as nonsense and defiantly raised her chin. 'As I am under your roof, I suspect I must obey. We can discuss this later. Your lessons in parenting can begin.'

Tylir's eyes crinkled at the corners. 'Your aunty Mel knows what is proper, young lady. Listen to her. Obey.'

Katla tugged Mel's hand after several men came up to Tylir to ask his opinion about the upper pastures and he went off to see about the cattle. A smile split her face and she batted her lashes, her mother come to life. 'See, he likes you. I can tell. He is going to want to kiss you soon. I can just feel it.'

Mel put her shawl about Katla's shoulders. 'You are getting cold. The day has turned chilly. We need to go in.'

'My mother used to say her arms went up in goosebumps when she successfully matchmade. Mine do as well.'

'I think it is time you had your supper, sweetling. And I want to hear these riddles first. Sometimes, Elkr's father used to teach him inappropriate things or rather things which little girls should not say.'

Katla looked like she was going to protest but then she smiled. 'Magic happens at feasts, doesn't it, Aunty Mel?'

Without answering, Mel led Katla into the hall. There was an obvious reason for why he wanted to speak to her—Katla's welfare and it had nothing to do with any attraction she might feel towards him. To think otherwise was to risk humiliation, and she'd endured enough humiliation for a lifetime. Humiliation was something she left behind in the North along with many other parts of her life. She was not going to go back to the woman she was then.

Chapter Eight

Mel took one glance at the peacefully sleeping Katla, her blonde hair splayed out on the pillow and her cheek resting on her new doll. She was innocence personified. She swallowed hard.

Before she sought out Tylir, she must remind herself that she was a realist, not someone who believed in dreams. Wasn't that what she promised on Elkr's grave? As a young woman she had spent far too long dreaming that someday someone would come and rescue her. That person wasn't coming. She did her own rescuing. The first step was getting to Islond. The next was finding a farm. She had to keep that in the forefront of her mind and not get distracted. A home of her own was the only way she'd achieve true safety.

She nodded firmly and turned her footsteps towards the main hall, not allowing them falter. The fire had flickered down to embers and the hall, which had teemed during supper, echoed to the faint click of *tafl* counters being moved. Remembering how her husband hated being interrupted when he was playing *tafl*, she hesitated on the doorstep, wondering if she should turn around and speak to him in the morning. She straightened her shoulders. She'd left that sort of behaviour behind in the North.

Tylir's brow was furrowed in concentration and his long fingers nimbly moved the various counters. Rather than taking an age to decide his next move, he placed the counter quickly.

Mel cleared her throat when she was ten steps into the hall. The game stopped. Both men stared at her. 'I can return another time.'

'I appear to be intruding on private matters, Sunbear. We finish this match tomorrow.' Stargazer gave Tylir an enormous pat on the back and her a look which made her feel as if she were undressed as his alcohol-laced breath wafted over her, making her stomach churn, before he strode out of the hall.

The giant hall suddenly seemed both far too large and far too small with just her and Tylir in it.

In the silence, she shifted from foot to foot and wished she had stayed next to Katla.

'You took your time.'

Mel pasted a smile on her face. 'I didn't mean to interrupt. You said that you wished to speak to me. It seemed urgent. We can speak in the morning if you wish.'

'I rarely sleep. Too many ghosts.' He shrugged and started to move the counters about. 'Stargazer was merely keeping me company while I waited for you. He has a woman who warms his bed and wanted to visit her.'

'I didn't realise he was married.'

He gave a half smile. 'He isn't. I've lost track of his

women. The man is nothing if not inconsistent in his affairs of the heart.'

The muscles in her neck relaxed. Tylir was subtly warning her about Stargazer. Sweet really. As if she hadn't figured out that the man thought himself a gift to women when his breath smelt, and he bore the same signs of indulgence that her late husband had. However, she refused to confess this. 'I suspected he was that type. I've encountered them before in the North.'

Tylir nodded towards the board. 'Do you play?'

'When I was first married, my husband and I used to play a lot. We fell out of the habit after Elkr was born. Babies take up a great deal of time. And he travelled a great deal.'

She held back the words about how her husband had loudly declared that she was no longer worth the effort in front of his assembled warriors and their wives and then laughed about it. Ever afterwards, she'd pretended to be too busy with Elkr or preparing her potions to prevent him from getting a second chance to humiliate her in that way.

'We must play sometime.' Tylir's gaze held hers for a fraction too long. 'I do enjoy a new challenge. I already know all the gambits Stargazer uses.'

A new challenge. Men preferred the pursuit, even if the quarry was unattractive. She pressed her lips together, more aware than ever of the intimacy of the place.

She swallowed hard. Her overactive imagination was running away from her.

'I doubt you will find me a challenging opponent.'

His smile was slow and did strange things to her stomach, starting warm curls which entwined and moved. She pressed her hands together. She was not some sort of giddy maiden, but a widow. She knew the games men played and how their attention wandered once they had captured a woman's attention.

'I suspect you are better than most.' He lengthened the words *better than most*, giving them an entirely different connotation.

'Your suspicions would be wrong.' She nodded decisively and attempted to take charge of the conversation. Stargazer might have a reputation with the ladies, but she did not doubt that Tylir could equally charm women when he put his mind to it. 'Katla wanted a story but rapidly fell asleep with a smile on her face. She is determined to have riddles at this feast you have planned. We practiced several so she could tell them perfectly.'

'What does she get if she tells them properly?' His eyes danced. 'A kiss?'

'No.' She silently cursed him for making her look at his mouth and wonder what it would taste like. 'Katla likes all sorts of things. In my trunk, I've some woven braid which would do as trimming for a new dress…if indeed there is to be a proper feast.'

Tylir began setting up the *tafl* pieces and patted the bench next to him. 'The invitations will go out to the neighbours tomorrow. Who will turn up remains a matter of conjecture.'

Mel remained standing. What she had to say would not take long and the intimacy of the darkening hall pressed down on her. She was aware of his bulk and the way his hair fell over his forehead and shoulders.

'Is my half-brother and his family included in the

invitations?' she asked quickly before her mind started
to go to places it shouldn't.

He set a piece down. 'I suspect he will have something else to do but the invitation will be sent.'

'I suspect he will.'

He pressed his hands against the table. 'I didn't start
the feud, Melkorka. Helm did that when he openly speculated about my wife's honour after I refused to yield a
portion of land to him at the funeral.'

Mel's stomach twisted. What had Helm known about
Ingebord? Like his mother he had a talent for ferreting
out horrible gossip in order to cause maximum mischief.
But it would seem Tylir's marriage to Ingebord was not
the idyllic love match Virin had portrayed. She hated
how her heart leaped at the insight.

'I've no doubt. He could start a fight in an empty
room. He would do if he was bored.'

Tylir laughed. It was the sort of laugh to make a
woman's insides become liquid fire. She concentrated
harder on her breathing and reminded herself that the
man was an expert in seduction. Had to be. Gradually,
her racing pulse slowed. 'Is there anything else?'

He sat up straighter, staring directly at her mouth. 'Is
there anything else you think I might need to know?'

'I hope you didn't think anything about Katla's request earlier. She has a little girl's notions sometimes.'

He watched her from under hooded eyes. 'Do you
mean about kissing you?'

'She meant nothing by it. Her way of saying that
she liked you and I should like you too. I suspect she
won't want to be parted from me, but she'll settle. She
is settling.'

He captured her hand and held it in his much larger one. 'I know what Katla is on about. Her matchmaking is transparent.'

She was tempted to pull away but somehow lacked the strength. 'I want to end any notion of matchmaking before it begins. I'm determined to live my life as I see fit, not as another dictates.'

'I see.' He released her hand. 'Sit. I wanted to speak to you about Katla, not to make good that kiss you promised.'

'I never—' She noticed how his eyes danced in the firelight. He was teasing her. 'What is it about Katla?'

'Why does she keep asking me about some kitten I am supposed to have rescued? Three times during the meal she brought this cat up. I've never kept a cat in my life. My mother might have but my late wife could not abide them.'

Mel sat down on the bench hard. She should never have brought up the kissing. He wanted to know about Katla and the kitten. It was not some attempt at flirtation, but a genuine desire to learn about his daughter. Her husband had never really been interested in Elkr beyond the fact that he had a living son.

'A confession—I embellished a few of the tales I'd heard about you. Katla adores cats. She also loves tales of Freya and the cats which draw her chariot.'

His crooked smile shone. 'Embellished. I like that. How often have I saved kittens?'

'Pretty much every time you see one, which is quite frequently, and you were given a kitten which some swore was from Freya because it grew and grew. It made her stop crying on the boat.'

'Ah, that makes sense. I suspect I shall have to acquire a large cat.'

'They help with the mice.'

He asked a few more questions about Katla and what she liked and what she was like. Questions which required Mel to think. It was clear he had considered what could be best for the child's future. Mel was pleased that she could answer the questions easily.

By the time they had finished speaking, the embers in the fire had burned to a low glow and the warm darkness felt uncomfortably intimate.

'Does that help?' she answered after he asked about which gods Katla preferred and why. 'I hope I am not boring you with all this detail. Sometimes I talk too much.'

He covered her hand with his for a heartbeat. 'I'd thought if I knew more about Katla's habits, I could suggest one of the women, but the more you tell me, the more I think the nurse must be a very special person for a very special little lady.'

Mel's neck relaxed. Tylir appeared genuinely interested in his daughter and finding the right person to look after her.

'One will be found.' She tried for a self-deprecating smile. 'In the meantime, you will have to put up with me—the person who airs wall hangings in your hall without asking. Most of the women were shooting daggers at me with their eyes and muttering dire predictions.'

'I suspect they wanted an easy life.'

'As long as they don't take it out on Katla. Virin appears to have taken an irrational dislike to her.'

'One might say the same about Katla towards Virin.' Mel sighed fondly. 'She is a minx, that one.'

'Takes after her mother.'

'Estrid enjoyed rearranging people's lives but she did so in such a charming way that few objected.'

Tylir picked up one of the counters and rolled it about in his palm before putting it down with a distinct thump. 'I have been thinking about your proposed farm.'

She concentrated on the highly carved *tafl* pieces, rather than tumbling into his gaze. He knew she didn't want to marry. 'Have you found a good location?'

'Several possibilities, but I refuse to tell you them until we have found this elusive nurse.'

'Are you trying to make it easier or harder?'

He put his hands behind his head. 'I am offering you an incentive.'

'I am as anxious as you are to find one. No incentive needed.'

'Let's say that I want to ensure you are not taken advantage of and I want it to be somewhere where my daughter can quickly visit. I'm under no illusions that she will want to do that.'

'I'm grateful for any and all help. I'm not expecting a large farm like you have, but something which I can work properly. I want ground under my feet which belongs to me.' At his look, she knew she had confessed too much. There was little point in telling him about how much she wanted to belong somewhere. She would never belong here. She rose. 'I should go. I've no wish to be the one who is sleepy. Tomorrow, Katla and I shall tackle the weaving shed.'

She waited for him to wave her on her way.

'Why didn't you stay in the North? You inherited a great deal of gold. You obviously have some skill as a healer. That ointment has done my leg much good in a short space of time.'

'Because my husband was the one who brought the putrid throat into the village. I couldn't stay after what he'd done to the village.' The words came out quicker than she intended. 'I considered myself a great healer, but I couldn't heal him or my son or anyone else. The tonic which seemed to help ran out, and I had not planted enough of the right herbs to recreate it.'

'Surely no one blamed you. It is the gods' will if people survive. And I know what the putrid throat does. It took my uncle and cousins three years before my family perished. My aunt also considered herself an experienced healer. She nearly went mad with grief, but my mother told her—no, you did your best and that has to be good enough.'

'I'd no idea.'

'It is why I know you mustn't blame yourself.' His mouth twisted. 'Recovery is in the lap of the gods.'

She pinched the bridge of her nose. A large part of her wanted to believe Tylir's words, but a little voice in the back of her brain kept saying over and over that she should have been better at nursing them, she should have planted more of the medicinal herbs when she had a chance and she should have never have allowed Elkr to greet his father when he was so pale and coughing, but her husband had demanded to see how big their son was getting and she'd complied. She took a steadying breath and allowed the sense of complete hopelessness to pass.

'I should be better at looking after people. I spent

most of my life trying to be useful,' she said when she trusted her voice. 'Before I leave, I must ensure that a proper medicinal herb garden grows on this farm. Virin told me the last one has been allowed to go to weeds. Until a new crop of sage and rue grows, I can't make any more of that ointment.'

He examined her from under his lashes. She suspected he was able to see into the dark depths of her soul and knew she wanted the subject altered. 'You lost your husband and your son as well as several friends. Surely that is punishment enough, even if I don't think the punishment was warranted. If you desire a garden, there will be a garden. I will hold you to the promise of more of the wonderful ointment.'

She closed her eyes and remembered the faces of her former friends, the ones who survived, and how they refused to meet her eyes as well as the eagerness with which they had given her things for the voyage. She'd known then that they wanted rid of her and were grateful that she was departing, never to darken their doorsteps again. Such a change from the day she'd arrived in the village.

'It was easier on everyone that I left,' she said around the sudden lump in her throat.

'I'm pleased you brought Katla here.'

'My word to Estrid. You don't break a deathbed promise.'

He rubbed the back of his neck and gave a rueful smile. 'Always back to Estrid. I tried to forget her, you know, after I heard she married.'

'You also married,' she reminded him.

His lips turned up into a humourless smile. 'The two

things may have been connected. Stargazer will tell you they are if you ask him. He has a brain for snippets of gossip, going back years.'

Mel ground her teeth. 'I've no plans on asking him anything.'

He lifted a brow. 'You haven't thanked me for the garden. Yours for while you are here and Katla's hereafter. If it will prevent sickness amongst my people, that is all I need to know.'

She put a hand over her mouth. 'I'm delighted. Thank you.'

His gaze held hers. 'Most women would give a more effusive thanks.'

Effusive? He meant kissing. She could just picture how Estrid would have done it, draping her arms about his neck and pressing her body against his. She pressed her palms into her gown. 'Perhaps I am simply unsure what has prompted such a generous offer.'

'Perhaps you shouldn't look for hidden meanings. Everything I do is for my people.'

One of the dogs gave an enormous yawn. Mel jumped. 'The fire has burned down to nothing. I should go.'

'I find it difficult to sleep. Too many ghosts.'

'They are my constant companions as well.' She tried for a smile and slowly started walking backwards towards the door. 'I had hoped in time I would get used to them.'

He drained his tankard and wiped a hand across his mouth. He rose and she stopped her slow inching towards the door. 'Tell me, does Katla value the truth?'

'I like to think so.'

'And do you?'

'I do.'

'Then I had best do this.'

He captured her face between his hands and his lips brushed hers. The instant the feather-light touch settled on her mouth, her lips opened and the kiss quickly deepened. He pulled her closer so that her breasts encountered the hard muscle of his chest. She looped her arms about his neck and gave into the pressure. At the insistence of his tongue, her mouth open further. Their tongues touched and then retreated. He drank deeply from her mouth, and she allowed him to.

A deep warmth curled about her belly, and she forgot everything except the sensation of his mouth moving against hers and his fingers roaming down her back.

One of the dogs gave a soft yelp and brought her jolting back to the present. She was standing, between his legs, pressed up to his chest, hands entwined in his hair, kissing him as if her life depended on it. She jerked backwards and he let her go. Her breath came too fast and too shallow. His was also ragged. And she knew if the spell had not been broken, she would have demanded more and more.

With a tentative finger she explored her swollen lips. 'What was that for? Why did you do that?'

'Mel?' he asked quietly. 'Should I apologise?'

'I suppose you wanted to tell Katla you'd kissed me like she required.' Kissed her once and never again. She forced a smile and silently resolved to leave as soon possible. Staying would endanger her hard-fought-for equilibrium. She didn't want to return to the young woman who had had dreams in her eyes and whose marriage quickly crushed them. There was no long-term future for her here. 'You are a good father, Tylir.'

'I am trying to become one,' he said in a low voice and without meeting her eyes. 'Melkorka, Mel, we must speak properly.'

She held up her hands and backed away. 'No need to apologise. I worry that Katla is stirring. I must go.'

His lips turned up into a heart-stopping smile. It would be so easy to really like him. 'I suspect you are an excellent *tafl* player if you give yourself a chance. We must play.'

Mel pressed her hands against the skirts of her gown. She knew what would happen if she stayed and played. She also expected she would be discarded after he obtained what he wanted. A small place inside of her protested that Tylir was not like her late husband. She silenced it. 'Katla will need me if she wakes. I am here at her request.'

'Tomorrow then. I'm sure Katla will insist on it, once I explain the situation to her.'

She wet her quietly thrumming lips and longed for the floor to open and swallow her. Her late husband had enjoyed teasing her like that before he humiliated her in front of everyone. 'I am sure Katla will want to learn the rules.'

The gleam in his eye deepened. 'There, you see. It was not so hard. Go and see my child.'

Without waiting to hear more, she picked up her skirts and fled back to the alcove she shared with Katla.

The little girl remained sound asleep, hugging her doll tight.

Mel lay down and tried to slow her racing heart.

She'd been kissing this man. His heart was interlinked with Estrid's and Ingebord's, the woman who designed this hall in ways she couldn't comprehend. She once vowed that she would not take second best. She had to start listening to her brain and not her heart. And she had to find somewhere new to live, somewhere where she wouldn't be tempted to make happy families in the air and instead be left with her ghosts. The trouble was that the ghosts were not that appealing and a friendship of sorts with Tylir was.

Even though his body thrummed with energy in a way that it had not done for a long time, Tylir allowed Mel to flee the hall. Her heels kicked up tiny piles of dust. The dogs moved closer to the fire. He ran his hand through his hair and willed his heartbeat to stop racing. Nothing would be gained through chasing after her.

Her excuse was pathetic and more transparent than a sheen on a polished shell after a rainstorm. But he had never forced a woman and did not intend to start with Mel.

Staring at the fire and trying to recall the precise shade of her hair, he wondered why he had initially thought she was less than attractive. The more he encountered her, the more he noticed little things about her such as the curve of her neck, the slenderness of her fingers and the husky quality of her laugh. Things he found difficult to stop turning over and over in his mind until he knew in his heart that she radiated temptation with each breath she took, even if she looked nothing like his usual type of woman. But more importantly there was something more—her indomitable spirit, the way she kept trying and how she saw good in him.

The kiss went further than he had intended it to. He had merely meant to tease and brush her lips, but the quick taste had proved irresistible, and he had drunk deeply from her mouth. He wanted more, much more but he did not want to scare her. He hoped for her friendship, and he needed her to look after Katla. His daughter adored the ground she walked on, and he refused to be the cause of Mel fleeing.

Tylir drummed his fingers on the table. 'What?'

The dogs gave a chorus of barks before setting their heads on their paws. Much more would have happened had one not barked and shocked both Mel and him back to their senses.

Tylir clenched his jaw. He had not had that sort of loss of control since he and Estrid were first together. But Mel was more skittish than a wild raven or a maiden before her first tumble in the hay. She was a widow who had lost her beloved son. He could guess what she had been through from what her half-brother had claimed and the little she had revealed.

'Someone treated you very badly, didn't they?' he murmured. 'And I need to find a way to undo the damage.'

The closest wolfhound woofed in agreement.

He wanted to unwrap all her layers and that frightened him. He leaned over and stirred the fire, watching the sparks rise and fall for a long while.

'Did Tylir kiss you last night?' Katla demanded when Mel opened her eyes.

Katla loomed over Mel with an eager expression on her face. Mel attempted to rub the sleep out of her eyes.

Her dreams had been full of the kiss they shared and what very nearly followed. She'd reluctantly concluded that he'd been the one to pull back not her, and she could remember how her late husband as he lay dying had taunted her about chasing after men. He'd been wrong. Until Tylir she experienced no attraction towards any man.

Katla continued to press her nose against Mel's and stare at her with eyes which mirrored Tylir's. Mel gently moved her away.

'Katla! A young lady does not ask those sorts of questions, particularly not so early in the morning!'

Katla scrunched up her face. 'But did he?'

She need not tell Katla that he had. She had already read far too much into it and allowed far too many dreams. Tylir would turn out to be like all the other men she'd encountered. Worse because his heart was given over to Estrid and what little proportion which remained lay buried with his late wife. He reacted in a male way to her evident interest in him, nothing more.

Mel stood up and rapidly dressed and tried to ignore Katla's further questions while she helped the young girl to dress as well. But Katla was having none of it and kept up a steady stream. A thousand and one ways to ask the same question.

'You need to hold still to have your hair brushed and stop asking so many questions,' Mel said finally.

'That means yes! I knew it! I had goosebumps. He will want to kiss you again. Kissing can be habit-forming.' She paused and her face fell slightly. 'My mother used to say that. Never out of season or fashion.'

'Your mother had a lot of sayings.'

'I keep trying to remember them all.' She held up her doll. 'I whisper them to Freya at night, but I know I keep forgetting a few. How can I make my mother proud if I can't remember her?'

Mel stared up at the rafters and blinked rapidly. Every day she stayed here, it was going to make it harder for her to leave when the time came. Katla had a growing hold on her heart and Tylir populated her dreams, making them more and more erotic and having her starting to believe that she was a beautiful and desirable woman. All she had to do was suggest a marriage, one of convenience.

She instantly rejected the thought. Tylir would never agree to such a proposition, and she'd experienced a loveless marriage before. Never again. She'd vowed before she left the North Country that she was never going to marry for convenience again. She needed a true place of sanctuary.

'Katla, there is nothing between Tylir and I,' she said a bit more sternly than she intended. 'Yes, he kissed me last night, but because you wanted him to, not because he wanted to. He has offered to teach you how to play *tafl*.'

Katla put her hand in front of her mouth and gave a yawn. '*Tafl* is boring. Boring, I tell you. Sends me right to sleep.'

'It can be. My mother and father used to play it, and I'd have to sit in the corner drawing with my stick in the ash, quietly.' Mel paused. She had not thought about those simpler days for a long time. 'Once someone taught me how to play it, I found it exciting.'

Katla paused in tying her couverchef. 'Did I make things more difficult for you, Aunty Mel?'

'Try not to matchmake. Allow Tylir and I the opportunity to choose our own lives.'

'But you like him, don't you?'

'He wants to be a good father to you and that is what is important. But yes, I do like him. More than I thought I would.' She hoped her heart would see sense and that she would stop daydreaming about the way his mouth had felt against hers. Kissing her was anything but habit-forming. The past had taught her that.

'Come on, you can do better than that.' Tylir held out his hand to the one man he'd knocked down after two blows in their practice sword fight. 'Keep your mind on your task.'

'I am, my Jarl,' the man said. 'I just wasn't expecting the blows to come so fast.'

'If we end up in a battle, you need to be able to defend yourself.' Tylir crouched down. It had been a long time since he felt this full of energy and alive. Mel's ointment had worked wonders in such a short time, far better than he dared hope for. Thankfully Mel had agreed to show Katla how to make the ointment as well as the other one Estrid used to make for keeping hands soft.

He tore his mind away from Mel's soft hands and tried to concentrate. 'Now again.'

'You are being too hard on him, Sunbear, particularly as you have no intention on raiding the rich monasteries in Alba or Wessex anytime soon,' said a languid voice, appearing beside the man. Tylir wondered when his old friend had developed this indolent sleekness.

'You should try sparring with someone who can match your skill.'

'Care to fight me?' Tylir asked between clenched teeth. Friend or not, Stargazer should know that he could take him. 'Care to have a real challenge? Is that what you are saying? I have never run away from a challenge in my life.'

Stargazer wiped a hand across his mouth. 'If you are willing, I will enjoy the fight. Your aim has been off these last few months. It will be good to teach you some humility. Maybe then you will consider going adventuring with me.'

'Your arrogance will be your undoing.'

Tylir tightened his grip on the blunt sword and nodded to Stargazer. Round and round they went with the men rapidly gathering around and placing bets.

Before his wife died, they used to spar frequently, but those bouts fell away. The memories came flooding back. Tylir enjoyed the cut and thrust, the pivot when the sword thrust forward and the way his muscles screamed. The contest continued for longer than he'd expected with neither gaining the upper hand. Slowly, slowly he could see Stargazer tiring and his movements became more rigid. He'd have him in another few strokes, but he wanted to savour the contest; it made a change from thinking about the kiss he'd shared with Mel.

Sweat poured down Stargazer and Tylir knew it was a matter of breaths before Stargazer called a halt.

'Anytime, Stargazer, you wish to end this, say the word,' Tylir said as Stargazer's planned thrust to his left side failed. He had seen the manoeuvre many times before always just before Stargazer gave in. One last sword thrust to finish. He drove his sword forward.

'Bed or wed her,' Stargazer said as their swords clashed.

Tylir gripped his sword tighter. Tried to remember the next move in the sequence. Up or down. He went for up and missed the sword clash. He wiped a hand across his mouth. 'No idea what you are talking about.'

He backed up two steps and waited for the charge.

'That woman who guards your daughter.'

'Melkorka? What about her?'

'You desire her. Don't deny it. Bed her or wed her to someone else. Get her out of your system.' Stargazer smiled and twisted his sword, flipping Tylir's out of his hand. 'Or I will keep being able to do this. Is that why you truly do not want to go raiding again? Is it because you no longer have any stomach for a fight instead of this limp which seems to have miraculously improved?'

Tylir watched his sword arch away and become embedded in the soft dirt. He could not remember the last time anyone had done that to him. 'How well you joke, Stargazer. Anyone else would think you had an eye on the leadership. You know I'll never give that up voluntarily.'

Stargazer put his hands on his knees and laughed. 'I've wanted to do that to you for a long time.'

Tylir picked up his sword. 'I've no idea what you are talking about. Melkorka is here for Katla.'

Stargazer clapped him on the back. 'Lie to yourself all you want, old friend. We know the truth.'

The men gave ribald laughs. Tylir gritted his teeth. He shoved Stargazer backwards. The man tumbled down into the dust.

'I told you once and I won't tell you again—keep a civil tongue about Melkorka. I won't have her disrespected.'

Stargazer picked himself up and dusted his tunic down. 'I believe my point is proved. But call a gathering. Show your new daughter off to your neighbours. Show them you are a changed man. Maybe that precious Melkorka will find a man who appreciates her talents, and that will solve all your problems.'

Stargazer walked away without a backwards glance.

Chapter Nine

'I will be fine here. Aunty Mel, you may go.' Katla made an imperious wave from where she sat in the weaving shed several days later. She and another little girl were helping sort the spindles.

Mel's neck relaxed. Katla appeared to be making a friend, even if she appeared to enjoy bossing the girl about, informing her that she knew the proper way to sort spindle whorls. The other little girl seemed to look at her with something akin to awe and wonder.

The mother promised to look after Katla if she had something else to do, particularly as the woman had found the new batch of hand-softening ointment Mel made really helped her and her sister's chapped hands. The woman's words sounded like dismissal and Mel refused to become one of those mothers who hovered about doing nothing. Helm's mother had been like that, constantly worried in the early days that she'd some-how lead Helm into mischief. She pinched the bridge of her nose. She was many things, but she wasn't Katla's mother, not even temporarily.

She forced a smile and accepted the offer.

'That would be lovely. Katla, be good. I will return shortly.'

'Take the afternoon,' the woman said in a loud whisper. 'It is good for my daughter to have a playmate. She has seen enough sorrow recently.'

'Katla as well,' Mel whispered.

Mel hurried from the room and went in search of Tylir. She had spent most of the last two nights composing her speech about why she needed to leave, sooner rather than later.

What had happened in the weaving shed between Katla and her new friend this morning showed that her instincts were correct—Katla was starting to settle. She was going to hold Tylir to his promise that he would help her find the right parcel of land, something he had not repeated since they shared that kiss. They had barely talked since that kiss.

'Independence is important to me,' she muttered as she walked along the loch. 'I miss my son too much to ever be a good carer for this girl.'

She knew he should be in the practice yard at this time of day, but she did not want to have the conversation where everyone could hear, including Stargazer, who kept making inappropriate comments which he passed off as being harmless banter. She had noticed that Stargazer was careful not to make the remarks around Tylir.

She cleared her throat. 'I want somewhere where I can have room to breathe. It is something I promised my son on his deathbed. I would go where I could breathe.'

'Aren't you able to breathe here?' Tylir's voice cut through her reverie. 'You appear to be doing it quite well. In and out. In and out.'

'I didn't see you.' Her feet skittered into each other, and she nearly slipped on the shingle which surrounded the loch. His hand went under her elbow steadying her.

'Can't have you falling.'

'I don't intend to.' She pointedly moved her elbow and he released her. The warmth from his hand had spread throughout her arm, reminding her of the heat-infused kiss they had shared. 'Make a point of it in fact.'

'Obviously. No one ever intends to fall.' His lips turned upwards. 'You appear to have lost your shadow.'

'Katla assists in the weaving shed. She has made a friend with a little girl.' Mel described the girl and her mother.

'Excellent news. I think I know who you are talking about—one of my men's wives. She has been looking after her cousin in the next valley. It is good that she has returned.'

'Why didn't you tell me about this woman and her child before?'

Tylir waved his hand. 'No idea when she would return and she is very busy running the small farm. She only helps out occasionally.'

Mel tucked a strand of hair behind her ear. 'Here I wondered if she might be suitable for Katla. Katla is settling, Tylir. She even allowed Virin to show her how to wrap the wool into a ball. It would be wrong of me to deny this.'

His blue gaze met hers. She thought she caught a glimpse of sadness. 'You want to leave as soon as possible.'

'It might be easier if I did.' She wrapped her arms about her waist.

Tylir's face became hardened planes. 'Because of the other night.'

'Already forgotten,' Mel lied, waving an airy hand.

'So quickly. I must be losing my touch,' Tylir murmured. 'Yet you keep avoiding being alone with me.'

'I have been busy with Katla.'

'An excuse, but as you say—Katla is with her new friend right now.'

Mel swallowed hard. 'I was coming to find you. To discuss what needs to be done.'

'By walking along the loch when you thought I'd be at the practice yard.'

'Getting my thoughts together.'

He put his hand under her elbow again and led her to where the bath hut was situated. 'There is no need for you to go. What passed between us won't happen again if you don't wish it, but I want you to tell me the truth.'

She wrapped her arms even tighter about her middle and tried to think of all the reasons that anything between them was an impossibility. But her mouth ached for the way his lips had moved overs hers.

She glanced into his eyes and her heart nearly stopped at the warm uncertainty she glimpsed. In that heartbeat, she knew she had to tell the truth or regret it for ever. What had she promised Estrid? She would seize life for the two of them. This was not about love, but attraction. She was not about to make that mistake again.

She carefully tucked a stray strand of hair behind her ear. 'No need for apologies. I enjoyed it.'

A smile split his face. 'You did?'

'I did, but I've no wish to demonstrate for Katla.

Katla should play no part in anything which passes between us.' She paused and hoped he'd understand— Katla must not build dream houses. 'We must be circumspect.'

'We will be.'

She closed her eyes. 'Thank you.'

His hand smoothed her hair back from her forehead. 'What if I enjoyed it as well? What if I wanted to keep on kissing you?'

She opened her eyes and stared directly at his mobile mouth. 'I might question your eyesight.'

He lifted her chin. 'Who did this to you, Mel? Who made you think that you were unattractive?'

Her mouth went dry. All she could think about was the curve of his upper lip and how high his cheekbones were. He was the sort of man who commanded attention. She suspected he must have been quite the sight with Estrid. Her dark beauty and milk-white skin complementing his blond hair and golden skin. She was nothing like that. She forgot that at her peril.

She focused on the door to the bathing hut, tried to still her racing heart and breathe normally. 'I know how I look. I've caught my reflection in a still pond before. I know what my late husband said. No false claims here.'

'What did your son say?' he asked in a low voice.

She pinched the bridge of her nose and tried not to remember how Elkr had called her his pretty mother. 'Unfair. He was a little boy.'

'It doesn't make it any less true,' he murmured, leaning forward so that their breath intermingled. 'I kissed you, Mel, not because Katla wanted me to but because

I wondered how your lips tasted. I wanted to see if they tasted like cloudberries.'

'You did?'

'I enjoyed kissing you, Mel. I keep thinking about it at the oddest of times. Shall we try again?'

'Tylir.'

Their lips collided. Instantly he drank from her mouth. The fire which had raged through her the other night and in her dreams leaped and filled her.

She entwined her arms about his neck and pulled his mouth closer. Their bodies collided, his hard muscle hitting her soft skin. The kiss intensified until the only thing she knew was his mouth roaming hers, his tongue sweeping along the edge of hers and the raging inferno which built up inside her in response. The rush made her feel gloriously alive in a way she never considered she'd experience.

His hands slid down her back to cup her bottom. He ran his hands over the soft curves before he pulled her more firmly against his erection. Her entire body quivered.

She tried to hang on to the last tendrils of sanity, but her entire body tingled from the passionate touch of another human being, the sort of touch she had thought would never happen to her, and she knew every fibre of her being required more. However, someone had to be the sensible one, because she knew what occurred when passion was spent. The thought acted like ice-cold water coursing through her, allowing her to make the correct choice.

She leaned back against his encircling arms and smiled up at him. His scar stood out from his ruined face.

'Are you sure this is wise?' She waited for his hands to fall away.

He slipped his hand further down her back and pulled her firmly back against the apex of his thighs. His lips traced a path to her earlobe. 'Why are you frightened of the passion which exists between us?'

'I've very little experience with men,' she admitted, listening to the steady beat of his heart. 'Only my late husband.'

Her heart thumped loudly as she said the words and she hoped she would have to explain about Elkr's view on her nonexistent charms.

He lifted her chin. 'You're going to have to trust me.'

'Sometimes I find it hard to trust,' she whispered.

'But you are willing to stay here with me and see where this passion leads.'

She wet her parched lips. 'I… I suppose so.'

He bent down and scooped her up like she weighed no more than a feather.

She splayed her hands against his chest. 'What are you doing? Someone might see. I've no wish for unwarranted gossip.'

'Taking you somewhere so that we can enjoy this conversation where we are unlikely to be disturbed.'

'But Katla—'

'Do not use my daughter as an excuse. She is being looked after with her new friend, according to you.'

'I suppose you are right.'

'No suppose about it.' He kicked open the door to the bath house.

A faint heat from yesterday lingered in the air and on the wooden benches. He lowered her down onto one of the smooth benches. She lay there, body thrumming, disinclined to move. Her mind reeled from the fact that he'd carried her in here like he could not wait to be intimate with her. She always considered that sort of thing happened to other women, never her. Elkr… Tylir wasn't Elkr, her heart firmly reminded her.

He closed the door with a firm click and removed his tunic, revealing a network of silver scars against golden skin. Her fingers itched to touch them, but she kept them rigidly at her sides, gripping the bench.

'Interruptions would be most unwelcome.' He gathered her hands into his. 'We need to talk, Mel. Us two together. Sensibly.'

'I… I…'

'You are free to leave anytime.' His tongue played with her earlobe, sucking it and blowing air against it until her body bucked. The heavy deadening feeling which had been her constant companion for so many months evaporated like mist before the hot sun.

She knew it was unwise, but she wanted to drown herself in these feelings of being alive and have those memories to ponder rather than continually being surrounded by ghosts. She also suspected it would be only this once, but she knew she needed this solace, this time to banish the ghosts.

She ran her hands down the scar-pitted skin of his chest, enjoying the silken smoothness of it. 'I want to stay.'

His mouth descended on hers again. She instantly opened her mouth and drank. Their tongues twisted and tangled.

His hand slipped down her front and palmed her

breast. The back of his thumb circled around her nipple, making it rasp against the cloth until its tip ached. Her back arched and a moan escaped from the back of her throat.

'Overdressed,' he rasped against her ear.

Undoing the fastenings, he quickly divested her of everything except her thin shift. He bent his mouth to where her nipple touched the cloth and drew it into his mouth. A stab of heat shot through her as his teeth gently nipped before his mouth started to nuzzle her. Round and round, making large circles on the cloth which permitted the dusky rose of her breast to peek through.

Small mewling noises emerged from her throat. He ran his hand down her flank, ruching the fabric up until he discovered the nest of curls at the apex of her thighs. His fingers entangled themselves and explored the slick hidden folds while his breath teased her earlobe. Round and round, teasing her with his slowness as if he were determined to explore every inch of that hidden region.

Her body bucked upwards, seeking release as the feelings grew within her and she knew only one thing could give her relief.

'Please,' she whispered, drawing his face down to hers. 'Please.'

'As you request, sweet Mel,' he murmured against her lips.

His knee parted her thighs and he drove himself into her.

Her body opened to accommodate him. When he was fully impaled, he lay on top of her. Acting instinctively, she began to rock her pelvis, faster and faster, calling the rhythm rather than simply following.

His groans matched hers. And she knew whatever she had experienced in her earlier life, no one had ever properly prepared her for the intensity of what she now experienced.

Tylir lay in the glow of the aftermath with Mel snuggled into his side, softly breathing. Her hair tumbled down over them. He had forgotten, if he had ever truly known, what it was like to feel this satisfied.

Once? He knew in his bones in this moment that once would never be enough with Mel. He wanted to bury himself deep within her again and again.

As he reached out to touch her half-naked shoulder and draw her closer to him, she sat and moved away.

'I need to get back.'

'Katla will be fine. Her new friend...'

She started to arrange her hair, retrieving the hairpins from where they were scattered on the floor. 'I know her better than you. She will panic if she thinks I have vanished.'

'If you think she will worry with you being gone for a little time, what do you think she will do when you actually go?' he asked to slow her down. He doubted he'd ever seen a woman dress as quickly as Mel did.

Mel paused in fastening her brooches. 'Katla will understand when I'm gone.'

'And you are determined to go as quickly as possible.'

Her fingers stilled. 'It seems best.'

He caught her hand. 'I'm asking you…no, begging… to stay for a little while longer.'

Her laugh rang false to his ears. 'Stay? What, for more of this? This doesn't change anything about my responsibility towards Katla.'

He let her hand go. She was hiding something. 'Are you going to say that you didn't enjoy it?'

She shook her head. 'That would be lying.'

'And you don't lie.'

'Saves having to remember.'

'You will be free to go when you like,' he said. 'But you did promise to make me that herb garden. My men will want your ointment. My leg has improved immeasurably since I started using it.'

He knew he was grasping at wisps of straw to keep her there.

'I will bear that in mind.' She straightened her skirts. 'I should find Katla.'

'This… What happened between us, it isn't over. It hasn't even properly begun.'

She gave the briefest of nods. 'You wish to…'

He captured her chin. Her eyes were far more haunted than he wanted. He silently cursed her late husband and wondered what he'd done to her to make her jumpy and frightened of being touched. 'One taste is not nearly enough. I want the full meal, Mel. I want to savour every bit of you.'

The sound of Katla's voice asking loudly where her Aunty Mel was echoed in the small chamber. Mel put her hand over her mouth and her eyes widened.

Mel started inching towards the door. 'I should go. She mustn't find me here, not with you. Alone. It would be too difficult to explain. Katla is a child who builds dreams. So much has changed for her.'

He nodded, hating that small stab of indecision. If Katla found them, would he be forced to make an offer and she forced to stay? Or leave? And if she stayed, would it because of Katla and not him? He kept his hands firmly by his sides and allowed her to slip away. 'Best to go on your own. You would not want to give Katla ideas or having her spinning false dreams. Gods know my life is littered with enough broken dreams.'

She gave him a sharp look. He had the uncomfortable impression that she was able to peer down deep into his soul and to see all the hidden spaces and mistakes. 'My thoughts precisely. Too many broken dreams in both our lives.'

With that she picked up her skirts and ran, slamming the door behind her. Tylir sat down hard on the bench. He'd made a terrible mistake in seducing her. It was all he could do not to haul her back against him and ask her forgiveness. He'd selfishly wanted too much and he had jeopardised their growing friendship.

In many ways. Mel reminded him of a wild raven he'd had as a child. He had worked very hard to tame it, offering it crumbs of bread until he overcame its fears, and its preferred perch became on his shoulder. The raven lived for several years after that, and he'd treasured the friendship.

Patience. He would have a second chance to enjoy her body. Another chance to get it right and show how good they could be together. Friends but lovers.

He tapped a finger against his mouth. He simply

needed to figure out what the breadcrumbs for Mel were and he knew just the person to enlist. He folded his hands behind his head and went over their joining again. Their next one would be even better, he promised himself. He would unwrap her fully and completely enjoy her.

Chapter Ten

Mel walked away with quick steps from the bathing hut and all it represented. She'd stayed far too long, lying in the warm circle of his arms, half dreaming that she too could be loved for the rest of her life. An impossibility.

'Aunty Mel! Aunty Mel! There you are. I worried something awful. It ate my insides like Fenrir the Wolf does when he eats the world.'

Mel opened her arms and Katla rushed into them, wrapping her arms about her waist, and burying her head into the folds of Mel's gown. 'What is wrong, Katla?'

'I worried you'd left. Without saying goodbye. And that I was all alone. Again.'

She raised Katla's chin. The girl's eyes were wide with genuine fear. 'Would I go without telling you goodbye?'

'But you went to talk to Tylir about that. I know it. You're going to go. The magic hasn't worked. Not one slightest bit. The boys were wrong about that.'

Mel frowned. 'What is all this about the boys? You're not making sense, Katla. Anyway, the gathering to celebrate you is coming up soon. Do you think I'd miss a chance to see you in all your glory, sitting next to your new father at the high table?'

Katla's eyes grew round. 'You won't leave before that?'

'Why would I?' Mel hunkered down so that her face was level with Katla's. 'My promise stands. I stay until you are settled, sweetling. I do want Tylir to keep his eyes out for a nice piece of land, somewhere close where you can visit because I can't stay for ever.'

Katla's eyes swam. 'My mother promised she would stay but she didn't. Was it all my fault? Wasn't I good enough?'

'Oh, darling, she wanted to.'

Mel hugged the little girl to her chest. It pained her that there were no easy words to tell the child that what happened to Estrid was nothing to do with Katla being good or bad and everything to do with the sickness Elkr had brought to the village. Even then, perhaps it hadn't been his fault. *Or hers*, a little voice whispered. The tight place in her chest eased slightly.

'What's brought this on? I thought you liked it here. You have the promise of a puppy for your very own.'

Katla scraped her toe in the dirt. 'I don't want to think about the North, but everyone keeps asking. Why my mother didn't bring me here and why you brought me instead. Until I couldn't remember properly.'

'By *everyone* you mean your new friend.'

'I do. I'm not sure she's a very good friend. She laughed at me about believing in the special magic.' Katla cupped her hand about her mouth. 'But Aunty Mel, you will never guess what—Tylir's late wife wasn't very nice. They did not get on.'

'Who told you that?'

'My new friend.'

'She is awfully little to know something like that.'

'She overheard it in the wool house. Her mother likes to chat while she spins. Nobody likes that horrible Stargazer either.'

'Women like to tell stories and gossip.' Mel rose and put a hand on Katla's shoulder. This new friend might be a mixed blessing. 'Shall we go and see where I am going to make the new herb garden for you?'

'New garden?'

'It won't be very much this year, but next year it will be really helpful to everyone.'

Katla frowned. 'I can't do it on my own.'

Mel put a hand on the little girl's shoulder. The storm had passed. 'I will help you. It will be a success. Something to show your...new friends and Tylir.'

Katla became all sunny smiles. 'I would like that. I like being outside instead of cooped up in that old shed anyhow.'

They had nearly reached the barn when Tylir appeared. He had clearly been in the loch for another dip.

He smiled, his whole face lighting up with warmth, and Mel's heart skipped a beat. 'Katla, are you ready to choose which puppy will be yours?'

'I'm not the sort of girl who likes puppies.'

Tylir's face fell. 'But—'

Katla raised her chin. 'Herb gardens and halls are for little girls. Puppies are for rough-and-tumble children.'

'And your other father said you might have one when you were bigger,' Mel reminded her in a soft voice.

'I'm still little.' Katla clung to her hand. 'I want to see this famous herb garden, Aunty Mel.'

He appeared confused but then smiled. 'The one your Aunty Mel is going to ensure we have.'

'The very same. We spoke about it earlier,' Mel said with heavy emphasis.

'Yes, we did.' He inclined his head, but the warmth in his voice trickled down to the base of her spine. 'I nearly forgot as we spoke of other things as well.'

The heat in her cheeks increased. Definitely flirting and not in a smarmy way, but in a way that she wanted the flirtation to continue and grow.

'Then it is all settled,' she said in her firmest voice to stop her veins fizzing with excitement and put an end to any flirtation.

The twinkle in his eye deepened. 'Settled. Very settled.'

'I plan to make a garden you can be proud of before I depart from this place,' Mel said.

'My mother's garden was a very good one.'

'Then the standard is set high.' She made a perfunctory curtsey and took Katla's hand. 'Come, Katla. We have much to do before we eat.'

'Somehow I feel you will exceed the standard.' His soft voice washed over her. 'As you have done with everything thus far.'

His intent gaze appeared to be focused on her face. She ran her tongue over her suddenly aching mouth. Her body throbbed with the memory of his touch. Mel gave Tylir her best hard stare and he raised a brow.

'I am pleased you think anything I do praiseworthy.'

'More than praiseworthy, Mel. More than praiseworthy.' He caught her palm and raised it to his lips. His tongue briefly drew a small circle on it. She swiftly drew her hand back and jerked her head towards Katla with a warning frown. Tylir's eyes danced even more.

Katla's eyes grew round, and her head bobbed back and forth. Mel could almost see the matchmaking plans spinning around in the little girl's brain. A reminder if she needed it that if Katla caught wind of the affair, its inevitable end would hurt her greatly. The last thing Mel wanted was to cause a greater wedge between Katla and Tylir. She wished she had never given in to her desire.

'We need to see this patch of ground, Katla, and then clean you up. The daughter of the hall must be presentable at supper.' She kept her voice firm and briskly cheery. Simply because she and Tylir had had sex once, she had a choice about it happening in the future.

'As my lady wishes. I look forward to hearing about your progress…tonight.' He turned on his heel and strode away. His backside looked every bit as good as his front.

It was all Mel could do not to cradle her hand to her cheek. He knew precisely what he was doing, assuming she would meet him at his say-so like some silly maiden in the throes of her first love. Except she wasn't. She was a widow and knew what the end of this sort of game-playing would be. She wasn't afraid of falling pregnant. Her knowledge of herbs ensured she knew how to avoid such an eventuality. But that was not the only thing at stake here. She straightened her spine and banished all thoughts of Tylir's bottom.

'Did you know that Tylir likes you? Likes you a lot,' Katla whispered, tugging at Mel's hand.

'Tylir was teasing me—that is all. Men do that sometimes.' She stared after him. 'And I am not overfond of being teased.'

'Oh, I think you quite liked Tylir's teasing even if you are pretending that you hated it.' Katla gave a mischievous grin. 'I saw the way your cheeks turned pink when my father spoke to you. Sure sign, my *mor* used to say.'

'You think that?' Mel tried to keep a stern face but failed. It was the first time Katla had referred to Tylir as her father as though she had no other and was satisfied with that. Progress surely, even if it did make her heart sink slightly. Soon she would have no excuse to stay. 'We need to see to this herb garden. A good garden with herbs can save people's lives.'

'Sometimes you are too serious, Aunty Mel. You really are. Freya thinks it is something you should work on—smiling more often.'

'Jarl Tylir! We must speak immediately!' One of his men from the outlying farms accosted him right before the evening meal.

Tylir stopped in his perusal of the yard and contemplation of how he was going to seduce Mel later that evening. Business before pleasure.

'Is there a problem?'

'I understand you have Helm's half-sister here. Under your protection, if you please.'

Tylir narrowed his eyes. The man had been one of his stalwarts but had often taken Ingebord's side in the latter days of his marriage. He had to wonder if the man was simply seeking to cause trouble. 'I wasn't aware that I needed to explain my decisions to anyone. Melkorka is a guest here.'

The man rubbed the back of his neck. 'Fork-Beard and his men were responsible for my boy's death.'

'Melkorka Helmsdottar was in the North when the brawl started and arrived after the General Assembly made its decree. She is under my protection.'

'But she is of the same blood.'

Tylir raised a brow. Blood feuds belonged in the North, not in this country. He might not have any time for Fork-Beard, but Mel had proved her worth in bringing Katla to him and for staying. In her own way, she was incredibly brave to defy her brother in the manner she had, and he owed her an incalculable debt. 'Do you doubt my wisdom in this matter? Would you like to challenge for the leadership of this *felag*?'

The man gulped hard. 'No, Sunbear. I merely mean to say that blood will out. Give it time.'

Tylir rolled his eyes upwards. Mel was entirely different to Fork-Beard. Anyone who spent a little time in her company knew this. He banged his fists together. 'We made peace at the General Assembly. Will you have me go back on my word?'

'But you are having a feast here and you've invited him. He and his men killed your wife.'

'Ingebord drowned in a hot pool. Misadventure. I accept the verdict. I would advise you to do so as well.'

The man's mouth tightened. 'With all due respect, it is not that simple. My son did not die for nothing in that brawl. He died defending your honour and this land.'

'Your son died with honour, but this has nothing to do with our guest.' Still the unpleasant memories rushed back into Tylir's mind. Fork-Beard had clearly arranged to meet Ingebord at the hot pool, as they had been conducting an affair earlier in the year. There had been tears when he discovered the affair, but Ingebord pleaded for a second—or was it a fifth?—chance. He'd lost count and any thought of jealousy had long since vanished. He accepted his wife for what she was, but they agreed to maintain a marriage partnership of sorts.

The lure of being desired even by a weasel like Fork-Beard had proved too great and when Fork-Beard sent a message, she had abandoned her duties in favour of continuing the affair. Stargazer had shown him the message after the body was discovered.

He had agreed with Stargazer's assessment. She'd been doing it to gain Tylir's attention, and openly consorting with one of his closest rivals had been her preferred method. He could still remember the upwards curve of her lips as she left that morning and her backwards glances. He'd thought at the time she was trying to entice him to come with her and enjoy the morning sun. He had not had the heart to tell her that any desire for her had been extinguished months before.

It had been a shock to discover her naked body in the hot pool later that day when he realised that she failed to return and Virin grew anxious about her lady.

The man pursed his lips together. 'I think you are running a risk having her here like this. Fork-Beard is the sort to take offence at nothing. And Stargazer told me that the woman was certainly the type to cause a stir.'

'Stargazer talks too much. And I fear no man, least of all Fork-Beard.'

'I see. I just wanted to warn you like. Helm is a man bent on revenge. I have heard murmurings.'

'No doubt you have.'

Tylir gritted his teeth. Now he was having an affair

with Helm's half-sister. He had not planned it and he would not have halted what had passed between him and Mel even if he had known about Helm's threat.

He hated to think how his relationship with Mel could be exploited. And yet, he knew he was not ready to give her up. He was counting the breaths until he could taste her again. He wanted her to be happy with him. And he had no idea how long it would last.

'Melkorka is here to get my daughter settled. I will not have rumours being spread.'

'Does this woman know about your wife and Helm?'

'I can't see that it is any of your business. The woman, as you call her, is looking after my daughter.'

'As long as Helm doesn't use her as a counter. I've already lost one son, Sunbear.'

'Is this the way you speak to your jarl?' Stargazer asked, coming up to them and clapping the man on his back.

'I will speak to him how I choose, Stargazer. No need for you to tell me what to do.'

Stargazer put up his hands. 'Merely trying to help out here.'

Tylir cleared his throat. 'I believe we are done here. We must speak later, old friend, but for now, drink and eat. Enjoy the hospitality of my hall.'

The man reluctantly nodded and Tylir moved away to speak with some of his other men. He listened with half an ear to their concerns and easily sorted minor squabbles while his mind kept returning to the one truth about his relationship with Mel. He should have told her before they made love about his wife and her brother, but he had not wanted to spoil the moment with such unwelcome memories. The last thing he wanted was for her to think he'd used her for some sort of revenge. But he was going to have to explain and soon. Only he wanted one more night with her. Just one where he could show her how good they could be together. Then when he did explain, she would understand how much he desired her and how the past had nothing to do with their future.

Mel practiced a dozen excuses before she went to the hall after she ensured that Katla was sound asleep. She had changed into one of her dark green gowns, the one that prompted Elkr to call her his pretty *mor* whenever he saw her in it.

She knew wanting to look desirable for this man was a foolish thing, but the thoughts kept coming even as she tried to dismiss them. She kept hoping Tylir would find a way for them to have some time alone, perhaps even with a flirtatious game of *tafl*. She knew precisely what she was going to ask for if she won—a kiss like the ones they had shared in the bathing hut.

To her slight disappointment, Tylir was in the hall with a group of men and women, obviously discussing something of great importance. He gave her a perfunctory wave. She hesitated on whether or not to join the group.

A man with a long moustache grabbed her arm. 'You must be the famous Melkorka Helmsdottar.'

His alcohol-soaked breath washed over her. Mel hated the way her stomach clenched. She forced the bile back down her throat. This was not the North, where feuds were rife. She was under Tylir's protection.

She pulled her arm from the man's grasp. 'That's right.'

'Your brother had my son killed. In a fight. He could have stopped the brawl before it started, but he egged his men on. They stamped on my boy's head.'

Her stomach knotted. Helm had a quick temper. Her late husband had shouted at her when he learned that she had hidden Helm and his family for a few days while they waited for a ship to flee the North, using words like *foolish*, *reckless* and saying that such a man would bring ruin down on all of them. She had to wonder if Elkr had been right for once in his life.

'When was this?' she asked, stuffing the fear back down her throat.

'Last summer. They said my boy's death was misadventure because no one could be held responsible for starting the fight, but I know different. I know who started it and why.'

'Has this been discussed at the Assembly?'

'Aye, it were. Said he slipped in the melee and was trampled. My boy had sure feet. I know that in my bones.'

'I was in the North then.'

He tugged at his moustache. 'Just wanted you to know. Just wanted you to know what your family was like.'

'What is going on there?' Tylir called out. 'You should know better than to speak to the women in my household without my permission. Do you seek to question my authority?'

'Sorry, Jarl Sunbear.' The man crumpled. 'It won't happen again.'

'Better not or I shall take it as a direct challenge to my leadership.'

The entire hall went still. The man rapidly backed up.

'I like having you as my leader. You brought us here and into prosperity. I've no wish to go back to plying the sea.'

'There was nothing Melkorka could have done about your son. She was not in Islond.'

'I wanted her to know, that's all.'

Tylir nodded. 'This is taking longer than anticipated, Mel. Can you wait a little until this is done?'

'Very well.' She firmed her mouth and damped down the sense of disappointment. What had she hoped for? That he would have cleared the hall for her again? That he would sweep her into his arms and declare some sort of undying love in front of his men simply because they had shared their bodies? Those sorts of thing only happened in the skald's tales, and she'd given up on believing in such things.

She turned on her heel, wishing she'd not given in to foolish sentimentality earlier when she changed into this gown.

'Were you looking for something, my lady?' Stargazer asked. 'Or someone to pass the evening with? Tylir has been singing your praises about this ointment of yours. Perhaps you would like to spread it around.'

Said with a leer and a slight sneer as he looked her up and down. She knew that sort of man—the ones who liked to insinuate and to make women feel uncomfortable to boost their own sense of self-worth. He probably thought his friendship with Tylir made him untouchable. She might not be able to stop the remarks, but she refused to give him the satisfaction of reacting to them.

'Who is with Tylir?' she asked. 'I don't believe I have met them before.'

'Some of his men have just arrived from the outer farms. Typical problems for this time of year.' Stargazer gave a smarmy grin, which seemed to take in the contours of her bust. 'I am willing to entertain you until Tylir is free if that is what you'd enjoy.'

Her flesh crawled under his gaze. 'That won't be necessary.'

'You know I am one of Tylir's oldest friends. We share everything.'

She tightened her jaw. 'One of my late husband's retainers said that to me as a young bride. He lied. An untrustworthy man. He was later set up by footpads.'

Stargazer dropped his hand. 'Sunbear trusts *me* implicitly. I know him better than anyone.'

'Then you'll know that there is nothing between us aside from care for his daughter. He is enjoying being a father—something which had eluded him for some time.'

Stargazer laughed. 'He is indeed. Speaks of nothing else. I suspect his wife, Ingebord, would be eating in the rushes in jealousy. She was desperate for a child to ensure she would always live in the style she had become accustomed to.'

Desperate to give her husband a child? Mel could understand that longing. She had seen so many women over the years when she was a healer who wanted a living child. That ache to hold your own went beyond all understanding. Or was Stargazer implying Ingebord was simply desperate to secure Tylir's wealth? That certainly fit with the rumours she'd heard in the weaving hut about her—that she was hard work, demanding with scarcely a kind word for any. In fact, the more Mel heard of the woman, the less she liked her. She doubted that Ingebord had made Tylir happy and was pleased Katla would not have to experience the woman's regime either.

'I've no wish to intrude on his business. Please inform the jarl that I have retired for the night.'

Stargazer gave her a penetrating look, one which seemed to peer into her innermost soul. He pursed his lips and narrowed his eyes further. 'You know Estrid took his heart with her to the grave. She tore it out with her dainty hands, leaving him bleeding and bereft when she married that husband of hers. I pity any woman who cares for him. I have witnessed what he did to poor Ingebord and how she suffered.'

Mel raised her chin. 'I wish to ensure Katla is settled and then I shall take my own lands. I want somewhere to grow my herbs, make my tonics and ointments and have peace. That is my entire purpose.'

The lie was evident in her tone, but she hoped this man would accept her words at face value.

'Ask old Virin if you do not believe me about the suffering and cruel games he played.' His mouth twisted. 'He used to send her with an herbal concoction to every woman he bedded so that no chid would be produced.'

Mel tilted her chin upwards. It surprised her that someone who was supposed to be Tylir's friend gossiped in such a manner. 'How interesting.'

A strange light appeared in the man's eyes. 'There were many women. Most lasted no longer than a night. No wonder Ingebord took comfort elsewhere.'

A vague pang of pity for Tylir's late wife passed through her. She knew what it was like when your husband had a wandering eye. She had never seen it as reason to seek solace in the arms of another man, but she knew plenty who did.

'The condition of Tylir's heart fails to concern me. The condition of his child does.' She hoped her words convinced Stargazer. Her heart easily heard the lie. 'The next occasion I make time to speak to him about his daughter, I trust he will be less busy.'

Stargazer's eyes narrowed. 'You really are a force of a nature.'

'I take that as a compliment.' She turned on her heel and marched firmly out of the hall without a backwards glance.

Chapter Eleven

Once the cool darkness of the yard had enveloped her and the sounds of merrymaking faded from the hall, she allowed her feet to slow. She struggled to take a deep breath. Why had she entered that hall with such expectation of Tylir? After everything she'd been through with Elkr, she'd vowed that she'd never allow a man to have that sort of hold over her again.

Her mouth twisted. What a piecrust promise that had been. All it had taken was a man with deep eyes and a gentle touch and she'd forsaken all her principles. For what? A few heartbeats of pleasure.

She reached the wall of the barn and sank down. 'Tylir is Katla's father. That is my sole interest in him. This afternoon was an aberration.'

She repeated the phrase six times, making it sound far more forceful each time. Brave words, but her heart did ache and protest that she was jumping to conclusions. After what had passed between them earlier, she wanted to believe it was something more than bodies colliding and seeking refuge from life's storms.

And it did bother her that her growing regard for

Tylir shone so brilliantly on her face that Stargazer had decided to mention Virin's special potions. She had considered that she was an expert at hiding her emotions. Her mother had always declared she was horrible at hiding her feelings, but it was a good thing because then no one would have to guess. She had not known that it was a liability until she met Helm's mother.

She had worked on it and thought she perfected it during her marriage while she was dying inside as her husband regaled his followers with his latest sexual conquests.

She firmed her jaw. Perhaps Stargazer was trying to be kind in his own way. After all, he understood what she seemed to have such trouble accepting—that Tylir could never have any real or lasting interest in her.

The cold from the ground slowly seeped into her bottom and she knew she would have to move before her limbs completely stiffened, but she didn't want to. She could not bear to return to her room and wait in vain once more for sleep to find her.

She pinched the bridge of her nose. What was she waiting for? When was she going to stop believing in dreams? She knew what she wanted from life—a small farm, and a door she could bolt firmly. Nothing grand or luxurious, simply somewhere she could live free without having to second-guess her actions.

She closed her eyes and imagined once again the snug house with the large garden and prosperous fields. It bothered her that she could see it looking a bit like Tylir's hall. She screwed up her eyes and tried harder.

'Mel? Melkorka, what are you doing out here? I waited for you in the hall. Too many people crowded around.'

Her eyes flew open at the sound of his voice.

Tylir's shape loomed large in the gloom. She rapidly stood, smoothing down her skirts and thanking the gods that he could not see her upset expression.

'I had trouble sleeping.' Her voice sounded far too strained and high to her ears, but she suspected he would only hear the lightness. 'It has been this way since my son died.'

She waited for him to mumble his apologies and leave her to her grief.

'Is that what this is? An attempt to rest on the cold ground?'

'I'd no wish to disturb Katla.' She caught her lower lip between her teeth. 'I left a message with Stargazer. My presence would have been an unnecessary intrusion. Your men wish me gone. They distrust me because of my half-brother.'

Tylir waved a dismissive hand. 'Next time, tell me yourself. My men will understand in time about your loyalty. I hope you don't mind but I told them about your ointment and its healing powers.'

'That was very kind of you.'

'In the meantime, I look forward to my lessons on… parenting.'

Mel pursed her lips. She'd rushed to judgement far too quickly. Maybe they were not as close as Stargazer liked to think.

He held out a hand. 'Come for a walk with me. Please. I wish to have company on my rounds. Your voice is far more pleasant than my thoughts.'

Her entire body tingled. He was asking her to go with him and if she did, they would make love again. Or was that merely spinning impossibilities again?

'At night-time?' She forced a hiccupping laugh. 'Far too dark to see.'

'The moonlight is enough to see by. Starlight adds a certain lustre to my lands. The first time I saw them bathed in silver, I knew that this was where I wanted to make my home. Allow me to show it to you.'

There was an eagerness to Tylir's voice which reminded Mel of her son's when he acquired a new skill which he'd been particularly proud of. She could almost hear his voice calling to her to look. How many times had she looked away or had been busy with other tasks which seemed more important? She could not undo the past, but she could go for this walk with Tylir.

'With that sort of invitation, how can I refuse?'

His hand tightened about her fingers and tucked her arm close into his side. 'I knew you were a sensible woman.'

'You were going for a walk, or is it something you are doing for me?' she asked, hating how her voice quavered.

'Helps to clear my head. A habit my first commander taught me. It means I don't take my troubles to my bed.'

'He sounds like a wise man.'

'He was. A far better leader than I am. He died in a scrappy battle in Alba.'

'And you inherited his men.'

'Some and gained some more. When I decided my fighting days were over, most joined me here, where the laws instead of feuding hold sway.'

They walked for a little way in silence. Mel considered various topics and rejected them as they would all lead to the one thing she wanted to avoid discussing—their encounter earlier and if it was going to happen again.

'I know there is opposition to me being here,' she said when the silver-touched loch came into view and she found the silence too difficult to bear. 'Is it why those men arrived unexpectedly?'

He stopped abruptly and appeared to grow several inches. A cloud went over the moon, casting his face into shadow. 'These are my lands. I have the final say on who resides here. You remain under my protection. No one will harm you here.'

She tucked her head into her neck. He was right, of course, but it didn't make it any easier if people were against her. 'I dislike causing friction. I truly had no idea about your feud when I arrived. And my half-brother did not consider it necessary to tell me. You can see where I fit in. I doubt I have ever fit in. My marriage was one of convenience rather than pleasure. My husband… He had little time for me after I had his heir.'

'Yet you continued to make a home for him.'

'I had my son. I thought he would be enough, and then he died. And I knew my skill with herbs was an illusion.'

Her heart knocked so loudly that she thought he must hear. At the same instant, the moon reappeared and the whole world became bathed in its cold light.

His lips turned up into a genuine smile. 'Your skill with herbs is unquestionably real. Let us go further.'

'It is too dark out. We should be sensible and turn back.'

'Keep tight hold of my hand.' His hand came under her elbow. 'Are you brave enough to do that, Mel?'

Brave enough? She was a coward, but her heart urged her forward. 'What is the harm in continuing on?'

She curved her fingers about his and felt his warm palm against her cooler one.

'I hoped you'd say that.'

'Only hoped?'

'I'd hate to presume on my daughter's companion. There—you see, if I keep saying the words, maybe I will start to believe it.'

'Who do you think I am?'

'The woman walking next to me is the same woman I enjoyably held in my arms earlier. Mel.'

She stumbled over a tree root. He put his hand on the small of her back. 'We should walk without talking.'

'Listen. You might hear an owl.'

As if on cue the faint sounds of an owl hooting were swiftly answered by another owl. 'Calling for her mate?'

'A good omen, don't you agree?'

'Do I need to be looking for omens? Can't we simply exist in the present without worrying about the future?' She hated the faintly plaintive tone in her voice.

'Some people seem to need them.' He started towards a stand of trees. 'Come. One of my favourite places is near here. When I first arrived, I had thought to build my hall there.'

'What happened?'

'My wife had other ideas. It would not have been imposing enough for the Sunbear and his lady wife and most importantly prestigious guests they would entertain.'

'You make it sound like the Sunbear is another person, not you.'

'A role. It enabled me to stop being afraid during my first battle. It enabled me to command my first *felag*.' His mouth twisted. 'It brought me my wife when I had lost everything as Tylir.'

'I never considered that you might be afraid.'

'Everyone gets afraid, Mel. It is what you do with that fear.' His hand rubbed a small circle on her back. 'Shall we return to the compound?'

It was on the tip of her tongue to ask if he wanted to take her to his bed. She doubted if she had the strength to keep resisting. 'Keep walking on this path.'

'As my lady wishes.'

They continued in silence with the owls hooting every few steps. Every particle of her was aware of him, the way he breathed, the length of his steps and how his hand felt in the small of her back.

'About what happened earlier…this afternoon, I mean, not in the hall,' she began. 'We need to speak about what passed between us, Tylir, and not pretend it never happened. It was a mistake for so many reasons.'

He stopped abruptly and turned towards her, putting two fingers over her mouth, while his other hand raised her chin upwards, forcing her to gaze into his starlit eyes. 'If you are going to apologise for what happened this afternoon or ask me to, forget it. I refuse to.'

He took a step backwards.

She wrapped her arms about her middle. 'I'm not going to ask for any more than this, if that is what you are worried about. My husband…'

He put a finger over her mouth, stopping her words.

'Your husband is dead and plays no part in our conversation. I never met the man but suspect I would have loathed him.'

'I know you are not him.' Mel silently cursed. She had explained it badly. Tylir was nothing like her husband, except he was a jarl.

'Then stop trying to make me be him! I know what I want, and I want to be inside you.'

'You do?'

He gave a soft laugh which warmed her down to her toes. He put an arm about her waist and drew her against his hard chest. 'This is not how I planned this evening would go.'

Now that her slender curves were snuggling into him, her earlier worries vanished like mist on the loch. 'Isn't it?'

'I thought a game of *tafl* with a suitable wager or three before we ended the evening pleasurably in my bed.' His mouth twisted. 'My men had other ideas. Not ideal but my duty towards them does come first. My men wanted to meet the woman who had developed such a wonderful ointment and improved my mood, but she had vanished into the night air.'

She tucked her chin into her neck. 'I didn't want to intrude.'

'Everyone remarked on how much better I walked. Hopefully you will grow more herbs as everyone will want some.' He lifted her chin, so she was forced to stare into his eyes. 'But I demand my share first.'

Her heart soared. Tylir had not been seeking an end to this thing between them at all. He had spoken about her healing skills to the men. He had merely been fulfilling his duties to his men. Not everything was about her and their relationship such as it was.

'The thing you should know is that I'm not looking for for ever,' she said before her nerves completely failed her. 'I want to explore this…this passion between us, but I won't see Katla hurt.'

His grip tightened about her waist, pushing her tighter against him so that their middles touched. His rampant arousal pushed firmly into the apex of her thighs, leaving her with no doubt about the strength of his desire.

'Life taught me a long time ago that no one has for ever, but I will take the right and the now. And my daughter has no place in this discussion. What happens between us is between us.'

'Good, I am pleased it is settled.' She held out her hand, hating how her stomach knotted. 'For as long as it lasts.'

Silently she prayed to any god or goddess who might be listening, but most specifically to Freya, who understood matters of the heart, that it would last longer than a few days but short enough for her heart not to be broken when it ended. She knew it would be badly bruised when the inevitable happened.

His laughter rang out. 'I can think of something more preferable than a handshake to seal our bargain.'

She deliberately fluttered her lashes. 'Do we have a bargain?'

'You make me want to be better than I am. Remember that.'

She gulped hard. 'For as long as it lasts and no regrets.'

He captured a lock of her hair and twisted it between

his fingers. 'As if I could regret anything which has passed between us.'

Giving in to temptation, she reached out and ran her hand along his cheek, feeling the faint stubble beneath the pads of her fingers. 'I shan't either.'

A small part of her wondered who she was trying to convince.

'Good.' His mouth lowered and claimed hers.

She gave herself up to the intensity of the kiss. Their tongues touched and tangled, retreated and probed again. And the flames from earlier which she had considered dowsed flared into an inferno. She intertwined her fingers in his hair, holding him there. His lips moving against hers made her greedy for more in a way that her late husband's kisses never had done. She'd promised Estrid that she would live to the full.

The thought of Estrid acted like cold water. She tore her mouth away and dropped her hands to her sides.

'Did I do something wrong?' he asked against her jawline, sending tingles coursing through her.

'Not you.' She wondered how she could explain her fears about not being able to measure up to her friend. How she wanted to be important to someone. She wanted to matter and greatly feared the only person she mattered to was dead. She might as well wish to hold a star.

No regrets. Start a new life. Live for both of us. That was what Estrid whispered at the end.

She took a deep breath and allowed her hands to tug at his shirt. 'Let me see you. Let me enjoy you and this time when all is bathed in silver.'

His soft masculine laugh filled the hollow. 'My lady

is insistent. I like that. I like that a great deal. Silver bathing it is.'

He helped undo the ties and strip his tunic from his body, revealing the wide expanse of his chest with its well-defined muscles. The moonlight had turned his skin to silver. She drew in a sharp breath.

'Let me make a bed before we properly begin,' he rumbled in her ear.

She smiled softly, suddenly secure enough to gently tease, something she never dared do with her late husband, but she could remember as a small girl seeing her mother do with her father. 'Have we improperly begun?'

He gently nipped her nose. 'I've no wish for your clothes to be stained with the moss.'

'How very considerate of you. I'm impressed.'

His laugh made her tingle all over. He carefully laid out the cloak and tunic, creating a nest.

She pretended to examine it critically by walking around. 'You would make a passable maid.'

'Only passable? Would you make alterations?'

Mel pretended to think. 'One or two. To provide maximum comfort, you understand.'

A smile tugged at his lips. 'If you require my trousers to make this nest more comfortable, you must undo them. My fingers are awkward, and I don't want to risk knotting the tie.'

Her palms itched to touch him there, but she also worried that she would make a mistake or be awkward about it. The words confessing about how little practice she had at such things rose in her throat. She concentrated on the pile of clothes and swallowed hard. Her fears and inhibitions had no place here. They had already agreed to no regrets. 'That sounds like an excuse. Hand them over.'

She held out her palm and averted her eyes.

'Your choice. I can keep them on, but it might inhibit proceedings later. My lady always has the final say on these matters.'

She nodded, understanding what he was saying. He was not commanding her to do things like her late husband had. And to her surprise, she wanted to undress him and reveal his erection. In fact, she knew she wanted to touch him and see what his member felt like in her hand. Things she had never dared to do with Elkr.

She knelt on the cloak. 'No, I will undo them. I just needed to get to the right height.'

'Full of surprises, today, my lady.'

Her hands worked quickly at the fastenings, and the trousers slipped over his slim hips, allowing his arousal to spring free. For several long heartbeats, she simply stared at him and his size. He was larger than she expected, jutting out at her. More proof of Tylir's desire.

'Is everything all right?' His voice held a faint hint of worry.

Her heart constricted. He wasn't entirely sure of himself either. They were a pair.

'Perfectly fine.' Giving in to temptation, she stroked the silky smoothness of him with her forefinger. He went very still. The darkness hid his face. She took his stillness and silence as an assent for her to continue. She curled her fingers about his member before taking the head into her mouth and sucking.

'Mel.' The word was half groan, half plea.

A sense of power filled her. His erection had increased in size in her mouth. She tasted a faint salty tang on the tip which was unmistakably him.

'You will unman me if I allow you to continue.'

'Unman you?' she murmured.

'I will lose control, and this will be over before it truly begins,' he said with a gasp between each word, but his hands were entangled in her hair, keeping her there in front of him with the lightest of touches.

She rocked back on her heels. His face wore an intent expression of wonderment. A renewed sense of power surged through her. She had brought this warrior to this state. She had pushed him to the brink of losing control. The woman her late husband had claimed no man could desire and certainly not more than once. Like so many things, he'd been very wrong about that.

'Do you like?' she asked, pushing all thoughts of her past and supposed failures behind her.

'I like very much but I want you to enjoy this as well. Giving you pleasure gives me pleasure.' He tightened his grip on her. 'Please.'

She ran a finger down the length of him and pretended to think. His flesh quivered at her touch. And the drop at the end of his head grew.

Her pleasure, not just his. Her body tingled at the thought. He was concerned for her.

'I've no wish for this to be over quickly,' she admitted and withdrew her hand from him.

'Thank you.' He collapsed down beside her, drew three shuddering breaths before he removed her couverchef, causing her hair to tumble down in disarray.

'Utterly gorgeous. So many colours.' He placed a kiss against a curl which had fallen between her breasts.

She'd always loathed her hair, but the way Tylir touched it and said those words, she was almost convinced that she had made a mistake in her earlier assessment about its beauty.

'I am pleased you like it.'

He put a finger under her chin. 'One day we will do this properly in my bed. Piled high with furs and the hours stretching out before us. And then I can worship the beauty of your body as it deserves to be.'

The image made her mouth go dry. A small part of her warned that they were pretty words which meant little. Men always said things in desire. But her heart refused to listen. The sense of being cosseted and treated like a precious jewel was one she wanted to savour. 'I will hold you to that promise.'

He entangled his hands in her locks, and softly kissed her temple. 'And I will hold you to it as well. No finding an excuse when the time arrives. You must agree to be there, even if people are begging for your herbs and ointment.'

'Depends on if there is an emergency elsewhere. You would want me to look after Katla or indeed help your people in a time of crisis.'

'Faultless logic, but you mustn't argue with this.' He gently eased her back until she lay in the nest he'd created. Above him the stars twinkled. He slowly lifted her gown and exposed her fevered skin to the cool night air.

'Argue with what?'

'My turn to feast.' Before she could object, he lowered his mouth to her nest of curls. Slowly and inexorably his tongue explored the hidden folds and nubs, making lazy circles, round and round. She had thought the inferno had consumed her earlier but now she knew it had been a prelude to this. She teetered on the brink. Her body bucked upwards, seeking the relief which she instinctively knew only he could give.

She clawed at his back, wanting relief as her body writhed under the ministrations of his mouth. 'Please. I need you inside me. Now.'

He glanced up and gave a wicked smile. 'My pleasure.'

He rapidly positioned himself between her thighs and drove into her. Her body opened fully, and with one forward motion, he sheathed himself deep within her. Slowly he began to move, thrusting forward and she responded, matching him. Their rhythm was perfection, and she began to understand why so many women enjoyed the experience rather than considered it their duty.

Afterwards lying cradled in his arms, listening to the soft sound of him sleeping and watching the way his dark lashes were splayed on his cheeks, she knew she had never felt this alive before. More importantly, she knew she had lied to herself—she cared about this man and what happened to him, particularly as he struggled to be a good parent. And she also knew that she'd never regret their joining. She simply had to figure out a way of ensuring that he never found out about her growing feelings towards him. She was not going to give him that sort of power over her heart.

As the silver grey in the night sky started to turn to a rosy-hued dawn, Tylir loosened his arms. He'd spent most of the night watching her sleep and listening to her soft breathing. Watching over her and wishing he

could be in truth the sort of man she deserved instead
of the man pretending to be that sort.

He knew what he'd done on the battlefield after his
first commander died as he desperately tried to turn
the tide and avenge that brutal hacking. How Ingebord
had turned from him when she discovered he had little
interest in social status or the niceties and was nothing
but a tired warrior who was sick of the mud and stink of
war. How Estrid, the woman who had promised to love
him until the end of time, had barely waited a month
before declaring for another if Stargazer's investiga-
tions held true. It was only a matter of time before Mel
saw that ugliness of his soul which he fervently wished
wasn't there. And how she'd understand that he had a
stone for a heart rather than being able to love her as
she deserved to be.

For as long as it lasted, even though he knew he
wanted it to last a lifetime. Except one dark day, she
would see into his black soul and recoil just as Estrid
and Ingebord had done in their own ways. But for now
she made him believe that he could be that better man,
simply because she had chosen to sleep peacefully in
his arms. And he did not dare tell her how much it had
meant to him.

'We should go. Dawn is coming. People will be stirring.' He kissed her cheek and pushed away all thoughts
about the day he'd discovered Ingebord's body or the
day Estrid had broken with him. He wanted to believe
that this time he could be the sort of man he wanted to
be. 'You wouldn't want Katla to be frightened.'

At his daughter's name, she instantly sat up and

started to smooth her skirts down, covering her slender legs. 'We wouldn't want that.'

He noted the slight catch in her throat. 'Mel, you know if what passes between us results in a child…'

'It won't. I know my herbs. You need not worry about that. No need to send Virin to me.'

He frowned. Sometimes, Mel made little sense. He had never asked Virin to do anything like that for him. He never would. Until he discovered Katla's existence, he had worried that he was barren and destined never to have children. 'Send Virin to you? Have I ever suggested such a thing?'

Her glorious hair covered her face, hiding her expression. 'My mistake.'

He gritted his teeth and wondered who had been telling her tales. More than likely Virin or perhaps just one of the women. He could never understand why they would gossip about such a thing. He had not been the one to cheat. That had been Ingebord, who delighted in trying to torment him, knowing that if he admitted it bothered him, she proved her point and he would have to return to her bed.

He stared at the rose-coloured horizon. A new day and thus far uncontaminated with the mistakes from the past. He took a deep breath. 'I wanted you to know that I am prepared to do my duty towards any child. Virin has never had anything to do with the women I bedded.'

As soon as the words emerged from his throat, he knew from the swift intake of her breath, they lacked a certain elegance.

'I don't speak about such things to Virin. My mother

brought me up to know my duty,' he said, trying again but knowing he failed miserably to explain it properly.

'Your duty has never been in any doubt.' Her voice resembled a frost giantess from the old tales—foreboding and inclined to give no quarter. 'You acknowledged Katla.'

'Mel. It came out wrong. I'm no skald. I am a warrior who has become a farmer.'

'Just know that I would never go to her. I am an accomplished herbalist in my own right.' She stood up and raised her chin. Her eyes were ice-cold. 'Should I ever decide to have another child, it will be my choice and I will not require a man to do his duty by me or the child.'

He rubbed the back of his neck and wished he could unsay the words. 'Mel, I wanted to reassure you.'

'As you said—we overslept. The household will be stirring. I want Katla to remain in ignorance about us. It is the one thing I must ask.'

'Best rest I have had in ages,' he said, keeping as close to the truth as possible. 'I will have to try the hard ground with a warm body next to me more often, particularly when it belongs to an accomplished herbalist.'

She turned her back on him. 'You make it sound simple. Like we are going to meet every night until whatever this thing is between us passes.'

He frowned, unable to discern her mood. He had the distinct impression that he had said the wrong thing from the time he'd woken her and had continued to say the wrong thing ever since. Women were complicated creatures. He tried and failed with Estrid and Ingebord. It would appear the intervening time had not improved his tongue in the slightest.

He'd only meant that she need not worry about any children. He had thought she'd be pleased that he was even thinking about such consequences and had a plan—he would acknowledge them but leave them with her until they were old enough. A large part of him had wanted her to say that she wanted to have another child, and particularly with him. He knew such a child could never replace the one she'd lost, but he wanted to think she'd welcome his child. Instead, she had dashed those hopes as well.

He curled his fists and tried to think of a way to restore the harmony between them. 'Simply because we spent the night under stars doesn't mean I intend to release you from the promise of spending a night in my bed. There are many more delights I wish to sample with you.'

To his relief, she gave a throaty laugh. 'One promise you had best keep. You have set high expectations about this bed and its many furs.'

She turned on her heel and disappeared into the light mist which was rising from the loch before he had a chance to say more, but he took the words as a sign that she was eager to spend more time in his arms.

Tylir picked up a flat pebble and walked over to the loch. As a boy he used to skim stones and make a wish if he managed to get the stone to skip more than seven times. Why had he foolishly let Stargazer get to him and invited so many eligible farmers to the feast celebrating Katla's arrival simply to prove he was not as besotted with Mel as his friend teased? They would see in the blink of an eye how much more pleasant this hall was and how Mel's herbs were helping everyone with various aches and pains. They'd see that but they would also hear her throaty laugh and her air of friendly helpfulness towards everyone and they would attempt to gather her into their households.

He knew he would want to shout to everyone that Mel belonged to him and him alone, but Mel had forbidden him from doing that. In private and for as long as the passion existed between them. It would make it difficult to romance her in front of everyone.

The first pebble skipped five times, the second three but the third went for nine. Tylir smiled. All he had to do was to find a way to enlist Katla in his scheme to get Mel to stay for a little while longer. Then he could show her why she was better staying with them than flitting off with some unknown who romanced her. How hard could that be?

Chapter Twelve

Mel arrived back in the chamber she shared with Katla to discover that the grey light of dawn well and truly peeked through the cracks in the wooden walls. At the sound of her footsteps, Katla sat up and rubbed her eyes.

Now that Mel knew Tylir better, she saw him in the curve of the child's bottom lip, the sleepy way she blinked her eyes open and her slow hesitant smile when she woke.

'Where have you been, Aunty Mel?' Katla clutched her doll to her chest. 'Freya wanted to know. She has been keeping watch for ever so long. She thought Fenrir the Wolf might have eaten you up, but I told her to stop telling stories.'

Mel took the doll from Katla and placed her on the pillow.

'Such a sleepy girl,' she said, instead of remarking on the doll's theory.

'Where have you been? Somewhere good? Did you meet anyone?'

'I woke early and went out for a walk. Down to the loch. You should see the morning mist rising. Best part of the day. The sunrise with its rose-pink tones made the entire sky look like ripe cloudberries.' Mel carefully kept all mention of Tylir out. Any mention of him would confuse the child. And she wanted to hug the sensation she had of waking up in his arms to herself for as long as possible. It was as precious as the first snowflake that she caught on her hand every winter, though it would be just as fleeting.

Katla reached for Freya and hugged the doll close. 'Next time, may I come? I have always wanted to see the sunrise just as I have always wanted to see the Bifrost. My *mor* used to say if you saw the swirling green lights of the Bifrost, your dreams were very likely to come true.'

'If you are awake when I see a Bifrost, I am sure that can be arranged.'

'Did you see anybody on your walk? You didn't say and Freya wants to know. She doesn't like that Stargazer man. He tries to look down your gown.'

'It was very quiet out,' Mel said in a firm voice which sought to forestall any awkward questions. 'As it should be.'

Katla's face fell slightly. 'Freya thought you might be with my father. He would take you on a walk. I am certain of it.'

Mel's heart panged. Katla's acceptance of Tylir as her father was proof—if she required—that soon she would no longer have any excuse for staying. Katla was settling in wonderfully, particularly as Tylir took the time to ask his daughter questions about the day and carefully explained his day to her, something her late husband had never done with their son. Tylir would be a good father to the little girl, the sort she'd hoped Katla would have.

'We had best get you dressed.' Mel bustled over to Katla's iron-bound trunk and started to remove fresh clothes. 'People will start arriving for this gathering your father has called. You will want to look your best. Do your father proud.'

'I will take that for a yes as my *mor* would say.' Katla's eyes gleamed. 'You changed the subject and your cheeks flamed bright.'

'You think too much, little one.' Instinctively Mel brushed Katla's hair from her forehead and placed a kiss, a gesture she'd often done to her son, but had resisted doing to Katla until now.

The little girl's face became wreathed in smiles. 'My *mor* used to do that when I said something very clever.'

'Your mother was a good woman.'

Katla frowned. 'Do you think we can stop Tylir feeling sad about her? I think he is better now that you and I are here. He smiles more.'

Mel put her arm about Katla. The last thing she wished to do was to make the little girl hope for something like that. And Katla's innocent words about Tylir missing Estrid were a timely reminder—what they shared was passion, not their hearts. She vowed that she'd never marry, not unless her heart was truly captured, and she knew that the man adored her back— truly something akin to impossibility. She had to know that she'd be cherished instead of being another useful tool in her husband's arsenal. Katla would not understand any of that. She looked at the world with a little girl's eyes and a steadfast belief in magic.

Her heart whispered that Tylir already held a corner of her heart and she should stop expecting him to behave like Elkr had. She chose to ignore the murmur.

'I will always be your friend, Katla,' she said instead. 'Whatever happens in this life, remember that I, Melkorka Helmsdottar, will always be your true friend. I swear by Var the god of oaths.'

The little girl stuck out her bottom lip. 'But a true friend is not the same thing as being my new mother.'

'Shall we go see the spaniel puppies? They will soon be big enough to leave their mother and you need to decide what you are going to call yours and which one it will be.' Mel knew seeing the puppies was an attempt at bribery and distraction, but Katla was far too intent on matchmaking between her and Tylir. She might even tell the wrong person and that would be a disaster. 'Tylir said that you were to have first pick of the litter.'

Katla wrinkled her nose, but her eyes lit up. 'My mother wouldn't like a dog in my sleeping quarters. She said that dogs smelt and should be kept outside.'

'Another way that Islond is different. Tylir will let you keep the dog here.'

Katla nodded. 'Perhaps there will be some good things here after all.'

Mel's heart sank when they returned from viewing the growing puppies for the fifth time in as many days and she spotted her sister-in-law, Helga, on the pier. Just what she did not need on the eve of the great gathering in Katla's honour, as Tylir had taken to calling it.

A deep frown was etched on the woman's face and her boot tapped the pier. 'Finally, Melkorka. I would love to think that it was because you were busy with the preparations, but somehow that fails to be the case.'

Mel kept tight hold of Katla, hating how Helga always made her feel inadequate. It was a trait she shared with Helm's mother. And she had nothing to do with the preparations. Tylir was most insistent on that. He wanted to give the women of his house a chance to show her that they were capable. As she had no intention of staying, she could understand the logic even if her hands itched to help with the preparations.

She smoothed her skirts. 'No one let me know you were here.'

Helga rolled her eyes and made a disgruntled noise like a startled pig. 'I told that awful woman Virin. She said she'd inform you. I've been left standing here for an age…like yesterday's loaf of bread. I should have known that she'd be a shifty one. She used to tell me the most dreadful untruths about all sorts of people by way of gossip.'

Always back to Virin and her little ways. Mel gritted her teeth and tried to be logical about the situation. She doubted anyone besides the stable hand who was looking after the puppies had known they were there. They had stayed a bit longer in the barn than she planned, but Katla had wanted to pick up each puppy and decide which one was hers. Finally, she picked out her favourite—one with a brown-and-white tail and several brown splodges in his back who had chewed the tip of her boot.

'We were looking at puppies.' Katla clapped her hands together. 'I'm getting my very own. I can't wait to tell the boys as they said girls couldn't get dogs. Did they come with you?'

'Not this time.'

'Maybe next time, they can look at the puppies and run around with me.' Katla twirled about. 'Like I used to do…before…before I came to Islond.' Her voice trailed off.

Helga lowered her voice. 'Melkorka, we have matters to discuss…without the child. You don't want to distress her more than necessary.'

'Katla is my responsibility.'

The woman scrunched up her nose. 'I'm begging you for the sake of peace in this valley—find someone else to look after her while we speak. It won't take long.'

'I can take the little girl, my lady.' Virin sidled up to them. 'I searched all over the yard for you and you are already here talking with that…that woman. The Sunbear has decreed no one from Helm's household should leave the pier without his say-so and he is… busy at present.'

Virin managed to put a distinct sniff into her voice as if Helga's unexpected arrival on the day of the feast was all somehow Mel's fault.

'I am here, speaking with my sister-in-law.' Mel frowned. She doubted that Virin had worked very hard to try to find her. And it did not surprise her that Tylir was busy. He wanted the feast to be perfect for his little girl. What was wrong with that? She hated how her throat constricted and how she wished that he might care a little for her as well. Despite all her promises about living in the present and not asking for more, her feelings for him were growing.

'But the little girl—'

Mel firmed her mouth. Tylir obviously had his own reasons for trusting this woman. And she noticed Helga listened to every word as if they were juicy titbits. The last thing she wanted to do was show discord or for Virin to have cause to think there was. 'Katla needs to return to the sleeping quarters and get her hair braided and clothes changed. I trust you are able to do that.'

The old woman straightened. Her eyes gleamed as if Mel had given her a treasure. 'Do you think the little girl will go with me? We did not get off to the best start.'

A momentary twinge of unease passed through Mel. It was perhaps not the best thing, but it was clear Virin was eager to help out with Katla and she could think of no other option. 'I am sure she will.' Mel crouched down until her face was at Katla's level. 'Can you go and get your hair braided with Virin and get into your special clothes?'

Katla squeezed her hand and nodded. 'I will be brave now that I am to have the puppy with the dark brown spots.'

Mel suspected the last said in a loud voice was for the benefit of Helga so she would relate it back to the boys.

Mel waited silently with her arms crossed until Virin had bustled Katla out of earshot. 'What did you come here about? Today of all days? Are you trying to make trouble?'

'Melkorka,' Helga said in a cold tone, 'I have come to mend bridges, not burn them.'

'Helm departed with furious words, but despite everything Tylir sent an invitation to tonight's feast.'

'My husband has an overly quick temper, and you

were less than truthful with him. You hid Katla's parentage.'

Mel crossed her arms. 'He was less than truthful with me about his relationship with Tylir and Tylir's late wife from what I understand.'

Helga rolled her eyes. 'Are you ready to accept some of the blame? You insisted on coming here.'

Mel clung on to the remaining shreds of her temper. Helga always refused to consider that Helm had done something wrong. Even back in the North when they were scurrying for their lives, it was always someone else's fault. 'Surely you did not come here today to discuss blame or lack of it about what occurred. I accepted that Helm will not take me in should I discover some reason to leave Tylir's protection. Currently, I am fine. Thank you for being concerned.'

'No, I came to discuss this.' Helga reached into her pouch and withdrew Mel's mother's torc, the one she'd been convinced Helm had quietly appropriated.

Her mind raced. There had to be a reason why Helga had suddenly appeared with it. She was pleased that Tylir had never made a giant fuss about it. Instead, he allowed for this to happen. 'Where did you discover that?'

'Buried in the grain store. It might have been lost for ever but one of the maids was clumsy and thought it would be easier to get the grain from the old store. She withdrew this and brought it to me. She didn't wish to be called a thief.'

'And you knew who it belonged to.'

An uncertain smile fluttered on Helga's features. 'I won't have bad blood between you and Helm. Helm is an honest man. He would never steal from you.'

'I never said he wasn't.'

Helga crumpled, aging several years before Mel's eyes. 'You do believe me, don't you?'

'My torc was not in my trunk when I arrived here. All the seals were done up the way I had left them. It is a mystery to me how it made its way to the grain store.'

'Then it is a mystery to the both of us on why it should appear in the grain store.'

Mel struggled to keep her temper. 'Does Helm know you are here?'

Helga quickly glanced at the boat where five of Helm's men lounged. 'He does. He couldn't come himself, Melkorka. Be reasonable. Think of the accusations that man Sunbear would shout at him.'

'Who do you think hid the torc?'

Helga raised her arms to the skies. 'I swear by Var, I have not the slightest clue. Does that satisfy you?'

'As you are swearing by Var, the god who holds all oaths sacred, I believe you.'

Helga let out a long, relieved sigh. 'Finally. And you believe it had nothing to do with your brother or me?'

'I am willing to entertain that notion.'

'I suspect it will be that little girl's fault. She probably took it and hid it to make some sort of mischief. She was leading my boys astray.'

'Why do you think that? Katla is a very honest little girl.'

'She likes leading my boys astray, I can tell.' Helga withdrew a small pouch. 'This I am sorry to say was there as well. It does not belong to my family, and I believe it bears the device of the girl's supposed father in the North. I want nothing to do with it. My family will not be made into scapegoats for someone else's shady doings.'

Helga's voice rose on the last word.

Mel frowned. Helga appeared genuinely frightened. 'I am grateful for it being returned. Estrid's late husband was very fond of Katla. He wanted her properly settled.'

'She is quite the little heiress, then. What with one thing and another.'

Mel carefully pulled at the cuffs on her gown. Was this was what it was about—trying to see how wealthy Katla had become? 'I suppose she is.'

'My lads said she bragged about it. Said how wealthy her father was. And now she has an even wealthier father.'

Mel weighed the pouch in her hand. The knots remained intricately tied in precisely the same fashion it had been in the North Country. She could not see Katla bragging about it. Her nephews did always like to embroider a tale.

'Estrid's husband doted on the little girl. He made certain that she was well looked after. This was just a small part of her inheritance from him.'

Helga did her best fish impression with bulging eyes and open and shutting mouth. She suddenly gave her body a great shake and stood taller. 'I wish you had confided in me, Melkorka, when you first arrived. Much could have been avoided. We shall just say that Katla is quite the little scamp, but the boys are quite taken with her. They wanted to impress her. You know what boys can be like.'

Mel kept a tight rein on her temper. The words asking why Katla would do something like that nearly burst from her throat. Helga had come with the peace offering for some reason and she needed to discover that reason, rather than picking a fight. She owed it to Katla and to Tylir. He truly did not want the feud to continue. She had seen that when he defended her against his man's accusations the other day. Tylir wanted to protect his people. It was a sacred duty to him, not lip service like some saw it.

'I assume you and Helm will be coming to the feast celebrating Katla. There will be games, skalds and riddles.'

'I regret that will be impossible.' Helga pressed her palms into her eyes for a long heartbeat. Silently Mel will her to tell the truth, instead of a polite lie. 'Helm has no wish to dishonour his neighbour and has seen more than enough bloodshed and feuding for one lifetime. It is why we travelled over the sea—to make a fresh start and leave all the old unpleasantness behind. I used to think we had. I used to think Ingebord and I could be friends, but it proved otherwise.'

Mel firmed her mouth. Leave all the old unpleasantness behind. She knew who bore some responsibility for that, quarrelling with everyone over land and livestock, not listening to reason. And that someone wasn't Tylir. 'Good to hear that Helm no longer desires to make war on his neighbours. Good to hear that he changed.'

Helga glanced over towards where Tylir's men had started to gather. 'I've no wish for an escalation and a return to what passed last year. People died.'

'I know my brother can be short-tempered in drink, Helga. I know what passed between him and my late husband at our wedding. How Helm had to run for his life from his neighbours.'

Helga patted her couverchef. 'Helm and Sunbear's wife, Ingebord, had a brief affair. I was recovering from a miscarriage at the time and Helm was entrapped. They used to meet by the hot pool.'

Mel murmured her sympathy and Helga gave a brief nod to show her appreciation.

'Helm is a man of appetites,' Helga continued. 'I knew that when we married, but that woman played him. Ingebord wanted Sunbear to notice her and he refused to. That marriage was over, I tell you. She flirted with any man old enough to carry a proper sword. I have lost count how many men she was linked with.'

Mel forced her face to appear disinterested. It said something of Tylir's character that he had protected his wife's name for as long as he could even with her. 'Helm always chased skirts.'

'He faced severe temptation and promised never again after he broke with Ingebord. I have forgiven him,' Helga said with pursed lips.

'Indeed. I hope for his sake that he keeps that particular promise.' She held back the sarcastic remark asking if Helm had been forced in the woman's arms. Helga never understood irony or sarcasm.

'Helm came to his senses and broke it off. He had nothing to do with that woman's death. She slipped on the stones beside the pool and hit her head. The Assembly agreed it was an accident.'

Mel struggled to keep a straight face. Her half-brother told a pretty tale wrapped up in an embroidered ribbon when the circumstances suited him. 'What happened to her? Precisely.'

Helga widened her eyes. 'Has no one here thought to inform you? Sunbear and that louche friend of his, Stargazer, found her, drowned and naked in the pool which occasionally churns with heat.' She gave a delicate shudder. 'Her flesh was very nearly boiled.'

Mel winced. It sounded like a horrible way to die. And it must have been equally distressing for Tylir to find Ingebord like that. His marriage might not have been the best, but he had stayed with her.

'Where was that?'

'Near where our two properties meet. The General Assembly said she must have slipped on the stones and the god of the pool decided to make it hot.' Helga wrinkled her nose. 'You can always tell about such places—they smell like rotten eggs. But she liked to meet her men there or so Helm confided to me. Later there was a fight about the whole thing and men on both sides perished. One of Sunbear's men had his head crushed and one of Helm's took a knife to his side. The General Assembly decided that no one was to blame.'

'Old gossip with little relevance to today,' Mel said and hoped her words were true.

Her sister-in-law did the slow blink of a codfish. 'I was merely trying to explain why Helm and I wouldn't be at this gathering. And why I wanted to show that we are not dishonest.'

'I am pleased to have my torc back and some of Katla's inheritance.'

'We have seen too much suffering as a result of a feud which was not of our making. Is it Helm's fault that Tylir was an indifferent lover and she was forced to seek solace elsewhere?'

Mel held back the words pointing out the obvious that, far from being indifferent, Tylir was superb, a man who cared about his partner's pleasure, something she doubted her brother was ever concerned about.

Helm had had a choice. No one had forced him to lie with Tylir's late wife and he certainly knew that it was an excellent way to instigate trouble. Neither did she think Katla had been playing games with the torc. Someone had deliberately taken it and hidden it.

For right now though she was willing to give Helga the benefit of the doubt and believe that some maid had indeed discovered it hid in the grain store like the remnant of a child's game gone wrong or it had moved under its own power.

'We are agreed on the need to end suffering. Hopefully one day, things will have improved, and we will be able to break bread together.'

Helga gave a pleased smile. 'I knew I was right to bring that torc to you straight away. You were always Helm's favourite sibling.'

'I would like to think we could be friends. I plan to take my own land and farm.'

'Ah, that could be the reason that Tylir has ensured all the eligible men in the neighbourhood will be at this feast. Helm and I speculated on it. A subtle thank-you to you for bringing his daughter to him.'

Mel did a slow blink and tried to get her mind to focus away from her circling thoughts. Was Tylir eager to get her out of his life? Did he think she would go to the highest bidder? Had he not even listened to what she said about wanting independence and sanctuary? Did he want rid of her that badly? She struggled to breathe and tightened her grip, which was suddenly slick with sweat.

'He has invited all the eligible landowners? Why did he do that?' Her voice sounded far too high-pitched for her ears.

'He is trying to be kind, Melkorka.' Helga gave her a pitying look as if she guessed that Mel harboured unrequited feelings for Tylir. 'Lots of women have tried for him, before and after his wife's death, but for some reason he always seemed elusive. Even when Ingebord flirted so outrageously, he never took a mistress. Some say his heart was buried with his first love.'

'Could be.'

'I presume Katla's mother is the woman in question.' Helga patted Mel's shoulder. 'You must not pant after him because he is single. Helm worried that you might do something like that.'

Mel stepped away and forced air into her lungs. Her sister-in-law's gossip on matters of the heart was normally accurate. She had not stopped to think how much the truth might hurt. 'I have never discussed the state of Tylir's heart with him. Why would I? I am here to get his daughter settled.'

Helga waved her hand. 'As you say, old gossip. I do hope you and that little girl can bring a lasting peace. It has been sore missed of late.'

'Why did Tylir blame Helm for the death?'

'Easier to blame Helm than to admit the truth.' Helga tapped the side of her nose. 'They say Sunbear is cursed never to be happy due to his actions on the battlefield in England. They say an old witch put a spell on him, which is why that woman left him. They say because of the curse he can never satisfy a woman either and he knows it. It was why he turned a blind eye to that woman's flirtation.'

Mel struggled to keep a straight face. She didn't care about a supposed curse. She knew he had more than satisfied her. But she refused to divulge any scrap of information about the relationship to Helga. 'So much talk of curses! Some people will say anything simply to fill the air.'

Helga gave a slight sniff and peered more closely at her. 'It is what I have heard.' She waved a hand. 'From Helm, who had it from…'

'From Tylir's late wife, who might have wanted an excuse as to why she left his bed.'

Helga played with the gold torc she wore. 'I hadn't considered it in that respect.'

Mel raised a brow. 'My late husband said many things about me to excuse his behaviour. The excuses some people will give never cease to amaze me.'

'I never did like her. Not really. She reminded me of a very expensive horse. There was no heart to her.' Helga licked her lips. 'But I would like us to be friends, Melkorka. Too many people have been hurt by this feud. That battle their men had after Ingebord's death solved nothing and left the same number dead on each side. Maybe in time, we can bring the two men together and they can see that Ingebord was the poison, not my Helm.'

Mel took a deep breath. It was hard with Helga looking at her like she could solve the problem. The villagers had thought she could cure the sickness and she'd failed miserably with that.

'It needs to end, but I doubt I will have any control over that. You must be realistic, Helga. I've no influence over Tylir or indeed his men.'

'I think you are wrong about that. I think you can do much.' Helga leaned over and kissed Mel's cheek. 'Sisters, yes? Helm believes in his family. He believes in you.'

Helm didn't but he and Helga had been willing to take her in when she arrived. She most certainly did not want any escalation of the feud. She scrunched her fingers together to keep them from trembling.

The family politics were as bad in Islond as in the North, it would seem. Same people, same tetchy tempers and temptations but a different location. She had to wonder how long Tylir would stand for her being here if things became bad with Helm again. She knew she didn't want to find out. She knew she wanted to leave before that day happened.

'If I can bring a lasting peace before I go to my own holding, I will be satisfied.'

Helga's mouth fell open. 'You remain intent on getting your own place?'

Mel forced her voice to be light. 'Why would I want to remain here? I want somewhere where I am treated like an equal and where I can find safety and sanctuary for always.'

Her heart protested at the empty words but she silenced it. She did want somewhere where she could grow her own crops. What she shared with Tylir was lovely, but it was not for ever. They both accepted that and she refused to ask for more than he could give. She hoped they would remain friends when they were finished, because she did value his advice.

'Helm thought…that is…'

She could imagine what the gossip had been, and why perhaps Helga had seen fit to suddenly bring her the torc. However, she wondered why someone had thought to spread the gossip so quickly.

'The gossip is wrong again. What a strange occurrence.'

Helga gave a weak laugh. 'I'd forgotten how sensible you are, Mel.'

'That's me—sensible to a fault.' Somewhere the old reliable Mel had to exist.

Chapter Thirteen

'Helm's wife arrived and is in close conversation with that woman, Sunbear.' Virin strode up to Tylir where he stood watching the horses, pretending that he was unconcerned about the woman who arrived at the landing just as he'd returned from the outer farm with three more sheep and a pig for tonight.

In his mind he could hear Ingebord complaining with a pretty pout that there was never enough food for the guests he invited and the entertainment lacked a certain refinement. He wanted tonight to be perfect for his daughter's sake. He wanted Mel to see him as a good father and a benevolent host.

Once that was accomplished, he would bring forward the next stage of his scheme to convince Mel to stay and be the mother Katla desperately required. And if he was being totally honest, a woman he wanted to keep in his life. She made him feel like the future had possibilities, instead of being something to endure.

'Tell me something I am unaware of, old woman.'

Virin opened and closed her mouth like a codfish or maybe just an old fishwife.

Fork-Beard and his wife were up to something; he knew that in his bones, but for Mel's sake he wanted to give them the opportunity to act like decent human beings. He wanted no contention between blood kin. Peace between neighbours—wasn't that what the General Assembly had decreed should happen?

Virin gave one of her sly looks, the sort she always gave before poison dripped from her lips. 'I considered it important, particularly after what the child confessed to me when I tried to brush her hair.'

Tylir frowned. A confession from Katla to Virin sounded unlikely. The old woman was seeking to cause mischief. He internally wished he'd never promised his late wife that he would look after her old nurse. But he'd given that vow when they were first married, before he knew what Virin could be like. He simply needed to find a place where she could live out her days in peace without stirring up mischief.

'Mel allowed you to look after Katla?' he asked, trying to figure out how Virin came to watch over Katla.

Virin preened. 'She wanted to speak to her sister-in-law alone. That's all I know. I was glad to be of service to your family, Sunbear.' She gave an overly dramatic sigh. 'My loyalty was accepted without question until she arrived.'

Katla stamped her foot and drew her brows together. 'You lie, old woman. You volunteered. You said you were going to braid my hair, not go and see Tylir, carrying some tale. I told you we need to wait for the deep magic to work and then we'd see whose word counted for the most—yours or Aunty Mel's.'

'You must tell your father what you did.'

'What? What sort of deep magic is the child talking about?' The words burst from Tylir's throat much more forcefully than he intended.

Virin tapped the side of her nose and said in a barely audible whisper, 'I told you Sunbear doesn't like un- truthful children. You must tell him immediately what you did and the tricks you have been playing or it will go worse for you.'

Katla visually shrank back. 'I do want to tell the truth, but the magic must have time to work. They told me that.'

Tylir ground his teeth. He refused to allow Virin to scare the child like that. Katla was beginning to trust him. 'I am the child's father and not some frost giant who can be used to scare a child senseless.'

Virin blinked. She obviously had not expected him to hear the remark. 'Did I say something amiss, sir? Katla needs to tell you the truth.'

'My father did not like how you spoke to me,' Katla loudly proclaimed.

Ignoring Virin's swift intake of breath, Tylir hun- kered down beside Katla. The little girl had called him her father. He blinked rapidly. He had never thought to hear the words from her lips, but she had said it with- out hesitation. And he wanted her to say it again and again. He doubted that he would ever tire of hearing the words coming from her lips.

He put out his hand and she unhesitatingly put her fingers in it. He curled his fingers about hers while a lump developed in his throat. He swallowed hard, be- fore turning towards Virin.

'I believe Katla can stay with me and watch the horses

go through their paces. A new hairstyle can wait. She will tell me about this tale in her own time.'

'First puppies and now horses,' Virin muttered. 'In my day, young girls stayed indoors and did not have smelly pets.'

Tylir swung Katla up onto his shoulders. The little girl instantly grabbed his hair like it was a horse's reins. 'Your day was a long time ago. I plan to do things differently with my child.'

Virin stalked off, muttering dire predictions. Tylir rolled his eyes at her sourness.

'Aren't you pleased, Katla, that it isn't Virin's day anymore? And what is this about you finally having chosen a puppy? I thought you didn't want one and wouldn't look at them.'

'That was 'fore I met him properly and he licked my nose.' She gave a merry laugh and explained that she had chosen her favourite spaniel puppy, the one with dark brown spots. 'I am so looking forward to having my own puppy. I'm going to teach him to do tricks. My…other father had a dog who walked on his hind legs when he was a boy.'

'Is that so? That must have been a smart dog.'

Katla tightened her grip on his hair. 'Maybe one day, I will get to show the boys my new puppy. Then they will believe me about the tricks a dog can do.'

'The boys?'

'Aunty Mel's nephews. They don't think much of girls. But a girl with a dog who can do tricks might be a different matter.'

'Possibly.' He set Katla down.

'I had to show them that I was brave so they would

tell me the secret deep magic of keeping Aunty Mel with me for always.'

'You want to keep Mel with you for always.'

Katla gave a solemn nod. 'We left before they knew I had done the brave thing they asked. I paid the price for the magic to work but it hasn't worked this far. Maybe because their mother is talking to Aunty Mel, the magic will start to work.'

Tylir frowned. The little girl's face was very serious. And he suspected that this brave thing those unruly boys had convinced her to do was the confession which Virin had tried to force her to give. 'What brave thing did you do, Katla?'

'I had to give them as much gold as I could lay my hands on to get the secret. It was the only way to unlock the special magic.' Katla held out her hands. 'I need magic, Tylir. Much magic. I can't bear losing Aunty Mel. They said I would surely do so, if I didn't do what they requested.'

Tylir frowned. He had never liked Helm's boys the few times he met them. Overindulged, mama's boys from what he recalled. He was tempted to say that he no longer believed in magic or the ability of the seers to influence the future. Katla had a little girl's understanding of the world, but he had seen far too many good men go to their deaths because of what a seer had read in the runes. 'Little girls in my experience don't have much gold. And a good seer costs dear. Better to trust your Aunty Mel to get you what you need.'

She drew her brows together and pursed her lips, looking so like his dead sister at that age but somehow completely herself that Tylir's heart squeezed. And he knew whatever the little girl had done, he would forgive her. He simply needed to know how much gold and to whom he owed payment. He fervently prayed to any god who might be listening, but particularly to Freyr that Katla had not taken the gold from his neighbour.

'Come now, how did you get this gold you required?'

'I went into Aunty's trunk and took her gold torc as they said the pouch my…other…father gave me would not be enough.'

'Your other father gave you a pouch of gold?'

'He showed me the pouch after my mother died. He said that it was mine to do what I wanted with when I grew up and no one should take it from me. When I saw the pouch in my trunk it was like my father had answered my prayer. The magic I longed for could happen.'

Tylir schooled his features. He had seen enough of life and how women without protectors could be treated to understand why the man had done such a thing, but Katla was a little girl. She did not understand about gold, seers or indeed that Mel as a widow might require gold. His blood ran cold and he prayed to the gods that his daughter had not done what he suspected she had.

'Then they said they needed more gold? These nephews of Mel's?'

'I saw the torc and took it.' She screwed up her face. 'They never gave it back or told me how to keep Aunty Mel with me for ever. I am frightened that she will go, Tylir, particularly if she knows what I did. I need her with me. Will you help me keep her here?'

Tylir ground his teeth. The gods enjoyed laughing at him. Just when he thought he could enlist Katla in a scheme to get Mel to stay, this happened. He was now going to have to find a way to get the torc back for Mel without inflaming the situation with Helm. And without giving Mel a reason to depart. He had to hope she believed in second and third chances.

'Why didn't you tell your aunty Mel?'

'I was afraid that she'd be angry with me and leave. I didn't mean any harm.' She chewed her bottom lip. 'But I think she is upset about losing her torc. She searched and searched for it in the trunks when they first arrived.'

'Has she asked you about it?'

Katla shrugged. 'She thinks it was her brother, I guess.'

'Why haven't you told her the truth?'

'She has been upset about her son. She cries every night and talks in her sleep, even though she thinks I don't hear her. Her pillow is often wet.'

'I see.'

Katla cupped her hand about her mouth. 'Her pillow wasn't wet this morning though.'

Tylir stroked his chin. He knew quite well why Mel's pillow wasn't wet. She had slept in his arms instead. He felt quite proud that no tears had been involved and he knew he'd do everything in his power to keep her pillow dry. 'We shall have to try and keep it that way. You and I.'

Katla beamed up at him. 'We will indeed. I knew you want her to stay as well as me.'

'Staying will be Mel's choice, but we must tell her the truth about the torc and the pouch of gold before this goes any further.'

Her brow furrowed in thought, reminding him of Estrid. Somehow the great ache he'd had from that woman's betrayal seemed to have vanished. The boy he'd once been had loved her with all his heart, but the man he was didn't. Therein lay the difference. 'Must I tell her about the torc…all by myself?'

'I will go with you.'

She grabbed his hand. 'Later, after we see the puppies. My spotted one should be ready to leave his mother soon.'

'I suspect now will better, then Mel will be able to get back her torc all the sooner, particularly if our visitor has not left. You can tell her where you and your friends placed it.'

Katla hung back. 'I am not going to like this.'

'I will hold your hand if it makes it any easier.'

She beamed up at him and he felt as if he had grown ten inches. It was the sort of admiration that he had never expected to see. 'Thank you.'

Mel stared at the boat as it pulled away from the quay. The waves which followed the boat had crests as the men put their collective backs into the effort to leave this place. She rolled her neck and arms, trying to ease the tight muscles.

How typical that this should happen today when everything was chaotic. But Helga seemed to be determined to let her know that it had not been Helm who had taken the torc. Probably she was concerned about what others might say, if the loss was inadvertently mentioned.

She did not believe for a heartbeat that Katla would have enacted such a scheme on her own. Her nephews had played some part of it, but she couldn't fathom the how or the why of it. However, nothing was gained crying over spilled milk or questioning the motives for returning torcs.

Helga had repeated her desire for better relations. She had no idea if she could improve relations between the neighbours, but she knew she had to try, and making unfounded accusations about her nephews would serve little purpose.

It bothered her that she'd been quick to blame Helm for the missing torc when there were several possibilities. Thankfully, Tylir had not confronted him directly. The question was how to explain her mistake to Tylir and to ensure that no blame was attached to Katla.

'Melkorka, Katla had something to say to you.' Tylir strode towards her holding Katla's hand.

Katla still had mud on her apron from where the puppy had jumped up earlier and her hair remained in a tangle. From the streaks on her face, it was clear she'd been crying. The last thing anyone needed now that the feast was nearly on them.

Mel frowned, trying to figure out what happened, why Katla was upset. 'Katla, did you run away from Virin?'

Katla slowly shook her head.

Tylir put his hands on Katla's waist, keeping her in place. 'Allow Katla say her piece, before judging her, Melkorka.'

The fact that Tylir had used her full name twice showed that whatever Katla had done was very serious.

'Is everyone all right?'

Katla ran over to her and hugged her about the waist. 'I'm so…sorry, Aunty Mel. I shouldn't have done it.'

'Done what, sweetling? Did you run away from Virin?'

'I took your torc and the pouch my other father left for me before we came here. The boys were going to tell me the secret of keeping you with me for always.'

Mel went very still. Katla had taken them? 'They were?'

'They never did though even if they did take the torc and pouch. They said I had to wait until the full moon to know if the magic worked, but it hasn't happened. And now you are going to go. I can feel it in my bones. I am going to lose you.'

'Those were not yours to give away, Katla.'

'I knew it was naughty, Aunty Mel, but I wanted us to be together. For always. I didn't know anything about my new father or the possibilities of puppies.' She scuffed her boot in the dirt. 'And Virin said that you were going to be leaving soon and I told her to wait for the magic 'cause I had paid for it with gold. She took me straight to Tylir.'

Mel glanced at Tylir, who shrugged.

Mel took a deep breath. That her nephews had taken advantage of Katla failed to surprise her. 'Thankfully, their mother returned the torc and pouch to me this morning.'

Katla's eyes bulged. 'She did?'

Mel held them out. 'Tylir will put them away for safekeeping. Helga was most disturbed as she did not want Helm to be accused of theft. He apparently has suffered enough.'

Tylir nodded. 'You will know for the future not to trust people when they ask you to do something that you know in your heart is very naughty, Katla.'

'Are you very angry with me, Aunty Mel?'

'No, sweetling, not angry. A little disappointed but not angry.'

Katla gave a tight smile which reminded Mel of the smile Estrid gave when she feared what was coming next. 'But I am not going to lose you, am I?'

'You love your new home. And you are going to have a new puppy to keep you company. Although I doubt a puppy will wriggle as much as you do in bed.'

'I love it only because you are here.' Katla glanced up at Tylir. 'You are not married—'

Mel quickly put two fingers over Katla's lips before she said the fatal words. She should have guessed from the gleam in Katla's eye that she was going to try to matchmake. She could not bear having to see Tylir lie, or worse, tell the truth that he didn't really care for her. She couldn't bear that, not when she knew she liked being with him, liked kissing him and most of all simply liked him. Hearing that those deepening feelings were not reciprocated was something she wanted to avoid today. 'I enjoy being a widow. I do forgive you, but next time, please ask before you do something like that.'

'I will, Aunty Mel. I swear to Var the god of all sacred oaths, I will.'

Tylir made a barely perceptible nod. 'I shall leave you two as I can spot another ship arriving. I will put the torc and gold away for safekeeping before that happens.'

He strode off, barking orders to his men about making sure the hall was fit to receive all the guests.

'I like my new father,' Katla said with a smile. 'But I would like it even better if you could stay here for ever.'

Mel gave Katla a quick hug. The child would not understand the agreement she had with Tylir. She'd learned her lesson with her late husband about asking for more than men were willing to give. This time she was determined to ask for less than she wanted. 'We need to get ready for the party.'

'People might bring me presents, Virin said.' Katla clung on to Mel's hand. 'I think that is exciting. Everyone will know I am the daughter of Sunbear.'

Mel curled her hand about Katla's. After the feast, would she truly have any cause to stay? Katla was well settled. And there was that farm she wanted to find, the one where she could shut the door and be safe. Funny how it did not seem as appealing as it had done.

She hated how her heart kept telling her to find excuses but prolonging something like that would only cause more heartache further down the road. Helga had been right in her warning—Tylir did not seek a long-term passionate relationship with her.

'Yes, it is. You never know who you might meet.'

Katla turned and smiled one of her Estrid smiles. 'I agree. My mother used to say that feasts were the perfect time for strengthening bonds and matchmaking.'

She said the words like she had learned them by rote, and Mel could almost hear her old friend saying the exact same thing.

'Quite the mouthful for a little girl.'

Katla gave a wide smile. 'My mother used to say to…to my other father that before every feast. She made me memorise it. I don't want to forget her, Aunty Mel.'

Mel ruffled the girl's hair and told her that there was plenty of time for making a suitable match when she became older.

Katla stamped her foot and looked ready to start screaming. Mel hurriedly scooped her up so that she wouldn't reveal her matchmaking ambition to the growing crowd.

She knew her heart could not take Tylir's refusal. She had to be content with what she had and not keep wishing for more.

Chapter Fourteen

After he returned to the loch, Tylir silently cursed at the various men who were arriving for the feast. Inviting all the eligible bachelors in the surrounding area for this gathering had seemed like a good idea when all he and Mel had done was kiss and he wanted to prove that he was not as smitten as Stargazer complained. Now, all he wanted to do was to growl at them, shout that she was already spoken for and for them to turn tail and run.

Katla had made it clear that she was intent on matchmaking. And why not? It wasn't that he loved Mel, he told himself, not with the same starry-eyed infatuation he'd had for Estrid, or even that desperate hunger for Ingebord at the start of their relationship, before he discovered what she was truly like. But he did have tender feelings of friendship for Mel, and if he was honest with himself he simply couldn't stop thinking about her, wanting her, feeling that magnetic pull towards her.

'Sunbear, just the man.' One of his former comrades in arms clapped him on the back. 'I hear you have a very wealthy widow staying with you.'

'News travels fast.'

'Wealthy widows with a well-turned ankle are few and far between. Stargazer says that this one is a beauty.' He rubbed his hands together. 'I am quite willing to try my luck.'

Tylir silently cursed Stargazer. Men were arriving to seek her hand, men who were probably better for her than he was. He knew all his many flaws and knew that he did not deserve Katla or Mel, not truly.

A quick scan of the shoreline confirmed his worst fears. The boats which were arriving did seem to be decked out to impress a potential bride. And a beautiful wealthy widow was just that sort of tempting prize, particularly one who had wrought many changes in this hall and brought it alive again.

His stomach clenched like it had the first time he encountered men being slaughtered.

'Sunbear? You have gone bright red.'

He forced the bile back down his throat. 'I have no wish for anyone to be made uncomfortable. Melkorka is my honoured guest.'

The man tapped the side of his nose. 'I understand. Discretion. But my children have been missing their mother so. A wealthy woman who is willing to work hard seemed a tale too good not to miss. And she is supposed to understand about herbs.' He puffed out his chest, making his tunic ripple. 'I have it on good authority that she has not had a good man in her life for a long time and will be panting for it. A ripe plum for the picking, eh?'

Tylir longed to remove the man's head from his neck for even daring to make those sorts of remarks about

Mel. Mel was a person with feelings. She deserved better. She deserved to be spoken about with respect and dignity. He took ten deep breaths and felt the control over his temper return.

Mel also possessed an incredible amount of good sense. She would see straight through men like this puffed-up loser. But she should not have to experience one heartbeat of unwanted scrutiny.

'When you speak about a guest in my household, I trust you to keep a civil tongue.' He bit out each word. 'Or leave. Immediately.'

The man hastily took three steps backwards, throwing up his hands as he did so. 'I'm only repeating what I heard, Sunbear. Perhaps I ought to return to my children and find another woman.'

Tylir allowed a grunt to emerge from his throat as he did not entirely trust his voice. The man hurriedly found a reason why he needed to be elsewhere immediately and had to leave. He repeated this several times, babbling to Virin and a variety of neighbours. He said it so many times that people started to look at him like he'd lost his wits. Finally, he jumped into his longboat and ordered his men to row as fast as the wind.

'What was that all about, Sunbear?' Stargazer asked, his voice dripping with innocent speculation.

'I have no idea. The man suddenly found he had urgent business elsewhere. Most peculiar.'

'Most peculiar indeed.'

Tylir tapped his fingers against his thigh while he waited to greet the next jarl and his wife. He needed to find a way to protect Mel from predatory men like that who would use her until she was worn-out like a limp rag. The only possible way he could protect her was to marry her himself. He had no choice. It was the best solution for them both. The suddenness and clarity of the thought surprised him.

He grasped the lady's hand. 'That's it.'

'What is it, Sunbear?' she asked in the tones of someone who was trying to gentle a wild animal.

Tylir let go of her hand. 'I am delighted to have so many people arrive at my estate in order to meet my daughter. You do me much honour. Please drink and be merry.'

The woman's cheeks went pink. 'Thank you.'

She and her husband hurried off to where Virin and her army of women stood with their welcoming horns.

Tylir stared out at the loch where the little white waves lapped against the boats. The tension went out of his back. He accepted the inevitability of what he had to do. He had no choice but to marry Mel. It was the best solution for her—and for him if he was being honest. He was the only man who would treat her in the way she deserved. They could have a decent life together.

He simply had to find a way to get her to accept the inevitability of the action. After all, the passion was there, and there was something else—a steadiness of growing friendship that he had not anticipated or looked for. He knew he kept collecting stories to tell her and questions just to hear her voice answer them. But his heart remained intact, encased in its shield of ice, though its traitorous leaps told him differently.

He swore to the first full moon after his wife's death that he would never be vulnerable to a woman again, not in the way he was to Estrid or indeed to his late wife.

And he intended to keep that vow. But he also knew he had to protect Mel from those who would take advantage of her and make her miserable.

He would only have one chance to explain it and he needed to make it count.

Out the corner of his eye, he spotted Mel laughing at some remark by Katla as they stood waiting to greet the guests.

She picked the girl up and swung her about in carefree abandon. His heart squeezed. Just once he wanted someone to look at him like the way Katla looked at Mel and be able to look back at them the way Mel regarded Katla. He wanted Katla to proudly call him her father and say it with love in her eyes. She might do it if he could get Mel to marry him.

But was this a way to getting Mel to understand why she had to say yes? Katla's happiness.

He tapped a finger against his lips. Katla's future happiness could be enlisted. Mel cared deeply for the girl. Seeing them together like that made him realise that Mel would do anything for the little girl. He was certain that she'd see the sense of it—no promises of undying love but unstinting protection instead.

He had to figure out a way to do it before any of these new arrivals induced her into another alliance. The problem was further complicated by the fact that he had promised not to put chains on her and that their affair would last for as long as it lasted. He knew Mel prided herself on keeping her word and he had to be seen to keep his.

Katla suddenly spotted him and waved to him. He waggled his fingers back at her. One of the warriors gave him an odd look but he refused to care. He was no longer Sunbear the Berserker, but Tylir the father to a lovely daughter.

'Tylir, Katla is here ready to greet your guests,' Mel said, coming up to him. She appeared serenity personified. Tylir wondered how he'd ever, even for a heartbeat, not considered her beautiful. She might lack the conventional prettiness of his late wife or Estrid, but there was an inner luminosity which shone out through her eyes. He was tempted to draw her into his arms and kiss her soundly, stamping his imprint on her, but retained a small vestige of control. Patience had granted him victory on the battlefield. It would ensure him victory now. He had to choose his time carefully and ask.

'Is my daughter excited about tonight?' he asked as Katla gave a twirl in the pathway of one of the wolfhounds.

'Nervous as well as excited,' Mel said in a low tone while Katla vaulted over the wolfhound, laughing as she did so. She landed on her bottom, stood up and wiped her hands on her gown.

'I'm ready to greet the guests.'

Mel leaned over and wiped a smudge from her nose. 'Now you are.'

'A little dirt won't hurt.'

Tylir stared in amazement. It was hard to believe that only a few short days ago the little girl had been terrified of getting dirty or interacting with animals. 'Are you sure that this is not some changeling?'

'It is me, Tylir, really me,' Katla cried, stamping her foot. 'What is wrong with me liking to play with dogs?'

Tylir hid his smile behind his hand. 'Nothing, little one. Nothing at all.'

'She wishes to do you and this house proud.'

He was tempted to roll his eyes at the thought that he would not be proud of his daughter.

He hunkered down so that he could meet his daughter's eyes. 'Are you ready to do this and help me greet our guests? The dogs will have to wait for a little while longer.'

She gave a tremulous smile. 'My mother would expect no less of me. I will be brave.'

Inwardly he sighed. The last thing he wanted was Katla doing it because of her mother and her expectations. He wanted her to do it because it was something she looked forward to. He wanted her to be happy.

'Your mother would be very proud of you, dear,' Mel said. 'She sent you to look after your father.'

Tylir raised a brow at that remark, but from Mel's hard stare he knew he should not question it.

'She did rather, didn't she?' Katla gave him a look under her long lashes and extended her hand. 'I hadn't considered that. I will greet our guests and leave the dogs until later. Do you think my puppy will miss me?'

'Your puppy will be tucked up nice and tight with his mother, away from the hustle and bustle,' Tylir said.

'You should think about your guests, Katla. Your *mor* knew your father would need someone like you in his life.'

'And you,' Katla added, batting her lashes furiously.

Tylir silently blessed her. The girl was unwittingly making his case for him. Between the two of them, he doubted if Mel would be able to withstand the assault.

Mel raised a brow. 'Me? I am only here to get you settled, little one. My dream of my own farm remains important. I told you that several times. You will be able to come and stay.'

'I know but—' Katla's lower lip stuck out and her hands trembled just like his sister's used to do before she launched into one of her screaming fits.

'Our guests are here,' Tylir said before Katla started screaming. 'Show me what your version of hospitality looks like.'

Katla gulped hard. 'I will try, Tylir, to be civil even if I find it hard.'

'Good girl.' He smiled back at her, but Mel's words had caused his heart to sink and for a fraction of a heartbeat, he had wanted to join in any screaming fit Katla had. It was as he feared—Mel was doing everything in her power to find an excuse and leave. He had to find a way to keep her here permanently and with all speed. For Katla's sake. A large voice deep inside him protested that it was for his sake and no one else's. 'We must endure the feast and our guests.'

Mel gave him a sideways glance. 'Endure?'

'Feasts are never my most favourite thing. But alas, the guests need our attention.' He turned on his heel and strode away before he was tempted to say more.

He regarded the people arriving for the feast. Stargazer had been right. The sheer number of unattached men threatened to overwhelm the women. Mel could have her pick of any of them. He wished them all into the sea. This was not the right time for this, but he also greatly feared that it was the only time he would be given. He could not allow Mel to slip through his fingers.

* * *

'I think you should wear your green gown,' Katla said with a shy smile when Mel returned to their alcove after they had spent most of the afternoon greeting the visitors. It appeared that nearly everyone in Islond had come to greet Jarl Sunbear's new-found daughter.

Mel was pleased that she had managed to deflect several marriage proposals. It surprised her how many men were bold in their approaches. It was almost as if they knew about her quest to have her own farm and were determined to gift her theirs in exchange for her hard work. She suspected the idea could have only come from one man—Tylir. Was Helga right about his intention to see her matched to someone else? Her heart wept at the thought of it.

But it was another indication that she was right to begin the process of distancing herself from Tylir and his schemes. She wanted somewhere of her own where she would not be beholden to any man.

'Why the green gown?' she asked lightly to distract her thoughts.

'Freya thinks you look ever so lovely in that. It makes your waist look very small. It was Elkr's favourite gown of yours. He said you were his pretty *mor* when you wore that one.' Katla gave a small smile. 'Tylir is bound to want to go for a moonlit stroll with you after the feast if you wear that.'

'Who said that we were going to go for a walk?' Mel asked, pushing away the feeling of sadness at her son not being there.

'You did. You asked him but he didn't answer.' Katla gave a little smile. 'It's fine, Aunty Mel. I know you and he go for walks and talk about me. It is a good thing, I think.'

Mel gave Katla a fond kiss on her cheek. How she was going to miss the child when she left. Seeing all these people arriving for the feast made her realise that she was living a fool's dream. Katla was self-assured now and didn't require her. 'I suspect you are right. Your father wants to know all about you.'

'If you say so.' Katla held her doll to her ear. 'Freya says that he likes spending time with you.'

'If Freya says so.' Mel forced a smile. There was little point in confessing that it felt like she had tumbled back into that period of her marriage when Elkr had tired of her but had not found the strength to utterly reject her. Katla would not understand.

Katla held the doll to her ear. 'Freya says not to worry. All will be well. The magic will happen. At the feast if not before.'

Mel wished she had the child's simple faith. One day Katla would grow up and realise that the world had a way of trampling on your dreams.

'I suspect he will be busy at the feast. And anyway, I have you to look after.' Mel held out a cloth. 'Now come here, while I get that dirt off your face.'

Katla scrunched up her nose but submitted to Mel's ministrations. 'I still think you should wear the green gown.'

Mel busied herself with rinsing out the cloth.

'My dark blue gown will be fine. I am far from being the star.' She touched Katla's nose with her forefinger. 'You are.'

'My father should think you are.'

Tears welled up in Mel's eyes. 'I am glad you acknowledge him as your father.'

Katla rolled her eyes. 'Best that I do 'cause it is the truth.'

Mel hugged the little girl to her. She knew when she left, she would be leaving a large part of her heart behind. But she also knew she wanted at least one more night of feeling like she belonged in Tylir's arms. Surely the gods could grant her that?

When Tylir discovered Mel kneeling alone in the small shed where the spaniel puppies were living, he heaved a sigh of intense relief. He had worried that he'd find her in close conversation with one of the bachelors, something Stargazer had implied with a smug grin, particularly as Katla appeared to be happily playing with the daughter of a fellow jarl. He should have known Stargazer was teasing him. Mel was not like his late wife or Estrid.

'Where is Katla?' he asked, his voice coming out far rougher than he intended. At her surprised look, he added, 'I wanted to ensure she wasn't hiding somewhere scared.'

She rocked back on her heels and glanced up at him with an eyebrow lifted. He winced. The excuse was pathetic. He had wanted to see her, pull her into his arms and drown in the warmth of her mouth. And he suspected she guessed it. It frightened him that he was vulnerable to a woman again.

'Katla has gone to play with some of her new friends for a little while before the feast actually.' Mel tucked a strand of hair behind her ear, revealing the length of her neck. 'I had to promise her that I would check on Ivar before she'd go. She has promised me that she won't get dirty.'

Tylir smiled back at her. 'I wouldn't mind and it is good that she is making friends.'

'She remains very much her mother's daughter and is interested in people. And I thought it excellent that she wanted to play rather than clinging to my hand.'

'Who is Ivar?' he asked instead of commenting about Estrid and her overly fussy ways.

'Her puppy, the one with the brown splodges on his back.' She gave one of her smiles, the sort which always warmed his heart. 'She worried that he might not be safe.'

'And is he?'

'Tucked up right next to his mother.'

'Shall we leave them to sleep? The feast will be starting soon.'

He tucked her arm in his and drew her towards him. Her lips parted. Giving in to temptation, he lowered his mouth and drank. Her arms came about his neck, and as he pulled her against him, her softness hit the hard planes of his muscles. He tried to pour everything into that kiss so that she would understand without him having to say the words about his growing feelings for her. He cupped her bottom and pulled her firmly against his erection.

She put her hands up against his chest. 'We need to stop.'

He put her hands between his. 'Why?'

Her smile trembled. 'If this continues, we will miss the feast and Katla will be upset.'

Giving in to impulse, he raised her hands to his lips. 'Marry me? We can announce it at the feast and then everyone can know why we were late.'

A myriad of emotions flitted across her face—fear, panic and terror. He went completely still. He had misread the situation.

'Why do you want to marry me?' Her voice was no more than a whisper in a howling gale.

'Because Katla will love it,' he said before any other reason spilled from his throat.

Her lips became a thin white line. 'Katla. That is the only reason.'

He swallowed hard, knowing he had made a mistake and not knowing how to make it right. If he confessed, his heart would be laid bare again like it had been with Estrid.

'We are both widowed, Melkorka,' he said, trying again. 'It is not as if we are young and believe in love. A practical marriage. It would suit us both, I think. We are friends.'

'A practical marriage between friends.'

When she said it like that, she made it seem like something weak and feeble.

'Yes, we are good together. Everyone has commented how alive the hall is now. You are a miracle worker. You brought about that change. We are friends after a fashion.'

She put her hand to his face. 'I am sorry, Tylir, I can't marry you. Not even for friendship.'

'What nonsense is this? It is the best solution for everyone, for Katla.'

'Katla is the reason you want us to marry, nothing else.'

He gritted his teeth. His heart screamed that he should tell her that he loved her. Whatever he had told himself, deep down, he knew it was true. But the other two times he had told a woman that he loved her, the relationship ended. Estrid had told him that she could not live on love and fresh air. While Ingebord had used his declaration to make a quick match and each time she wanted something, she had thrown the declaration back in his face until he no longer felt anything for her except contempt. He had vowed on her grave that he would never feel that weak and out of control again. He was not going to risk his heart again.

If he did not say anything, then maybe he could keep this woman in his life. 'Surely there are worse reasons for marrying than my daughter's sake. She will be able to go on about how the special magic worked. Finally.'

'I have always been perfectly clear, Tylir. I want my own farm. My own house where I can bolt the door and sit, safe from the storm.' She ticked the points off on her fingers. 'My late husband offered me a practical match. I know what sort of marriage we had. I can't go back to that. I won't go back to that.'

'I am not him! When will you accept that?'

'But you don't pretend to love me either.'

He ignored the sudden lurching of his heart and the swift sense of foreboding which filled him. His mind went back to when he asked Estrid to marry him, and she'd refused. He'd been nothing but a fling to her really, some fun before she settled in a sensible manner. But that was not it with Mel. He knew it in his bones.

'Why can't you have this sort of marriage with me? Infatuation does not make a good basis for marriage. I tried that with Ingebord and it was a disaster.'

She wrapped her arms about her waist and turned her face away from him. 'Because I just can't.'

'And that is the only answer you are willing to give?' The words burst from him in a great roar. 'What is wrong with you?'

'Nothing is wrong with me. I have been clear and forthright about my intentions.' She kept her face firmly turned away him and spoke to the spaniel. 'Nothing has altered to make me change my opinion. I leave when Katla is settled.'

'She is settled now.'

She turned back to him, her face white with fury and pain. 'Then I shall soon take my leave. Now, if you will excuse me, I need to find Katla. I just heard the gong summoning everyone. This feast is hugely important to her even if you see it as tiresome.'

'Wait!' He ran his hands through his hair. 'I never said that it was that!'

She left the hut without a backwards glance. Tylir stood there, stunned. Mel had refused him. Refused to even consider his proposal. She wanted something more.

'Where did I go wrong?' he roared. 'Can't you see I care for you? That you mean everything to me? Why do I have to say the words?'

The silence was deafening.

The spaniel and her puppies made soft snuffling noises in sympathy.

'It is better I discovered this now, instead of later.' He fondled the spaniel's ears. The great ache in his middle grew. He had made a mistake and he had no idea how he could recover. It was as if all his shields had buckled and he was about to face a death blow, but he knew he wanted to live. He wanted to keep feeling rather than being forced to live a half-life where he merely existed. 'I will find a way of getting her to stay. There must be one. I need time. I want her in my life. If she goes now, I will lose everything.'

The spaniel simply looked at him with sorrowful eyes before turning back to minister to her brood, going first to the one Katla called Ivar. Tylir took it as a good omen.

Mel didn't risk a breath till she was beyond earshot of the shed. She doubted he had ever been told no and she had shocked herself by being the one to tell him. She quickened her steps and refused to let her resolve weaken.

His marriage proposal had been mealy-mouthed at best. Marry because it would make Katla happy? She had been in a marriage of convenience before. And it had made her utterly miserable. She thought she'd made that clear to Tylir.

She hated the great hollow which formed in her middle now. She hated that Tylir had made her feel again. She hated that she wanted more from him than he was willing to give. But she refused to compromise. She deserved more. How had it taken her so long to realise that? Ironically, it was her time with Tylir that had made her see it, see her worth. She knew that now with all her heart and soul.

She glanced up at the sky and tried to regain control

of her emotions. Elkr had been a master at putting her off balance before a feast. She coped then. She could cope now. She pushed the hurt and anguish down into a space deep inside.

'Aunty Mel, is something wrong?' Katla sneaked up and put her hand in hers. 'I heard the gong, and you were not here. Tylir isn't here either.'

Mel squeezed the girl's hand and used her other to wipe away a tear. Idiotic things. She had sworn that she was never going to cry over a man again. Her promises to her heart were so easily broken. 'He will be here. He is the host.'

Katla's brow furrowed. 'But you look upset, Aunty Mel.'

'A cinder in my eye. Nothing more than that.'

'Here he is.' Katla dropped her hand and ran up to Tylir. 'Good, we can all go in together like we are a real family.'

Tylir raised a brow, but his scar showed vivid scarlet against his face. 'A real family?'

'It is best you go with your father, sweetling, without me. I am a guest here, not a member of the family.'

Katla glanced several times between them with an increasingly puzzled expression. 'If I must, but you could come as well. Tell her, Father, tell her to come with us.'

'I am afraid you must go as a pair,' Mel said with a catch in her throat. 'It is the right and proper thing to do.'

Tylir gave her a perfunctory nod and held out an arm to Katla. 'Come on, daughter. Shall we be a family of two together?'

As they went into the hall, Katla gave her an anguished backwards glance. Mel forced her hand to lift and wriggled her fingers at her.

When they had gone in, Mel made her feet move towards the hall. Somehow, she was going to have to figure out what to do with the rest of her life, a life she knew would not include Tylir or his daughter.

Chapter Fifteen

The hall teemed with people who all fell silent when Mel entered. Her heart sank. It was the last place she wanted to be, but it was also the place she knew she had to be. She was not some coward to skulk away, hiding her face, ashamed to be seen. It was far from her fault that Tylir had made an unacceptable proposal of marriage. And it was better that she knew it was unacceptable rather than hoping that some miracle would happen.

She suspected that this feast would be one of the longest she had ever endured, even longer than one where Elkr had told her that he no longer wanted to share her bed, preferring the arms of another woman.

Katla brightened and whispered something to Tylir, who nodded. Katla held out both her hands, but Mel turned away. She had to begin as she meant to go on.

It was clear Katla had found her home here and it was time for her to depart. She refused to go back to Helm's and eat crow. The only place for her was her own place, something small but hers. And she didn't need to rely on anyone else to find it.

She noticed that Virin was attentively serving both Tylir and Katla. Katla appeared content to speak to the old woman while she poured more drink into Tylir's goblet. Tylir saluted her with the goblet.

Mel examined the wall hangings which shimmered with gold and silver. Someone had attached many gold and silver foils to the pillars. The hall felt like it was the abode of a king, instead of the homely place she had grown to love.

Standing in the doorway for the entire feast would only call attention to her and cause unwanted speculation. And she had unfortunately told Virin and the other women who were doing the serving that she trusted them entirely to get the task completed.

Mel pointedly sat on one of the lower benches, next to several women from the weaving hut, women she was friendly with but had never spoken to at length. They scooted over and made her a place.

'Is everything all right, Mel?' one of the women whispered after the food had been served.

Mel ignored the continuing glowers from Tylir and tried to concentrate on the food. It all tasted like ash and sawdust. She pushed the trencher away.

'We thought you'd be on the top table.' The woman signalled to one of the maids for more drink.

'I even put a wager on it,' another said with a pretty frown. 'I wonder what Sunbear has done this time.'

'It seems Stargazer was correct,' a third said. 'Pity, I wish he wasn't.'

'He got you as well.' The second woman rolled her eyes. 'I thought I was the only one, but it was either that or he'd prevent me from finishing up washing the wool.

I had already a tongue-lashing from Virin about being work-shy. My husband really wants to expand his lands. I can't afford to get into trouble.'

'I wonder how many women he wagered with.' The first woman tapped her knife against her teeth.

'He'll be a lucky man tonight.'

'For the next few days and weeks, I reckon.' The second woman knowingly tapped her nose. 'If you know what I mean.'

'We all thought we were on to a sure thing as well. Goes to show.'

Mel examined her hands. 'What does that man have to do with me sitting here?'

'Nothing. He simply wagered me a kiss that you wouldn't be up on the top table when the feast came. I'd really hoped that for once, he'd lose.'

Mel pursed her lips. Stargazer had made wagers about her relationship with Tylir. It failed to surprise her. She wondered if Tylir knew or cared. Elkr wouldn't. He probably would have thought it funny. He might have even wanted to assist his friend.

Her heart protested that Tylir was nothing like that. She'd seen his worth in the way he cared for his daughter and how he listened to her suggestions. He had genuinely asked her to marry him. It had nothing to do with helping Stargazer with some silly wager with women.

'When did this happen?'

'Several days ago, when the feast was first proposed. Never forgets a wager does our Stargazer,' the first one said. 'Even our jarl's late wife…'

Mel sat up straighter. 'Stargazer had a wager with Tylir's wife. A sexual wager? When?'

The women exchanged glances. 'Someone might have an idea. A rumour, you see. Nothing more than woman-talk.'

'Keeping silent protects no one, least of all poor Ingebord,' she said before she lost her nerve.

'They might have had one just before she died,' one of the women whispered, looking down at her food. 'All the women in the weaving hut knew what she was like.'

Knew what she was like including having an affair with Helm. 'She liked the attention.'

'And the risk,' one of the women said, slapping her hand on the table. 'If we are speaking home truths.'

'Finally,' the second woman murmured. 'I don't think Sunbear knew. Stargazer is good at keeping things quiet and away from the people in power.'

'A conspiracy of silence then.'

The first woman covered Mel's hand with hers. 'It tore the Sunbear terribly it did when she died. He blamed Fork-Beard. No need to mention Stargazer, you see. No need to get our men punished. The jarl has been happier since you arrived, Mel.'

The other women murmured their agreement.

Mel banged her hand on the table. 'Keeping quiet only helped Stargazer.'

'One day, the gods will punish Stargazer. I firmly believe that.' The woman gave her hand a squeeze. 'We thought that perhaps with you around…well, Stargazer's influence with the jarl might wane.'

'Somebody has to do something.' A righteous anger grew within Mel.

The women glanced at each other. 'Maybe you can do something about Stargazer and his loathsome wagers if you stay. The younger women often feel pressured to accept his wagers. He is an expert at this game and we women always lose.'

'I've always been quite clear that I would go when Katla was settled. I have put my life on hold for long enough.' Her mouth tasted like ash by the time she was done.

All the women's faces fell. And she knew she had disappointed them. But she couldn't simply abandon her dreams.

'While there is life, there's hope,' one woman murmured. 'The gods must be ready to act soon.'

Mel pointedly changed the subject to the weaving of sailcloth. The women seemed to accept that she didn't want to talk about it anymore and the conversation soon moved on.

Mel allowed it to ebb and swirl about her. She needed time to consider what to do. Staying here and hoping that Tylir would somehow grow to love her in the way she cared for him was folly. Besides, it was too late. She had already rejected his offer. Tylir was not the sort to propose marriage twice. And she refused to start regretting her decision, however much doubt nagged at her.

'Katla is tired now. She was asking for you.' Tylir appeared with Katla held fast in his arms. Katla's head was nestled against his neck.

He carried the little girl as if he was carrying the most precious object in the world. Behind him stood various jarls who were obviously waiting their chance to speak to him. Her late husband would never have done that. She couldn't remember if Elkr had ever carried his son after he had dangled him on his knee and declared him as his. She doubted it.

It would be far too easy to confess her love to this man, which was why she had to leave. Mel tried for her brightest smile. 'Asking for me? Surely she enjoys being snuggled up in her father's arms.'

'She wanted you to settle her, but I could do, I guess.' He paused and said in a barely audible whisper, 'I don't know how, Mel. Show me. Help me, Mel, be the father you think I could be, the one I want to be for Katla's sake.'

Her heart squeezed. He always seemed to want to do the right thing. He wasn't like Elkr in the slightest. Maybe it was time to stop using her past as an excuse. Maybe it was time to try to see if her future was destined to be different to the past. All she had to do was to seize the opportunity. Running never solved anything.

Mel rose with as much dignity as she could muster and nodded to the women, who smiled in unison. One day soon she'd figure out what to do with the treacherous Stargazer, who she instinctively felt had something to do with Tylir's wife's death. But she couldn't say anything without proof. Right now, she had to figure out a way to fight for the future she deserved, a future with Tylir in it.

However, a good leader knew when to advance and when to tactically retreat. Confronting him now would make matters worse. She would go slowly and see. Her nerves tingled like she stood on the edge of something exciting, forcing out the earlier gloom.

'I will take her. No need for you to leave.' Mel forced

a smile. 'You can learn about settling her some other night. There is a specific routine she likes to follow.'

'I will hold you to that. Remember I am a slow learner and take pity on me,' he said but his arms continued to hold Katla tightly. His eyes seemed to indicate that there was a hidden meaning to his words.

She hated the leap of hope in her breast that maybe she had not destroyed everything and that maybe there would be a chance for them to rebuild. If she explained to him about her fears, would he listen? Would he give her the space to explore this growing friendship? Intellectually she knew it was probably too much to ask, but her heart wanted to believe.

'It will be easier for Katla if I look after her tonight. Your men will look for you to be here for a while yet.' She gave a little laugh. 'I know what happens at feasts.'

'Some other night then. I will hold you to that promise.'

'I try to keep my promises, to see through all my plans.'

'Of course, though some plans are best altered.'

'Perhaps. Such things are not straightforward though,' she said and tried to keep the wobble from her voice.

He transferred the sleeping Katla over. Mel held the solid weight in her arms. Katla murmured slightly and put her arms about Mel.

'I had such a nice time, Aunty Mel,' she whispered. 'But Tylir was sad that you were not with us. Next time. Promise.'

'Whatever you say, darling girl,' Tylir said, giving Mel a significant look as if to warn her to keep quiet about any plans to leave.

'A thought for another day.' Mel shifted Katla's weight a little. 'Now you are getting heavy, young lady. We had best be off.'

'Mel…'

'It is just as well Katla is tired as I am exhausted.' She forced a yawn and turned away.

'We must speak.' He put a warm hand on her back. 'Soon. There is much I want to say.'

'Not tonight. We agreed on that.' She gestured towards one of the jarls who stood nearby, clearly impatient to get to some topic of great importance. 'You have other duties and responsibilities.'

She silently prayed that he would accept the excuse, but on the other hand, her heart wanted him to shout he'd made a mistake earlier and asked her for all the wrong reasons and he wanted to ask for the right ones if she'd let him.

He allowed his hand to drop and gave a tight smile. 'As ever, duty calls.'

Her heart screamed she'd done it wrong. She should have thrown her arms about his neck and confessed her feelings, given him a chance. She bade her heart to be quiet.

She shifted Katla in her arms again and started to walk back.

Katla sighed and snuggled closer. 'Aunty Mel, why were you with the women?'

'Because you needed to be with your father.'

'He wanted you with us. I think he is worried that you might leave. He said that the magic might not work but if I tried very hard, maybe it would.' Katla put a hand to Mel's face. 'Do you think it will work after all? Now that you have the torc back and everything? I thought magic worked differently.'

'We can talk about that tomorrow.'

Katla kept quiet for the rest of the journey back to the alcove.

'Aunty Mel, you are going to stay, aren't you?'

'With you tonight? Of course.'

'If something bad happened and you weren't there, where should I go?'

'Nothing bad is going to happen.' Mel gave a little smile. She could remember her son having the same sorts of fears. 'You can always go and see your puppy, Ivar, if you are worried and I am not there. His mother would look after you both, I'm sure.'

Katla nodded solemnly before she snuggled under the furs, hand firmly grasped about Freya. 'I will go there. You always have the best ideas.'

'Sweet dreams, sweetling.' Mel stood watching the little girl for a long while, knowing that she was going to get very little sleep. Her mind was far too busy making plans about what she could do to try again with Tylir to settle.

From under hooded lids, Tylir watched Mel and Katla go out of the hall while pretending to have a conversation with another jarl. The feast which had gone brilliantly in many ways had failed spectacularly. The old heavy and yet strangely familiar weight of the curse seemed to settle on his soul again. He twitched his neck. The curse wasn't real, and he could work out a way to keep Mel here. Teaching him how to settle Katla was a threadbare excuse for keeping Mel here, but it was the only one he could think of quickly.

And after that? his mind asked as he gave a nonsensical answer to the jarl.

Virin appeared to want to speak with him. He mentally sighed but nodded to her, indicating that she would be next. Virin had been overly attentive all night, insisting on serving him and Katla. He expected she might want to gloat or to offer some more unwanted advice or to tell him that his goblet needed refilling. Again. She'd been remarkably persistent about it. Almost as if she was listening for Katla to ask about the problem with Mel, a problem he was certain everyone had seen.

'I am surprised your little bird has flown.' Stargazer clapped him on the back before he could investigate what Virin required. His smile was wider than Tylir had seen for many months. But there was a shiftiness to his eyes and a swagger to his step.

Tylir frowned. He'd known Stargazer since they were boys, but Katla hadn't warmed to him. And he refused to allow Mel to be abused in that sort of way.

'Keep a civil tongue.'

'Did I say something wrong?' Stargazer looked about him as if he were playing the fool for the crowd. 'Everyone knows you have been having an affair with the woman, Sunbear. You just think they don't.'

'I told you not to speak about Mel in that way.' Tylir allowed the righteous anger to build within him. He'd accept a lot from Stargazer but not this. The man knew when to back off. He had always done.

Stargazer gave another look to the growing throng. He seemed to be enjoying himself. 'Right.'

'In fact, you are not to speak like that about any woman under my protection.' Tylir hauled back his hand and hit Stargazer firmly on the jaw. Stargazer tumbled backwards.

'Your temper remains.' He rubbed his jaw. 'I'll give you that.'

'Do you wish to challenge for the *felag*?' Tylir asked. 'Or do you wish to leave?'

The colour drained from Stargazer's face and he scuttled backwards. 'Remember who I am? Remember how close we were before she arrived?'

'Do you mean Mel?'

Stargazer rubbed a hand across his chin. 'Yes, her.'

Tylir regarded Stargazer, the signs of heavy living and bullying. He'd ignored it for many years. He could no longer ignore it. 'We took different paths years ago. Long before Mel. I was far too blind to see it. I will ask you to go in peace.'

Stargazer's mouth dropped open. 'For me to go?'

'You have your own lands. You may attend to them. Leave in peace, but I will not have my leadership challenged in this fashion.'

He started to turn. Out of the corner of his eye, he spotted a flash of silver. Stargazer had drawn a knife and made a downward arc.

Reacting instinctively, he reached out and grabbed Stargazer's wrist, forcing the knife away from him. The knife fell to the ground with a clatter.

'If it is a challenge you want, ask for it honestly. You are drunk, old friend. Go find somewhere to sober up.'

Stargazer wiped spittle from his mouth. 'No. You and I. Here and now. It has been a long time coming, Sunbear. This *felag* should have belonged to me by rights. Your wife should have been mine. You took everything from me, but there is someone under your roof who will help me take it back.'

The entire hall went silent.

A sudden cold settled over Tylir. Stargazer was serious, deadly serious. He had been planning this for a long time. 'Very well. You have challenged and we shall fight. I will allow you to choose the weapons.'

'Swords and no quarter given.'

'Melkorka, Melkorka…' Virin's rough whisper made Mel sit up.

Mel shielded her eyes against the light from the torch which Virin carried. 'Is there a problem?'

'Sunbear is about to fight Stargazer.'

Mel quickly sat up. All tiredness vanished. 'Fight him?'

'A dispute over you spiralled out of hand, if you must know.' Virin made a clicking noise in the back of her throat. 'Now Stargazer is vying for control of the *felag*. My lady predicted this would happen on the day she died. She warned me to be on the lookout for Sunbear's jealousy of Stargazer. I failed to believe her.'

Mel rolled her eyes. Evenings at Elkr's feasts often devolved into a series of rolling brawls. And Tylir knew he had no reason to be jealous of Stargazer. She loathed the man. But maybe there was something she could do to stop it getting out of hand. She grabbed her shawl. 'I had better go then. I will wake Katla.'

Virin shook her head. 'The child will sleep. Let us

go together now.' She lowered her voice. 'They intend to fight to the death.'

A cold crept into her soul. She could not rid herself of the notion that this was some sort of plan. 'To the death?'

'Sunbear has gone berserk. I just thought you would want to know.'

Katla murmured in her sleep and called for her.

'Let me settle her,' Mel said.

Virin gave a vigorous nod. 'Best not to have her there. Her father in full berserker battle cry will only upset the child.'

Mel made a pretence of tucking the furs about Katla. She bent so her mouth was right next to Katla's ear. 'Katla, listen carefully now. After I've gone, count to thirty and go see your puppy. Stay there. Tylir and I will find you. Squeeze my hand to show me you understand.'

Katla's hand returned the faintest of squeezes.

Mel bit her lip and prayed to all the gods that Katla truly understood. If Tylir was killed, they would come searching for Katla as his sole heir. Her life was in danger.

'Melkorka, we need to go,' Virin said with real urgency in her voice. 'He needs you there. You might be able to bring him back from the madness.'

'All set,' she said in a steady voice. 'Shall we go?'

'You don't seem as surprised as I thought you might that a rift such as this has come about,' Virin commented pointedly as they walked quickly back towards the hall. The growing sound of people placing their bets filled the torchlit darkness.

'Your lady wagered with Stargazer and lost. Inge-bord was trying to meet the terms when she died. This friendship has been dead for some time, if it was ever real in the first place. If Stargazer has challenged Tylir for the *felag*, this is an issue of Stargazer's jealousy of Tylir, not the other way around.'

Virin missed a step. 'How did you come by all that gossip?'

Mel waved an airy hand and tried to bid the knots on knots in her stomach to go. 'I listen to the stories and try to see what is behind them.'

Virin harrumphed. 'Then you will want to know Stargazer intends to kill your man.'

'He might want to, but I doubt he will succeed.' Mel stared at the ring which had been created just outside the hall. More people than she considered possible crowded around it. 'Where are the opponents?'

'Getting ready. I dare say someone is trying to sober Tylir up.' Virin gave a hiccupping sort of laugh. 'He certainly was downing the mead tonight. Must have been upset about something. Always tries to drown his sorrows.'

A distinct prickle went down Mel's back. She should have known that Virin was up to no good. However, it was best to play along and pretend wide-eyed incredulity. She had to be able to seize any opportunity which came along. 'Did Tylir ask for me?'

'No, Stargazer wanted you here by his side.' Virin put an arm about Mel and shoved her forward so that Mel nearly fell into the ring. The crowd closed around her, many eyeing her with suspicion and drunken anger. If she tried to escape now, she feared she would not get far. 'He wanted you front and centre. Something for Sunbear to get an eyeful of. Thinking that you are in league with his enemy will drive him over the edge of insanity.'

'In league with Stargazer?' Mel resisted the urge to laugh. The idea was madness, but then Virin did appear to only have a nodding acquaintance with sanity. 'Have you both lost your mind?'

Virin's mouth became a thin white line. 'You are Fork-Beard's sister after all. Stargazer considers you a gift from the gods. And I believe finally the gods will avenge my lady's death. She would still be alive today were it not for her miserable marriage to the Sunbear.'

Mel reached behind her and grasped the woman's wrist. Virin gave a muffled cry and struggled to free herself, but Mel held fast. 'You can stand next to me and watch as well.'

'Why should I want that?'

'It is what I want that matters, and I do not wish for you to give any word to anyone that you have separated me from my charge.'

Virin glared at her but stopped struggling. Mel knew her hunch was correct—Virin had been tasked with getting her here so that someone could spirit Katla away. She silently prayed Katla understood the whispered message and was now with the spaniel and her pups. 'On reflection, I will do as you suggest. I too wish to see this fight.'

Mel's gut instinct told her that she and the old woman wanted a very different outcome. She had to hope that Tylir fought with all his heart and wanted to live.

'Delighted you have seen sense.'

Chapter Sixteen

Tylir concentrated on practising his swing with the sword in the relative privacy of his chamber. There was a comfort in the familiar moves. He had faced challenges before but nothing like this.

Stargazer was right about one thing—this fight had been coming for a long time. He was pleased that he'd barely sipped from his goblet during supper. Instead, he'd carefully poured most of it on the rushes, an old trick he'd learned from the first jarl he'd served—*Let the men think you are merry as then they will be more willing to confide.*

He wondered if Stargazer had remembered that advice or not. He doubted it. But did he truly know what the man thought?

He made a few practice swings with his sword. He wished he'd been able to let Mel know about the fight and to tell her to have Katla ready to flee if he was killed. He wished he'd told her properly why he wanted to marry her, instead of the pathetic excuse he'd given. He wished he'd told her how important she had become to him.

He did one more practice swing. If he survived, he would put it right. It bothered him that he did have a reason to live. He'd always fought before as if he were already dead. But he needed to fight today to ensure Mel and Katla remained safe and in his life.

'Jarl, are you ready?'

He wanted to scream—is a man ever ready to fight his supposed best friend to the death?

He'd done everything he could to avoid this moment and ignore the increasingly blatant betrayals. He had sought the expedient explanation rather than the truth. He bore a great deal of responsibility for Stargazer and his behaviour, but he intended to change that tonight.

'Am I ready?' He picked up the shield. 'I am eager for it.'

He walked out into the cleared area in front of the hall. Loud cheers rang out from the crowd. A host of torches illuminated the growing throng of faces. He spotted Mel with a shawl about her, standing rigidly next to Virin but no Katla. Mel's face was set white, and an air of grim determination hung about her.

He narrowed his eyes. Mel stood far too close to Virin, almost as if she was being forced to watch. An ice-cold finger went down his back. The rot went far deeper than he'd imagined. If Virin was involved in the plotting with Stargazer, then Ingebord must have been as well. She had wanted him to follow her that day. She had left all the clues. She wanted him to think that she renewed the affair with Fork-Beard when in fact, she had been plotting with Stargazer all along. It finally made sense.

He quirked a brow upwards to Mel and she gave a decisive nod back. He breathed out. Katla had to be safe somewhere. He trusted Mel implicitly. She would be clinging on to Virin for one reason and one reason only—to keep Virin away from Katla. He'd hang on to that thought and fight for both Mel and Katla.

Stargazer swaggered out into the ring.

A much smaller cheer than the one which had greeted Tylir erupted. Stargazer obviously had garnered support beforehand.

Tylir set his jaw. He had not even considered this when he agreed to the gathering to celebrate Katla's arrival. Stargazer obviously had. He wanted to provoke this fight.

'Shall we begin?' he asked through clenched teeth.

Stargazer wrinkled his nose. 'You are set on this. You could cede control.'

'Why would I want to do that? We are in Islond now, rebuilding our lives. No need to go adventuring or whatever you have planned.'

Stargazer shrugged. 'Have it your own way then.'

Stargazer raised his sword and began his attack. Tylir pivoted and deflected the sword blow.

'You will have to do better than that.'

They circled round and round each other. Occasionally Stargazer thrust his sword forward and Tylir deflected each thrust, watching and waiting for an opening. Stargazer always made a mistake. Patience would win the day.

Metal hit the wood of the shield and then the metal of the sword. Round and round with onlookers on both sides calling out helpful suggestions.

Stargazer appeared to drop his shield to the left. Tylir thrust forward.

'Give up, Tylir, old friend. You are only making it worse. You will be going to Valhalla today.'

'Same back at you.'

Tylir brought up his shield and hit Stargazer squarely in the stomach. They both retreated.

Sweat poured down Tylir's face. More than he expected from the exertion. He gritted his teeth and wondered if someone had altered his food or drink.

'Drank a lot at supper, Sunbear?' someone yelled with a laugh.

Tylir narrowed his gaze.

There was something in Stargazer's manner which was overconfident. As if he expected something to happen or something to kick in. Tylir silently blessed their first commander.

The time had come for Stargazer and the others to think he had drunk more than he should. The time had come to finish this fight.

He readjusted his grip on the sword and pretended to stumble, causing his shield to buckle. The crowd groaned.

Stargazer brought his sword down heavily on Tylir's shield arm. The sharp touch from the metal caused his arm to ache and his grip on the shield to loosen further.

Stargazer twisted his arm, and the shield spun free. The shield bounced several feet from them.

'You appear to be losing. Are you going to beg for mercy, old friend? Ask me to spare your pathetic life?'

Tylir wiped his hand across his mouth. 'I never beg. But I am going to live.'

Stargazer laughed, the laugh of someone who had spent too long in the company of Loki the trickster. 'Not so fearless now, Sunbear, without your shield. Not so invincible. I've no idea why we even followed you. You have become yellow and a coward. There are riches for the taking across the seas and we are stuck here.'

'You were free to leave.'

'I needed your men. My men. Men who would follow me if you weren't there. Ingebord swore it.'

Ingebord, his wife with ambition. It made sense. She had decided he was not the sort of man she required to further her ambition, but was reluctant to give up the trappings of being his wife. 'Were you planning on killing me that day?'

'Of course, you fool. We planned to blame it on Fork-Beard—win-win. But Ingebord was dead when I arrived. A real shame—we had enjoyed our little games behind your back.' Stargazer wiped an arm across his mouth. 'There was no time for the setup we had planned after that, and you were hot on my heels. Still, Fork-Beard remained a convenient scapegoat.'

Tylir spat on the ground in disgust. 'You couldn't even challenge me like a man, could you? Do you really think you can command my men? That they will follow you off on some needless adventure over the seas?'

Stargazer tossed his sword in the air and caught it. Confident of victory. Tyler gritted his teeth. Stargazer always had enjoyed the flashy tricks. 'Isn't that what I am doing?'

'You have to come through me first.' Tylir crouched, knowing that he would have one final blow and he would have to make it count. He had to succeed for Mel and Katla's sake.

Stargazer drove forward. Tylir pretended to stumble and kicked out his foot, catching Stargazer off guard.

The man fell to the ground. Tylir rolled sideways and rose before Stargazer managed it.

As Stargazer tried to right himself, Tylir placed his sword so that the point was against Stargazer's throat. 'Move another muscle and you are dead.'

'Ready to die.'

Tylir kept his hand steady and the point against Stargazer's throat. Many in the crowd urged him to finish the job. 'No, you are not. Yield.'

'I yield,' Stargazer whispered.

'Grim called Stargazer has yielded. I have won,' Tylir called. He gestured to two of his men to bind Stargazer.

'Why are you doing this, Jarl?' someone in the crowd shouted. 'Why have you not killed him? He planned on killing you.'

'We live in Islond now,' he answered in a ringing voice. 'We live in a land where there is a rule of law. The time of feuding has finished for me. The General Assembly needs to judge this man and his crimes. It is the only way justice can be seen to be done.'

The crowd cheered.

Tylir calmly stepped over Stargazer's now bound and gagged body and raised his sword. 'Would anyone else care to challenge for the right to lead this *felag*? I am waiting.'

The entire crowd went silent.

He nodded. 'No more challengers. Therefore, I remain in charge. We obey the rule of law here.'

'Jarl Tylir,' Mel's lone voice pierced the silence. 'Jarl Tylir.'

The crowd took up her chant.

Tylir held up his hand. 'I am proud to continue as your leader.'

The cheers grew louder.

He gestured towards where Mel stood making a large sweeping gesture with her arm while her other hand held tight to Virin. 'I believe Melkorka Helmsdottar wishes to speak.'

Mel came forward, dragging a struggling Virin by the arm. 'I ask that this woman be brought to justice. She revealed to me that she was working with that traitor Stargazer. Thanks to their plotting, things were set in motion with my half-brother which should never have happened.'

'This is Fork-Beard's sister,' Virin said in a ringing voice. 'She is the one who was in league with Stargazer! You know me. I've no need to lie.'

'I should have looked much closer to home before now. My wife and her lover, Stargazer, plotted against me. Now only the old nurse, the facilitator, remains.'

Mel looked up at him and mouthed, 'Thank you.'

Virin made a disgusted noise. 'How could I do such a thing? Your wits are addled, Sunbear.'

'Are they?'

'How much have you drunk tonight? It seemed to me that I refilled your goblet many times.'

'Amazing the amount of liquid the rushes can absorb.' Tylir kept a straight face.

Virin went white and appeared to age rapidly. He should have guessed that she would be behind some of the trouble. He had known that Ingebord was unhappy, but he hadn't realised her unhappiness had extended towards murder. 'I am innocent of whatever you think I did.'

Tylir snapped his fingers and asked for the old woman to be put under guard. 'The Assembly will try you, Virin, along with Stargazer.'

'I'm so sorry,' Mel said in a low voice to Tylir after Virin had been removed. 'You did not deserve such a terrible betrayal.'

The scar pulsed on Tylir's face. 'I was blind. We had been friends so long that I never considered the betrayal would come from Stargazer.'

'But it did.'

His eyes became bleak. 'It will take time to understand the reasons, but I'm glad to be alive.'

'Better than the alternative.'

He laughed. Laughing made his arm ache. He pushed away the pain and tried to concentrate on the important things. 'Where is Katla? Is she safe?'

Mel's lips curved up into a smile. 'Shall we go and see her? Or can I bind up your arm first? I've no wish for you to lose any more blood.'

'I yield to your expertise.'

At his words, two bright spots appeared on her cheeks. It was all Tylir could do not to make a declaration for her there and then. The words of love threatened to spill out, but he held them back. Patience. He knew the value of the prize he sought, and he was certain they would have the rest of their lives together.

After ensuring Tylir's arm was properly bound, Mel led the way to the small shed and tried not to think about what had just nearly happened. When he stumbled before Stargazer, Mel had been certain that he was going to die. 'In here I hope.'

'You only hope?'

'I only had time to whisper my instructions, but your daughter is a brave little girl. Takes after her father.'

'My daughter is a brave girl but she has had an excellent example in you.' Tylir's voice dripped with such warmth and sincerity that Mel's heart started spinning impossible dreams.

Lifting the torch, Mel peered into the shed. Katla was curled up with the puppies with her doll cradled close and her thumb in her mouth. The spaniel gave a soft woof as if to say she was guarding the little girl as well as the puppies.

Tylir put a heavy hand on her shoulder. 'You were right, Mel. She did as you suggested. My daughter is a resourceful girl.'

'I think so as well. Shall I carry her back to bed? You have hurt your arm.'

'I would carry her, but I am grateful for the help. Mel, I am grateful for all your help.'

'I was pleased you were able to put your ghosts to rest tonight, Tylir.'

'It is you that has truly freed me, Mel.'

Rather than answering, Mel softly called Katla's name so as not to startle the girl. Her eyes blinked open.

When she saw them, Katla jumped up and rushed towards them. 'I did it right, didn't I, Aunt Mel? I counted to thirty and everything.'

'You did everything right, sweetling.'

'Oh, my stars.' Katla put her hand over her mouth. 'The Bifrost is out. Behind you. Something wonderful is about to happen. I can just feel it. Your son always said so, Aunty Mel.' She clasped her hands over her mouth. 'I'm sorry.'

'Did he?' Mel smiled at the memory of how her son had reached out to grab the light in the sky the first time he had seen it, and that ache deep inside her, while not gone, was more manageable. She could think of her son and remember the good times like watching the Bifrost.

The Bifrost with its undulating colours of bright green was as good an excuse as anything to take a chance.

'Thank you for telling me that it was there.' Mel threw her arms about Katla and savoured the little-girl smell.

She let her go and stood tall. 'I was wrong earlier, Tylir. I want to marry you.'

'No, you were right earlier. I was wrong,' Tylir said. 'I failed to be honest with you. I gave you the wrong reason why I wanted to marry you.'

'Oh?' Mel hated how the hope grew in her breast.

'I love you, Mel. I want to marry you because you make my life a better place to be. I want you in my life and yes in my bed. That is the only reason. You gave me my daughter, but more importantly you gave me my life back.'

'I did? You do?'

Tylir gave a hesitant nod. 'And I want a marriage of equals. A true partnership. Marriage is a lifetime's work and I want to spend the rest of my life working on making ours the best possible one with you. Shoulder to shoulder and marching forward to create our sanctuary. How does that sound to you?'

A true partnership like she had always dreamed about. 'It sounds like you read my mind.'

'Oh, my goodness. Oh, my stars,' Katla said. 'The magic does work. All it needed was the Bifrost rainbow. I will have to tell the boys that.'

Mel laughed. 'No magic, sweetling, unless you count the glory of falling in love with absolutely the right person.'

'Will you be my wife and my equal partner in life? Can I hope that you will allow me some small corner of your heart?'

'Yes, yes, I will,' Mel said. 'I love you, Tylir, already. I love that you try with your daughter, and you are willing to keep on trying. I love that you care about your people deeply. I want to share my life with you whether that is long or short. Equal partners.'

Tylir brushed her lips and Mel gave her mouth up to his kiss.

'Maybe one day, I will get a brother or sister,' Katla said in a little voice.

'Maybe you will, but for right now, you need to let the puppies sleep.' Mel turned to look at the little girl who she loved like her own. 'Time for bed. Tomorrow is another big day.'

'Will we have a proper wedding? Freya loves weddings.'

Mel exchanged glances with Tylir. 'Maybe we can get Helm and his family to be here for it, and our family can start building bridges with our neighbours.'

Tylir tightened his grip on her hand. 'I would like that. Our family. What sweeter thing could there be? All my family are with me now and that is enough.'

* * * * *

If you enjoyed this story, why not read Michelle Styles's Vows and Vikings miniseries?

A Deal with Her Rebel Viking
Betrothed to the Enemy Viking
To Wed a Viking Warrior

And make sure to pick up her story in the Sons of Sigurd collection,

Conveniently Wed to the Viking.

Author Note

The reasons for people in the Viking Age deciding to settle in Iceland varied. What is clear is that when they did settle, they set up one of the oldest forms of civil democracy. Indeed, Iceland's parliament continues uninterrupted to this day.

The *Laxdaela Saga*, which mainly focuses on the experiences of female settlers, makes it clear that most were seeking land. Several of the warlords retired to Iceland after making their fortune in the seas around Britain and France. It is also obvious from that saga, and the 'Halfdan Eysteinsson' saga in the *Seven Viking Romances*, that women were able to hold land in their own right. As Price makes clear in his book *Children of Ash and Elm*, various 'accepted' ideas about Viking culture, including the roles of men and women, do need to be re-examined.

As ever, any mistakes—including the inadvertent ones caused by my not studying the latest archaeological reports—are mine.

If you are interested in this time period, can I recommend the following books?

Ferguson, R. (2010) *The Hammer and the Cross: A New History of the Vikings* Penguin Books

Jesch, J. (1991) *Women in the Viking Age* The Boydell Press

Magnusson, M. KBE (1969) *Laxdaela Saga* Viking London

Magnusson, M. KBE (2003) *The Vikings* Tempus Publishing

Oliver, N. (2012) *Vikings a History* Orion Books

Palsson, H. and Edwards, P. (1985) *Seven Viking Romances* Penguin Books

Parker, P. (2014) *The Northmen's Fury: A History of the Viking World* Jonathan Cape

Price, N. (2021) *Children of Ash and Elm, A History of the Vikings* Basic Books, Hachette

Skie, T. (translated by McCollough, A. 2022) *The Wolf Age: The Vikings, The Anglo Saxons and the Battle for the North Sea Empire* Pushkin Press

Williams, G. ed. (2014) *Vikings: Life and Legend* British Museum Press, London

Get 3 FREE REWARDS!

We'll send you 2 FREE Books <u>plus</u> a FREE Mystery Gift.

FREE Value Over $20

Both the **Harlequin® Historical** and **Harlequin® Romance** series feature compelling novels filled with emotion and simmering romance.

YES! Please send me 2 FREE novels from the Harlequin Historical or Harlequin Romance series and my FREE Mystery Gift (gift is worth about $10 retail). After receiving them, if I don't wish to receive any more books, I can return the shipping statement marked "cancel." If I don't cancel, I will receive 6 brand-new Harlequin Historical books every month and be billed just $6.19 each in the U.S. or $6.74 each in Canada, a savings of at least 11% off the cover price, or 4 brand-new Harlequin Romance Larger-Print books every month and be billed just $6.09 each in the U.S. or $6.24 each in Canada, a savings of at least 13% off the cover price. It's quite a bargain! Shipping and handling is just 50¢ per book in the U.S. and $1.25 per book in Canada.* I understand that accepting the 2 free books and gift places me under no obligation to buy anything. I can always return a shipment and cancel at any time by calling the number below. The free books and gift are mine to keep no matter what I decide.

Choose one: ☐ **Harlequin Historical**
(246/349 BPA GRNX)

☐ **Harlequin Romance Larger-Print**
(119/319 BPA GRNX)

☐ **Or Try Both!**
(246/349 & 119/319 BPA GRRD)

Name (please print)

Address   Apt. #

City   State/Province   Zip/Postal Code

Email: Please check this box ☐ if you would like to receive newsletters and promotional emails from Harlequin Enterprises ULC and its affiliates. You can unsubscribe anytime.

Mail to the Harlequin Reader Service:
IN U.S.A.: P.O. Box 1341, Buffalo, NY 14240-8531
IN CANADA: P.O. Box 603, Fort Erie, Ontario L2A 5X3

Want to try 2 free books from another series! Call 1-800-873-8635 or visit www.ReaderService.com.

*Terms and prices subject to change without notice. Prices do not include sales taxes, which will be charged (if applicable) based on your state or country of residence. Canadian residents will be charged applicable taxes. Offer not valid in Quebec. This offer is limited to one order per household. Books received may not be as shown. Not valid for current subscribers to the Harlequin Historical or Harlequin Romance series. All orders subject to approval. Credit or debit balances in a customer's account(s) may be offset by any other outstanding balance owed by or to the customer. Please allow 4 to 6 weeks for delivery. Offer available while quantities last.

Your Privacy—Your information is being collected by Harlequin Enterprises ULC, operating as Harlequin Reader Service. For a complete summary of the information we collect, how we use this information and to whom it is disclosed, please visit our privacy notice located at corporate.harlequin.com/privacy-notice. From time to time we may also exchange your personal information with reputable third parties. If you wish to opt out of this sharing of your personal information, please visit readerservice.com/consumerschoice or call 1-800-873-8635. **Notice to California Residents**—Under California law, you have specific rights to control and access your data. For more information on these rights and how to exercise them, visit corporate.harlequin.com/california-privacy.

HHHRLP23

Get 3 FREE REWARDS!

We'll send you 2 FREE Books plus a FREE Mystery Gift.

FREE Value Over $20

Both the **Harlequin® Desire** and **Harlequin Presents®** series feature compelling novels filled with passion, sensuality and intriguing scandals.

YES! Please send me 2 FREE novels from the Harlequin Desire or Harlequin Presents series and my FREE gift (gift is worth about $10 retail). After receiving them, if I don't wish to receive any more books, I can return the shipping statement marked "cancel." If I don't cancel, I will receive 6 brand-new Harlequin Presents Larger-Print books every month and be billed just $6.30 each in the U.S. or $6.49 each in Canada, a savings of at least 10% off the cover price, or 3 Harlequin Desire books (2-in-1 story editions) every month and be billed just $7.83 each in the U.S. or $8.43 each in Canada, a savings of at least 12% off the cover price. It's quite a bargain! Shipping and handling is just 50¢ per book in the U.S. and $1.25 per book in Canada.* I understand that accepting the 2 free books and gift places me under no obligation to buy anything. I can always return a shipment and cancel at any time by calling the number below. The free books and gift are mine to keep no matter what I decide.

Choose one: ☐ **Harlequin Desire** ☐ **Harlequin** ☐ **Or Try Both!**
(225/326 BPA GRNA) **Presents** (225/326 & 176/376
  Larger-Print BPA GRQP)
  (176/376 BPA GRNA)

Name (please print)

Address   Apt. #

City   State/Province   Zip/Postal Code

Email: Please check this box ☐ if you would like to receive newsletters and promotional emails from Harlequin Enterprises ULC and its affiliates. You can unsubscribe anytime.

Mail to the **Harlequin Reader Service:**
IN U.S.A.: P.O. Box 1341, Buffalo, NY 14240-8531
IN CANADA: P.O. Box 603, Fort Erie, Ontario L2A 5X3

Want to try 2 free books from another series! Call 1-800-873-8635 or visit www.ReaderService.com.

*Terms and prices subject to change without notice. Prices do not include sales taxes, which will be charged (if applicable) based on your state or country of residence. Canadian residents will be charged applicable taxes. Offer not valid in Quebec. This offer is limited to one order per household. Books received may not be as shown. Not valid for current subscribers to the Harlequin Presents or Harlequin Desire series. All orders subject to approval. Credit or debit balances in a customer's account(s) may be offset by any other outstanding balance owed by or to the customer. Please allow 4 to 6 weeks for delivery. Offer available while quantities last.

Your Privacy—Your information is being collected by Harlequin Enterprises ULC, operating as Harlequin Reader Service. For a complete summary of the information we collect, how we use this information and to whom it is disclosed, please visit our privacy notice located at corporate.harlequin.com/privacy-notice. From time to time we may also exchange your personal information with reputable third parties. If you wish to opt out of this sharing of your personal information, please visit readerservice.com/consumerschoice or call 1-800-873-8635. **Notice to California Residents**—Under California law, you have specific rights to control and access your data. For more information on these rights and how to exercise them, visit corporate.harlequin.com/california-privacy.

HDHP23

Get 3 FREE REWARDS!

We'll send you 2 FREE Books plus a FREE Mystery Gift.

FREE
Value Over
$20

Both the **Romance** and **Suspense** collections feature compelling novels written by many of today's bestselling authors.

YES! Please send me 2 FREE novels from the Essential Romance or Essential Suspense Collection and my FREE gift (gift is worth about $10 retail). After receiving them, if I don't wish to receive any more books, I can return the shipping statement marked "cancel." If I don't cancel, I will receive 4 brand-new novels every month and be billed just $7.49 each in the U.S. or $7.74 each in Canada. That's a savings of at least 17% off the cover price. It's quite a bargain! Shipping and handling is just 50¢ per book in the U.S. and $1.25 per book in Canada.* I understand that accepting the 2 free books and gift places me under no obligation to buy anything. I can always return a shipment and cancel at any time by calling the number below. The free books and gift are mine to keep no matter what I decide.

Choose one: ☐ **Essential Romance**
(194/394 BPA GRNM)

☐ **Essential Suspense**
(191/391 BPA GRNM)

☐ **Or Try Both!**
(194/394 & 191/391 BPA GRQZ)

Name (please print)

Address   Apt. #

City   State/Province   Zip/Postal Code

Email: Please check this box ☐ if you would like to receive newsletters and promotional emails from Harlequin Enterprises ULC and its affiliates. You can unsubscribe anytime.

Mail to the Harlequin Reader Service:
IN U.S.A.: P.O. Box 1341, Buffalo, NY 14240-8531
IN CANADA: P.O. Box 603, Fort Erie, Ontario L2A 5X3

Want to try 2 free books from another series? Call 1-800-873-8635 or visit www.ReaderService.com.

*Terms and prices subject to change without notice. Prices do not include sales taxes, which will be charged (if applicable) based on your state or country of residence. Canadian residents will be charged applicable taxes. Offer not valid in Quebec. This offer is limited to one order per household. Books received may not be as shown. Not valid for current subscribers to the Essential Romance or Essential Suspense Collection. All orders subject to approval. Credit or debit balances in a customer's account(s) may be offset by any other outstanding balance owed by or to the customer. Please allow 4 to 6 weeks for delivery. Offer available while quantities last.

Your Privacy—Your information is being collected by Harlequin Enterprises ULC, operating as Harlequin Reader Service. For a complete summary of the information we collect, how we use this information and to whom it is disclosed, please visit our privacy notice located at corporate.harlequin.com/privacy-notice. From time to time we may also exchange your personal information with reputable third parties. If you wish to opt out of this sharing of your personal information, please visit readerservice.com/consumerschoice or call 1-800-873-8635. **Notice to California Residents**—Under California law, you have specific rights to control and access your data. For more information on these rights and how to exercise them, visit corporate.harlequin.com/california-privacy.

STRS23

HARLEQUIN
PLUS

Try the best multimedia subscription service for romance readers like you!

Read, Watch and Play.

Experience the easiest way to get the romance content you crave.

Start your **FREE TRIAL** at
<u>www.harlequinplus.com/freetrial</u>.

HARPLUS0123